ALAN JUDD

INSIDE
ENEMY

SIMON &
SCHUSTER

London · New York · Sydney · Toronto · New Delhi

A CBS COMPANY

First published in Great Britain by Simon & Schuster UK Ltd, 2014
A CBS COMPANY

1 3 5 7 9 10 8 6 4 2

Simon & Schuster UK Ltd
1st Floor
222 Gray's Inn Road
London WC1X 8HB

www.simonandschuster.co.uk

Simon & Schuster Australia, Sydney
Simon & Schuster India, New Delhi

A CIP catalogue record for this book
is available from the British Library

Hardback ISBN 978-1-47110-250-9
Trade Paperback ISBN 978-1-47110-251-6
eBook ISBN 978-1-47110-253-0

Typeset by M Rules
Printed and bound by CPI Group (UK) Ltd, Croydon, CR0 4YY

Also by Alan Judd

Fiction

A Breed of Heroes

Short of Glory

The Noonday Devil

Tango

The Devil's Own Work

Legacy

The Kaiser's Last Kiss

Dancing with Eva

Uncommon Enemy

Non-Fiction

Ford Madox Ford (biography)

*The Quest for C: Mansfield Cumming and
the Founding of the Secret Service (biography)*

First World War Poets (with David Crane)

The Office Life Little Instruction Book

To John, Jan, Tom and Ben.

Prologue

The clock repair shop closed early on Wednesdays. The keeper, in his forties with greying hair and gentle brown eyes, secured the door and window grilles with padlocks. The shop was the front room of a terraced cottage, with the back room as the workshop and a bath and toilet in an extension beyond. Upstairs were two rooms and a box room which the shopkeeper shared with a woman and her twelve-year-old son. That day, the boy was at school and his mother was out cleaning the houses of richer people. That suited the man's purpose.

Grilles were needed in that part of Hastings, up on a ridge away from the sea, although there was little in the shop for local thieves. They might think it had cash, but there was little enough of that. Businesses like his were always marginal but trade had slowed since he had learned it in prison, years before. Few people had mechanical watches or clocks worth repairing now and there were days when his only interruption was someone wanting a battery replaced. But that at least allowed him to get on with restoring antique timepieces he could still pick up cheaply in junk shops. In other towns, such establishments had long since elevated themselves into antique shops, but here they clung on amidst the rusting cars, boarded-up buildings and neglected dogs, serving a drab and poor population. The man sold his restorations in the auction rooms of Rye, Eastbourne, Lewes, even London, and increasingly on eBay.

It was a living, just, though not one that would have paid for his two-year-old Triumph Sprint 1050 in the lock-up a mile or so away in the industrial estate. But no-one associated him with the 160 mph motorcyclist in his black full-face helmet and belted Belstaff Trialmaster jacket. A man needed something to supplement a meagre living, he would tell himself on rare occasions when he felt the need for self-justification. The bike had paid for itself already and the work he did with it added variety to life.

It was unseasonably warm and bright that day, which made choice of cover easy. He put on a crumpled blue beach hat, white T-shirt, blue jeans and old trainers, carrying under his arm a rolled-up towel and small black rucksack.

Outside the shop, where he could keep an eye on it, was his Ford Fiesta van, twelve years old and sufficiently scuffed not to stand out on that street. But the tyres were nearly new, the interior was spotless, it started instantly and ticked over quietly. Like all his kit, it was in good order

He cruised into town, keeping to the speed limit, slowing before traffic lights, anticipating zebra crossings. In the underground car park beneath the promenade he chose a space in full view of two CCTV cameras. He got out without his hat, bought a ticket from the machine, returned, collected his towel and rucksack, locked his van, went a few steps, then returned for his hat. If the cameras were working they could not fail to register a man in no hurry, a relaxed man with nothing difficult or dangerous on his mind.

He sauntered along the promenade towards the Old Town where the fishing boats were drawn up on the beach. Although it was autumn, the day was warm enough for a few young people to sit on the shingle and for children to play on the never-to-be-completed harbour groyne. The sea was calm and sparkling and the tide was in, with its usual offering of plastic detritus. There were even a couple of hardy aged swimmers, which also suited his purpose.

He picked his way between the winched-up fishing vessels and the tall black net huts, stepping over wires and buoys en route to the public lavatory. There he entered a cubicle and emerged a few minutes later wearing brown corduroy trousers, a blue long-sleeved shirt and a black wig. His rucksack and other clothes he carried in a green Marks & Spencer's bag.

Walking briskly now, he bought a return ticket to the Silverhill industrial estate from the machine by the bus stop, paying cash. He got off outside a tyre-fitter, a car-parts warehouse and a block of flats behind which were two rows of lock-up garages with black doors. Some had cars, others the overspill of various businesses. Amidst the coming and going, loading and unloading, no-one heeded the man in the sober blue shirt who unlocked number seventeen and stepped quickly inside, lowering the door before switching on the light.

Half the garage was filled with the long cases of absent grandfather clocks and other bits of usable wood. In the other half, beneath a black plastic sheet, stood the gleaming black Triumph, its battery connected to a trickle charger. He uncovered it, disconnected the charger, tested the ignition, then took a screwdriver from the toolbox on the floor and removed the number-plate. Next he went to the up-and-over door and unscrewed the reinforcing panel surrounding the lock. Beneath it, pressed against the inside of the door, were three alternative number-plates. He selected one, fitted it, and hid the original with the others. Then he took off his wig and put on the boots, Belstaff and full-face helmet that hung from hooks on the wall. After checking the contents of the large pannier box and adding his wig to them, he opened the door and pushed the bike out. At the Silverhill traffic lights a BMW abruptly changed lanes, cutting in front of him and forcing him to brake hard. He did no more than wave his gloved finger once. When on a job he was a stickler for road manners.

He headed out through Battle and after some miles turned off into the Weald, wooded country with narrow winding lanes, small farms and high hedgerows. He cruised on little more than tick-over until a series of tight bends where he turned off again into a single-track lane, which eventually became an unmade road leading to a farm. He cruised along that through a chestnut coppice and a meadow until a rutted earth track which took him left through a field and shaw into a smaller field of rough grass. On the far side was an old black barn, recently thatched and painted with black double doors approached by a brick step. The track led past it to a gate and stile, with a rising field beyond.

The man parked his Triumph behind the barn, then took his time unzipping his jacket and removing his helmet and gloves. He looked about him, taking in the neglected apple trees down the slope in what had been a garden, the three beehives and the bramble-covered remnants of a ruined cottage. His gaze lingered on a post and rail pen to his right, with a small shed that looked like a pig-sty.

He walked round to the front of the barn and swung open the doors. Inside it was dark and clean with a brick floor and sandblasted rafters. Around the walls were posters describing flora and fauna and in a corner were piled plastic chairs and a couple of tables. A notice explained that the owner had restored the barn for free public use. The man took a packet of cigarettes from his jacket pocket and went outside to light up. On the small terrace was a round table with three plastic chairs. He rested his foot on one while he smoked, seemingly absorbed by the shallow grass-filled pond before him.

After a minute or two he ambled down through the rough grass to the remains of the cottage, the walls just a couple of stones high now. When he had finished his cigarette he flicked it into the hedge and walked back up to his motorbike, keeping clear of the beehives. After another leisurely look round, he took a collapsible trenching tool from his pannier, climbed into the pen and ducked through the low door of the pig-sty.

The floor was loose dry earth, with a few weeds. He knelt at the back, away from the door, and probed the earth with the pointed end of his trenching tool before beginning to dig. Within less than a minute he was brushing soil from the lid of the buried Army surplus ammunition box.

Inside was a bundle wrapped in old jeans and a box of 12-bore shotgun cartridges, number 4 shot. Inside the jeans was a dismantled sawn-off shotgun, its brutally shortened barrels extending only just beyond the stock. He reburied the box, reassembled the gun, put it to his shoulder a couple of times, dismantled it again, wrapped it in the jeans, put the bundle in his pannier and rode back the way he had come.

At the village of Bodiam he waited patiently in the short queue of traffic at the bridge over the Rother while two coaches pulled out of the National Trust car park by the castle. When the traffic moved he kept a steady pace out of the village before turning right. Two cars followed him. He continued all the way to the village of Sandhurst, noting without turning his head the cattle grid at the start of a gravelled drive, shortly before the 30 mph signs and the church. Reaching the village, he turned left as soon as the following cars indicated right. Once they were out of sight he turned round and headed back to the drive with the cattle grid.

It led up a short steep hill to reveal, hidden from the road, a Georgian house with floor-to-ceiling ground-floor windows and a beach-pebble turning area in front. It overlooked a fenced paddock which fell away towards the lane below. The few grazing sheep ignored the motorcyclist weaving his way between the gravelled ridges and holes.

He parked at the steps leading up to the wide front door. With his back to the house, he opened the pannier and assembled and loaded the shotgun but left it in the pannier, the protruding end of the barrel covered by the jeans. He took out a clipboard with a printed form and a handwritten address, pushed up his visor, mounted the steps and pulled the iron bell-pull.

The door was opened by a tall middle-aged man with grey crew-cut hair and gold-rimmed glasses. He wore green corduroys and a thick rust-red shirt, open at the neck.

The motorcyclist glanced at his clipboard. 'Mr Line?'

The man shook his head. 'No, I am sorry.'

'Mr C. Line? No-one else here of that name?'

'There is no-one else here. I am Dr Klein. Is it possible there is some confusion?' He spoke careful, accented English.

'Maybe. If you check the address, sir, I'll get the package.' The man handed him the clipboard and returned to his motorbike.

The man studied the form, looking up as the motorcyclist came up the steps towards him. 'I am sorry but I do not understand. This form does not have my name or address and appears to be for applying for a refund from the railway—'

He must have seen the gun, just, but would have had no time to react. The blast, point blank into his face, lifted him off his feet and flung him backwards into the hall. A clamour of rooks rose from the trees around the church and the sheep in the paddock scattered like minnows before reforming into a huddle, facing the house.

The man did not bother to confirm death. He picked up the clipboard and pulled the door to with his gloved hand. He dismantled the gun, wrapped it in the jeans and tucked it and the clipboard neatly back in the pannier. Then he pulled down his visor and rode carefully back down the rutted track.

Back in his garage with the door safely closed, he unplugged a pay-as-you-go mobile from its charger behind one of the clock cases and texted *Job done*. By the time he had finished covering the Triumph there was a reply which said *Thank you. Collect as before after 2200 hrs.*

When the man got home he hung his dry towel and swimming trunks on the line in the back yard. The woman was back and the television was on upstairs, which meant her boy was also back. He called up to her. 'Put the kettle on. I'm coming up.'

'Where've you been?' she called.

'Went for a dip. Colder than I thought.'

'All right for some.'

'Bloody freezing.'

Later that night, after she'd cooked for them, he said he'd had enough of television and computer screens and was going for a drink. She was ironing in one corner of the room and didn't object to having him out of the way. They'd been together over a year now. It was about three minutes' walk to his local pub where he read a *Daily Mail* someone had left and sipped at a pint of beer until the landlord called time. The place still adhered, more or less, to the old hours. He put his empty glass on the bar and called goodnight to the landlord, who was in the back somewhere. Once outside, he turned into the alleyway at the side of the pub and went into the Gents. He locked himself in the cubicle, lowered the lavatory seat, took off his shoes and stood on the seat to lift the top off the ancient cistern above. Taped to the underside was a fat package wrapped in black plastic. He replaced the lid, then sat on the lavatory and opened the package. The notes were used tens and twenties, the amount correct.

He walked slowly back to his shop, the cash distributed between the two back pockets of his jeans. The sense of a job well done was always pleasing. He would get the woman a treat tomorrow, some sexy underwear, perhaps. That might please her. There hadn't been much going on in that department recently. He would get the boy something, too. That would definitely please her; she'd want to show her gratitude.

1

'Just shows – while there's death there's hope. Right as usual, the old fraud.' George Greene, the Foreign Secretary, chuckled, straining his checked shirt against his stomach. It was a grey day and he was sitting on the leather sofa in his unlit office overlooking St James's Park, one arm along the back and one plump leg crossed over the other. His audiences often failed to appreciate his quotations and allusions and he knew they were a political liability, since a reputation for cleverness was usually equated with arrogance. But he relished life too much to permit the sensitivities of others to interfere with what he enjoyed. 'Disraeli, that is,' he added. 'It was he who said it. Can't think of whom.'

He looked at Charles Thoroughgood. 'Your late and unlamented predecessor, Nigel Measures, must have been the first Chief of the Secret Service ever to be killed in a road accident, wasn't he? And weren't you and he rivals for his widow at Oxford? Now your wife, of course?'

'Not exactly rivals but we all knew each other.' The story was too complicated to explain briefly and Charles had long since given up trying. 'But Sarah and I are now married, yes.'

'So two-in-one, then? You inherit his job and his wife? Like Wellington and Napoleon's mistress.' It wasn't a very precise analogy but it was good enough for George Greene.

'If that's a formal job offer, yes.'

'And if that's a formal acceptance, it is.'

The two men grinned. They were relaxed with each other, having served together at the embassy in Vienna many years before when Charles was a junior member of the MI6 station and George a rising star in chancery. But he rose too fast for the constraints of the Foreign Office and left to begin a political career as speechwriter for the shadow Home Secretary. Now, after entering Parliament and enduring years in opposition, followed by two brief junior ministerial posts, he had at last plucked the plum he cherished.

Charles was relaxed, too, with the other half of George's audience, Angela Wilson, the Foreign Office Permanent

Secretary. Clever, like George, but without his careless joviality, she had overlapped with them both in Vienna on her way to the top of the tree. She and Charles had once hovered on the brink of an affair, or so it had seemed to him. Looking at her now, a soberly dressed woman in her fifties with grey hair cut severely short, he couldn't help wondering whether it would have changed either of their lives. He had no regrets, and doubted she did. He was sure she wouldn't even remember it as a hovering. She certainly gave the impression she would have no time now for such frivolity.

'The point, Secretary of State,' Angela said, emphasising his formal title, 'is what the press will make of it when news that Charles is to be the new head of MI6 gets out. Cosy, incestuous Whitehall cronyism, that's how they'll see it. Which is what it is, of course.' She sounded exasperated. 'At the very least we should give the press desk a line to take.'

George shrugged. 'Sure, they can have an LTT. It'll be a nine-minute wonder.'

The lights came on, illuminating the paintings and panelling and casting homely inviting pools on the Foreign Secretary's desk. Then they flickered and went off again. No-one remarked on it.

'Part of my plan to drag the Foreign Office forwards and upwards towards a glorious past' – George Greene waved at the nineteenth-century paintings of naval battles that had replaced his predecessor's choice of Brit Art – 'is that, along with restoring our linguistic and subject expertise, we should avoid openness as far as legislation permits. You can have openness or you can have government, but you cannot have open government. Not effective government, anyway. It is therefore my intention that the reconstituted secret service you are about to command, Charles – MI6 or whatever you want to rename it and note I say command, not manage – keeps mum, shtoom, says sod all in public. No chiefly interviews or speeches, no PR, no profile or social media presence or nonsense of that sort. The secret service will do its work in secret. Your name and head office will be announced, of course – that can't be helped – but that's about it. The same will go for GCHQ. What happens with MI5, I don't know. That's the Home Secretary's business. Are you okay with that?'

Charles was.

'The Intelligence Services Committee may have views,' said Angela. 'They will expect to be consulted, at the very least.'

'They will be. I'll tell them. Get the chairman in for a briefing.'

'The chair is a woman, George. You've met her.' Angela emphasised 'chair'.

'Chairwoman, then. Nothing wrong with that, is there – no shame in being a woman? Why hide it?'

George Greene grinned again. He enjoyed baiting Angela, or indeed anyone baitable, but his off-the-cuff comments masked a powerful and unresting intellect. As a young man he had not come across as obviously ambitious, Charles reflected, but he could not have got where he was without ambition. Assuming he still had it, there was only one place to go.

George turned to Charles again. 'I know you were expecting this to be a selection interview rather than confirmation of appointment and I know you weren't looking for the job, so it's only reasonable that I should give you time to think about it despite the formality of my recent offer and your kind acceptance. Ten minutes? Two? You were always a cautious chap.'

'I've thought.'

'Good. Start on Monday. There's a nice new office. Well, a new old office, different office, probably not to your taste. I haven't seen it. Angela will tell you all about it. Any questions?'

The door opened and the private secrety said, 'Secretary of State, the Israeli Ambassador is here.'

'Wheel him in.' George bounced up from the sofa and held out his hand. 'Thank you, Charles. Look forward to working with you again.' The lights flickered and he smiled at them both. 'Good to have the old team back together, isn't it? Funny how things turn out. Only one problem: no money. Angela will tell you all about that too.' He pointed at the lights. 'She'll also tell you it's part of your job to sort out these bloody power failures. And she'll be right. Get that sorted and there'll be coffee and biscuits next time.'

Angela walked briskly down the corridor without pausing to check that Charles was following.

'You look cross,' he said.

'I am.'

'What did he mean about me sorting out the power failures? I'm not exactly technical. Nor is the job, is it? I hope.'

'I'll brief you. Meanwhile, you should know that we went to no end of trouble to set up a proper appointments procedure for heads of the intelligence agencies, getting agreement from the Cabinet Office, the Home Office, the MOD, the Treasury, Number Ten, everyone. Everything was to be open and above board, posts advertised, candidates interviewed by the heads of major customer departments, two to be put up to the Foreign Secretary, one to go forward to the Prime Minister for approval. All transparent, rational and defensible.' She paused while they passed two very short women pushing a trolley laden with old paper files. 'You see what we're having to do now, go back to paper because of all these power cuts? Hopeless. Anyway, then – heigh-ho – a cabinet reshuffle and a new secretary of state who says he doesn't need any damn committee to tell him what he wants, picks up the telephone to you and says come in for a chat and it's done, wham, bang, thank you, ma'am. Just like the old days, as if we'd never modernised at all.'

Charles knew all about George's views. The call to his mobile had come that morning when he and Sarah were moving into their Westminster house. Charles was lingering in his old rooftop flat in the Boltons, mentally saying goodbye to the gardens and plane trees below as the removers struggled with boxes of books and the heavy oak desk his father had made. George Greene had been characteristically brisk.

'Charles, it's George Greene. Long time no speak. You've heard about my new job? Well, I've got one for you. Is this a good moment?'

'No, I'm in the middle of moving house.'

'You'll have heard that we're disbanding the Single Intelligence Agency and reverting to its original constituent parts, the three intelligence agencies as were. I want you to head your old bit, the MI6 bit. Smaller than it was, of course, money being what it is, but at least the chain of command and responsibility will make sense again. Daft idea to have the SIA answering to a single junior minister who knows sod all when all the fruits of its work – and all the dog-turds – land in the laps of the foreign and home secretaries. Typical of the last government. I've got Tim Corke to take over GCHQ. You know him? Good. Anyway, the officials here had set up some balls-aching appointments procedure for senior posts in the SIA which they fondly imagine we're going to be using for the new heads of agency. Expect us to advertise the jobs and open them to anyone in the EU, if you've ever heard such crap. I'm ignoring it, of course. With the Prime Minister's support. Come in and have a chat later today, unless you want to say yea or nay now.'

'I can't. I'm in the middle of moving house.'

'Two minutes. This afternoon will do. Just two, I promise.'

Angela stopped in her outer office to say something about the permanent secretaries' meeting, waving Charles on. Her office was about the size of the Foreign Secretary's but lacked his double aspect. There were three paintings, one of a life-like turnip, one a green-and-white-striped rectangle and the other a medley of muddy colours with a single pinpoint of white just off-centre.

'My predecessor's choices,' she said, closing the door. 'I

suppose I should find time to change them. It was the first thing George did, of course, on his first morning. He chose sea battles against the French and Spanish as – quote – reminders for Johnny Foreigner – unquote. His very words. Hardly *communautaire* for a foreign secretary.' She dumped an armful of files and papers on the desk. Even as a young second secretary in Vienna she was always hurried, as if everything she dealt with was by definition important and urgent. Presumably it was, now. For a moment, however, the determined busyness of her expression softened into lined weariness. She looked older.

'One damn thing after another,' said Charles. 'Life, that is. According to the Duke of Wellington. Surprised George hasn't used it.'

'He will if he hears it.' She looked down and jabbed her keyboard but the screen remained blank. 'So much for the paperless office.'

'The lights are back on. Why isn't it working?'

'There's more to it than that. You'll hear soon enough. I won't go into it now.' She sat, indicating a chair to Charles. 'I've got the perm secs' weekly meeting in ten minutes. What began as an informal update, exchange of views, KIT – which is what we now have to call keeping in touch – and coffee, has grown into something with an agenda that has to be minuted. It's becoming a bureaucracy.

Next we know it'll be a department.' She yawned. 'Sorry, Charles. I've been trying to sort out my ailing mother, get her into a decent home. If there are any. Keeps me up half the night and awake the other half. Of course, it's not clear whether you'll be there or not.'

'Not yet, I hope.'

She smiled wearily. 'Perm secs', I mean. No-one's even thought about your grading. Your predecessor was grade 1, like the others, but the SIA was much bigger than your MI6 slice of it will be. You can come if you're 1a but there are no 2s there. Don't know whether there are any precedents. I'll have to ask the Cabinet Secretary. Congratulations on your marriage, by the way. I'm not sure I ever met your wife when she – when she was—'

'Married to Nigel Measures. Possibly not. They kept their professional lives quite separate. Her name's Sarah.'

'Bad business about Nigel's treachery and attempted cover-up. Can't say I ever took to him, frankly, but he was able. She is your first wife – you weren't married before?'

'No, a late marriage. Hope for us all.'

She looked down again with the slightest shake of her head. When she looked up her expression had resumed seriousness and purpose. 'There are various things to sort out. I take it your vetting's up to date?'

'It will have lapsed after I was kicked out of the SIA.'

'Of course, Nigel had you arrested, didn't he? Evil man. But the vetting can be quickly reinstated. I'll get someone on to it.' She made a note. 'And there are briefings, of course. You'll be briefed by your own board, which is already in place' – she did not look at him as she said that – 'and you should arrange early sessions with your main customer departments – MOD, Home Office, Treasury, Cabinet Office, the Bank – us, of course. And various others. Also there's a meeting starting in two hours which you should come to. I won't say any more about it now, it's – well, we're all sworn to secrecy. I'd better let the Chair indoctrinate you. Meet me outside the Cabinet Office and I'll get you through security. You don't have any passes now, do you? Finally, there's your head office – Rosewood House, part of the old Home Office empire in Croydon.'

'Croydon?'

'Money's tighter than ever and with so much of the Whitehall estate sold off and somewhere needed quickly it was a case of grab it while we could, I'm afraid. Nowhere else on offer within the M25.' She looked as if she was suppressing a smile, just.

'But we'll spend half our lives on the train, coming up to see people. No-one will come to see us.'

'Well, you are supposed to be a secret service, aren't you?'

'What about the former SIA building in Victoria Street? A few floors would do.'

'Sold to Gulf developers. Luxury apartments. Plus affordable housing, of course.'

'Where are MI5 and GCHQ?'

'MI5 are returning to their old home in Thames House on the Embankment and GCHQ remain in Cheltenham but they're getting a new London office as well, somewhere in Curzon Street. I dare say if MI6 had had a chief in place during the negotiations you might not have ended up in Croydon, but they didn't and you have. You could always turn the job down, of course.'

Charles crossed Parliament Square in bright cool sunshine, cutting through Dean's Yard into the quiet streets behind the Abbey. With a pleasing sense of novelty, he unlocked the door of the small terraced house – the smallest in the street – and picked his way between the packing cases and haphazardly placed furniture. Most of it had been moved in only the day before but already there was crockery on the shelves, food in the fridge, there were clothes in the wardrobe, flowers on the kitchen table and a platoon of pot plants in the tiny back garden. It was different, being married.

He texted Sarah, who had been called into work that afternoon. City lawyers, Charles was learning, were never off duty. He told her the job was agreed, which would please her, and added a moan about Croydon. She texted congratulations, had a client just arriving, would speak later. He had just put the kettle on when Angela rang: the Cabinet Office meeting had been brought forward, could he come now. He set off back through Dean's Yard, where the trees had lost nearly all their leaves but the grass was strikingly green. Already it felt good to be back in harness, to be wanted again. Except for Croydon.

2

Sarah was in her office off the Blackfriars Road, billing clients. Hitherto a task for a secretary or clerk, billing was now complicated and multinational, even for part-time solicitors who did only private client work. And now, for no reason she could discover, a whole tranche of bills suddenly had to be done by yesterday. She had not responded to Charles's moan about Croydon, partly because she had a new client arriving but partly too because she didn't want to betray irritation. He had only one thing to do that afternoon, so far as she was concerned: meet the Foreign Secretary and get himself appointed. Well, he had got the job, a great thing after finding himself on the scrapheap or worse, yet all he had to say about it was that he didn't like Croydon. Now, lucky man, he could spend the rest of the day arranging things in the new house.

She wished she had the leisure to do that. The moment they had walked into the little house, she had felt it was one she could love. Snug, charming, secure, in a quiet, almost private, street, it was within walking distance of nearly everything they wanted in London. But instead of having a delicious few days to potter and domesticate, she had to return to the office and get all the wretched bills out while catching up on other business and handling their own conveyancing. She also had to complete the agreement on the Sussex cottage they were renting, an absurd extravagance given that they had between them an embarrassment of properties, each with an unsold country place on the market. It was too late to get out of the agreement now but she was determined they must not renew it unless their other properties were sold. Secretly, she was glad she still owned her Cotswold house and suspected Charles felt the same about his Scottish eyrie. So far, it was a conversation they had avoided.

Naturally, the conveyancing took longer than it should have, with the Land Registry seemingly in chronic decline. They blamed their computers, of course, perhaps this time with more justification than usual. Now, on top of the move, the conveyancing and the clients' accounts, she had to see a woman whom one of the partners had wished upon her as 'a potentially significant private client opportunity'. Charles, meanwhile, who only ever seemed to do one thing at a time, appeared blithely unaware of how much she was doing. That was really why she had shown no sympathy over Croydon.

Her secretary buzzed to say that the client opportunity had arrived. Sarah looked again at the name, Katya Chester. It was faintly familiar, associated with Charles, with something he'd said. She checked herself in her mirror and waited.

Katya Chester was tall, blonde and beautiful, with high Slavic cheekbones, green cat's eyes and pouting lips. She was expensively dressed in a light grey suit, the jacket tailored. Her white blouse, open at the neck, revealed a large sapphire surrounded by diamonds on a gold chain, with matching earrings. She wore no wedding ring but had a diamond band on her wedding finger. Her handbag was expensive, probably Mulberry. She looked in her late twenties, possibly thirty, the sort of woman whose entry anywhere was an immediate provocation to her sex. When they shook hands her American celebrity smile showed a too-perfect set of too-white teeth.

'It is very good of you to see me. I know how busy you must be but I hope I shall not waste your time.'

It was an educated foreigner's English, careful, precise and overlaid by an American accent. She declined coffee, disappointing Sarah who had delayed her second cup in anticipation, and sat with a crossing of her elegant legs and susurration of tights. It was bad luck for Ms Chester, thought Sarah, that she wasn't received by a man.

'I am buying a house, a house in Belgravia. Just a small house, not extravagant. I should be very grateful if you would handle the conveyancing for me. I also have a friend who is very rich and who wishes to buy other properties in London and who will need a good lawyer. I should like to introduce you to my friend.' Her introductory paragraph ended with a wide smile.

Sarah opened her notebook. 'That's very kind of you but so far I have only your name and work telephone number.' It was a 219 area code, which she remembered from Nigel's political contacts included the houses of parliament.

Katya Chester was happily forthcoming. The house was perfect for someone like her, an American citizen on her own in London where it was necessary to be so careful. Belgravia was a nice area. The house needed improvement, of course, but that was to be expected. There were so many beautiful old houses in England, not only in London, but there was always a price to pay for charm. Fortunately, she was able to pay it. Another smile. She was a cash buyer, her husband, Mr Chester, having left her with more than enough money for her modest needs. Fortunately, too, she had an interesting job working for a member of parliament, a perfect sequel to her postgraduate studies in politics at university in New York. The MP she worked for was a very good MP, quite well-known, Jeremy Wheeler. His constituency was in Sussex – Sarah knew him, perhaps?

Sarah knew him; he had worked for her late husband and was the owner, she had discovered only that day, of the Sussex cottage they were about to rent. Charles, who had served with him in MI6, would be horrified. But she wondered why Katya Chester should associate her with Sussex. She had only been there once, to see the cottage. And she worked under her maiden name, Bourne, not as Mrs Thoroughgood.

'Were you born in America?' she asked conversationally.

'My parents were Russian. I was born there.'

'Your English is excellent.'

'Thank you.' Another smile.

'You'd better give me details of the house and the estate agent.'

She claimed to have enough money in the bank to buy the house outright. No need to sell shares or get anything from Mr Chester.

'Sorry, I'd assumed from what you said before that he was dead,' said Sarah.

'In his mind he is dead. His body still functions. He is in a special home. He is older than me. I have what you call here power of attorney.'

'He was – is – a very rich man?'

'He was a banker.'

'I must give you a statement of our charges and conditions. There's a paper copy here – somewhere – yes, here – but I'll email another anyway. I must ask you to sign and return it when you've read it.'

'I can sign it now.'

'I think you should read it first.'

'I am quite sure it will be all right.' She took the form and signed in a large loopy hand with a slim gold pen.

Sarah took it reluctantly. 'I won't act on it until you've had a chance to read the copy I'm emailing, just in case you change your mind. Where is your current home, by the way?'

She gave an address in Hans Crescent, behind Harrods. There was no tenancy agreement, so she could leave when she wanted. 'It belongs to my friend. He lent it to me until I could find something to buy. That was two years ago and this is the first house I have looked at.'

The winsome smile again. It struck Sarah that the woman was probably a one-track charmer who as a pretty little girl had learned a way of pleasing that life had reinforced ever since, with the result that she had become a prisoner of her own beauty. She might never have had to get her way by argument.

'A generous friend.'

'Yes. He is the man I wanted to talk to you about.' Her green eyes widened and she leaned forward, elbows on knees. 'He is Mr Mayakovsky, a Russian billionaire who has moved to London and wishes to invest in valuable properties. I would like, if you wish it, to introduce you to him. He could bring you much business.'

'That's very kind of you, Mrs Chester. I am sure I – and the firm – would appreciate that. Meanwhile, you'll see on the form you've just signed that there's a question—'

'He could bring you so much business that they would make you a partner.'

She ignored that. '– a question asking how you came to us for this business.'

Sarah expected her to say that she knew the partner who had dumped her on Sarah's desk. But there was a moment's silence, just the wide green eyes and eager-to-please expression. 'I heard – someone told me—'

'For example, was it by personal recommendation, or through an advertisement, or professional research—'

'By personal recommendation, yes, someone told me that you were very good.'

'Me? Or the firm?'

Another hesitation. 'Both. You and the firm.'

'Well, that's very gratifying.' Sarah smiled. 'Mr Mayakovsky, I imagine?'

'No, no, it was not him. It might have been Jeremy, Mr Wheeler.'

She seemed emphatic that it should not be Mr Mayakovsky. Sarah made a note to ask the partner concerned, though she wasn't sure that she would hear from Katya Chester again. She seemed the sort who might be on her way to call on another firm with the same story, then engage a third before changing her mind about the house at the last minute. They parted with handshakes and smiles. Sarah felt suddenly weary.

The phone was ringing before she returned to her desk, there was an urgent email flashing on her screen and her mobile was vibrating. She could see that the landline call was from the estate agent who had sold Charles's flat and who kept ringing with queries she had already answered. The email was from the managing partner asking her to stand in for him at a meeting that afternoon. The mobile message was from Charles.

She took that first. 'We should go out to dinner tonight,' his voice said, 'to celebrate the move. Somewhere good. There's not much food here anyway and you've probably had a rotten first day back, with all the house stuff on top of everything else. I'll book somewhere unless you're exhausted and would rather not.'

Her weariness evaporated. *Book now*, she texted. *Anywhere but Croydon. Champagne before we go.*

3

ngela Wilson was waiting at the Cabinet Office
Whitehall entrance.

'Sorry to keep you,' Charles said. 'Lot of people and police outside Barclays at the bottom of Victoria Street. Either a mass run on the bank or a mass raid. Getting a bit ugly.'

'Cash machines have stopped working.'

'All of them? More anonymous hackers?'

'Something like that.' She took him to the front of the short queue and signed him in with a day-pass.

He followed her along a corridor he had once known well. 'Not heading for a COBR, are we?' The acronym for Cabinet Office Briefing Room had come, through official shorthand and initial media misunderstanding, to stand for any ad hoc ministerial and official body summoned to take charge of crises. Charles's few attendances in his earlier MI6 days had been in connection with British hostages seized overseas.

'The COBR, not a COBR, if you see what I mean,' she said. 'The only room that's free. In fact, there's just been a COBR which you should have been at but no-one apart from me knew of your appointment in time.' She nodded and smiled at two young women they passed. 'No, but this cash machine business, it's not surprising it's getting ugly. Accounts are debited but no cash is forthcoming. I didn't want to say any more about it in front of people in the queue but it's not just a case of anonymous hackers who've got lucky. It's more serious than that, as you'll hear.'

It was a large basement room with a long table and smaller rooms opening off it, like satellite pods. There were more screens and IT paraphernalia than Charles remembered and the lighting, though bright, was no longer the unremitting strip-lighting glare. A wall-mounted screen showed the continuous BBC news-script. There were two or three people talking at the far end of the long table and some coming and going through the door beyond. The atmosphere was that of a place in which whatever was happening had happened. Someone at the end of the table laughed.

He followed Angela into the first pod on the right.

There, at a round table festooned with plugs and leads and overlooked by three screens on the wall, sat three men. One of them he knew, Tim Corke, new director of the newly independent GCHQ. Tall, with black hair and eyebrows, a ready smile and an easy social grace that made his past as an academic mathematician a surprise to most, he had once worked with Charles on an operation to bug an embassy cipher room in South America.

Tim stood to shake hands. 'Welcome to the Cabinet Office Future Estimates Committee. COFE, we call ourselves, which in our case we have not got. Nice boring title so it can appear in calendars without attracting attention. We're in fact a sub-committee of the National Security Committee.'

Angela introduced the others as Michael Dunton, new head of MI5, and Graham Wood, head of the Civil Contingencies Unit. 'We're just about a quorum but we're lacking Home Office and MOD. They were both at the COBR this morning, along with the money men and CNI – Critical National Infrastructure – people. I briefed them on you afterwards so everyone's up to date.'

They shook hands. Michael Dunton was a short, balding man with a broad red face and heavy-framed glasses that gave him an owlish look. Graham Wood was easily the youngest, probably in his thirties, slight, with sandy hair and cheap reading glasses from Boots, the sort Charles himself used.

They sat. Tim leaned forward, elbows on table and hands clasped. 'I don't know how much Angela's told you about what's going on and what we're here for—'

'Virtually nothing,' said Angela.

'Good, that makes it simple. I'll keep it short so as not to waste everyone else's time but you can follow up with me later if you like. I'm in London virtually all the time now.'

Charles took out his black leather pocket-book. Tim shook his head. Charles put it away.

'Intermittent power cuts, cash machines and traffic lights out of order, erratic mobile reception, banking and Internet failures, computer-driven stock market highs and lows, chaos in international corporations, interference with police and military communications, power cuts to hospitals, water-pumping stations, gas and electricity supplies, supermarkets, airport delays, disappearing trains, unresponsive government departments, tax and social security computers going haywire – though the two latter are nothing unexpected, perhaps.' He smiled. 'The stuff you've seen and heard a lot of in the past few weeks, often attributed to anonymous superhackers directed by an unknown Mr Big, the devil's version of Sir Tim Berners-Lee. You can't have missed it, even in your Scottish eyrie.'

Charles nodded. The past few weeks had indeed been characterised by random IT and power failures, short-lived but very disruptive. The only consistent feature was that they were confined to Britain. Other media theories included al-Qaeda sympathisers in Birmingham and Chinese maths students in Shanghai with time on their hands. 'I doubt I'd be here today if I'd been up there recently. Wouldn't have got down. The whole country seems to be stuttering to a halt.'

'Believe it or not, it's more serious than people think. It's not random and it's not hackers. It's coordinated systematic attacks on the CNI – power, water, gas, communications, money supply, transport, food distribution, police and military capability. Especially worrying are recent DOS – denial of service – attacks on financial systems, especially the wholesale banking system, exchanges between banks and other banks and banks and governments. If that goes, everything goes. Worse than the near-collapse of 2008. There'd be no money for anyone, anywhere. Fortunately, they've not really tried to bring it down yet. Each time they do just enough to prove to themselves – and us – that they can get in, then they move on. If news got out it could create a run on the banks, with all that that implies. The City is doing what it can to protect itself, with advice from us, but the more people get to know of it, the more likely it is to get out. However, their most recent tactic is this week's attack on the Internet itself, at least the routing that covers most of the UK. You may have noticed it went down for a while a couple of days ago. That's what this morning's COBR was about.'

Charles had been packing books at the time but heard about it afterwards. 'Who's doing it and how?'

'Can't say for sure but we're pretty certain it's state sponsored. Has to be, on this scale. No individual or group could coordinate the degree of computing power they used the other day. Which means Russia or China.'

'But why? Not in the run-up to war, are we? China's got a lot of investment here, wouldn't benefit them to bring us to our knees.'

'Despite which they've been attacking our government systems for years, partly because they can and partly to refine their techniques in case they ever need to go all out. They've a clever way of making it look like common hacking attacks when actually it's technically more – I don't suppose you'd like me to go into the technical aspects now? Finding the light switch was about your limit, I seem to remember, Charles.' The others smiled. 'Also, they've been supplying the components of our IT infrastructure for years, all the micro stuff you never see. We warned successive governments that they may have designed bugs into some of these things so that they can switch them on and off at will but, as ever, cost and convenience overruled security.'

'But why now, if that's what they're doing? What do they gain?'

'That's partly why my money's on the Russians. They don't much like us and don't give a damn anyway. We're a useful surrogate for the US. They don't want to take on America but they can beat us up a bit without serious consequences and see if their techniques work. Also, there are indications that they're still feeling their way with what they can do, still experimenting, which suggests that their ability to do it may be recently acquired. If there were a long-laid Chinese plot to turn our inbuilt on switches to off and all the rest of it I don't think they'd risk blowing it on a trial run.'

'How are they doing it?'

'I'll explain later, save wasting everyone else's time. Meanwhile, there are two other aspects, less obvious as yet but just as serious. One is that they could be working up to bringing down the Internet over the British Isles for a period. It doesn't need to be permanent to be catastrophic. If they could do that they wouldn't have to bother with our power, water, gas and fuel distribution and banking systems because they're all Internet-dependent. No-one in electricity substations or telephone exchanges diverts things by throwing a few switches any more, no-one opens valves in pumping stations. It's all done remotely via the Net. And because we're creating truly national grids, so that an excess in one area flows to another, it's much harder to seal off an area. Hitherto you could – say – isolate a region's power or water supply because it was independent and self-sustaining. Now it isn't. The benefit of joining up all the different bits is that everything works better. The cost is that the whole system is much more vulnerable. Get into one little corner of it and you can get everywhere.'

'With the Internet, they need only bring enough of it down for long enough for the world to see the UK as vulnerable and unreliable. Investment dries up, the City is finished as a world financial centre, government income collapses, borrowing increases and we're in a mess. Worse mess than usual, that is. Much worse.'

Charles had long since given up any pretence of IT literacy. He was beginning to wonder whether it might now cost him his job, or whether he should resign first. Incapable of asking the kind of informed question that might demonstrate understanding or provoke insights, he had to rely on the obvious, simple, big ones. 'But can anyone bring the Internet down?'

'Well, they had a pretty good trial run this week, albeit for only part of the country and for just over an hour. But they proved they can do it. We got government scientists into this morning's COBR and asked them whether it's possible for anyone – any state or group or whatever – to bring down the entire Net. Yes and no, was the answer, as with many things scientific. They reckon that a big enough attack, well thought out and organised, could probably collapse the entire Net, but not for long. That's because it's so big and so uncoordinated and anarchic that, like water, if you block it here it will find its way through there. There would be massive disruption but it would recover and go on working patchily, after a fashion. But what you could do, as the Russians demonstrated in Estonia a few years ago, is attack a country or part of a country for long enough to send it back to the pre-Internet age. You'd stop it functioning as a modern state, with all that that implies.'

Charles could grasp that. It was detail he feared. 'So what do we do about it?'

'That's what we're here to decide. But it's only one aspect, as I said, the one everyone knows about. Everyone in government, anyway. But there's another aspect that adds venom to the first.' Tim sat back, leaving his palms flat on the desk and looking at Charles. 'We believe – in fact, we're convinced, though we don't know how they've done it – that there is repeated penetration of our most sensitive government systems, yours – MI6's, that is – included.'

43

There was another burst of laughter from the end of the larger room. They were waiting for him to respond. 'The Russians again?'

'Most likely. Certainly a hostile intelligence service. We're sure of that because of the nature of their penetration. They don't advertise themselves, don't want us to know they've been in and are very selective in what they try to access. With your people, for example, they're looking for sources, identities of sources. They're most interested in Russian or Chinese sources, which is clever because it keeps us guessing as to which they are. They want to know others too but seem least interested in terrorist sources. If it were a terrorist group, of course, it would be the other way round.'

'Have they identified any?'

'Frustratingly, we can't say. We know they've been into your system because they leave – if you like – an electronic version of footprints in snow. We do regular trawls of sensitive systems, looking for footprints, and they probably don't realise we've seen them. But we can't say for sure what they could see from where they last stood, as it were. It's more complicated than that sounds – I'm over-simplifying.' He smiled.

Charles smiled.

'They're never in for long – two hours twenty-three minutes is the longest – and access is intermittent, mostly evenings and weekends. Access to other closed systems – MI5, our own in GCHQ, some of the MOD, Foreign Office and central government systems – is less extensive and more spasmodic. But – and this is the killer point – they penetrate other systems only when they're already in the MI6 system.'

They were all looking at Charles. 'So we're the problem?'

'Something or someone in you is the problem. More likely someone. Someone on your system is giving them access via his or her computer. Not necessarily knowingly.'

'But the MI6 system is a closed system. Can't be accessed from outside.'

Angela smiled ruefully. 'Was, Charles, not is. You've been away a while. Welcome to joined-up government and joined-up Whitehall. All part of modernisation, joining the real world – that is, the virtual world – and all that. You'll understand why I couldn't say any of this before you took the job.'

'Do ministers know – George Greene?'

'They know the obvious, of course – power cuts, threats to banks, Internet failures and so on – and they know the secret bits in outline,' said Michael Dunton. 'They also know we're investigating it and that, as a security threat, it's primarily an MI5 responsibility, though for the actual technical sleuthing we depend on Tim's people. And they know that this committee exists to oversee the investigation.

But they don't know all the grisly detail. We'll have to tell them. Sometime.'

'Before they read it in the headlines,' said Graham Wood.

They went over the ground, with Graham giving more examples of CNI attacks. Tim leant forward again, elbows on table, hands clasped as before. 'Of course, your immediate problem is how to investigate your own people without any of them knowing there's an investigation. It could be any of them, including your own security people. The only person in MI6 we know it couldn't be is you, since you haven't had access to any MI6 computer systems and therefore can't be the one who's letting the attackers in.'

'What do you suggest I do?'

'Be our eyes and ears, let us know of anything remotely suspicious. I now have people in Cheltenham accessing your systems to try to find the source but it would help no end if you could let us know of any weaknesses you spot, human or system. And keep us informed, day or night.'

Charles nodded. He had taken over a few odd jobs, he reflected, but nothing quite like this. Certainly nothing in which ignorance was an advantage.

'There is one thing you could do, though, something that maybe only you can do. But, again, you'll have to make sure no-one else in your service knows. You could recontact an old friend of yours, Configure, and see if he can help. He gave us a lot of help in this area in the past. Don't worry, everyone around this table knows about him.'

'Everyone except me. Who's Configure?'

'You knew him as Lover Boy,' said Michael. 'Russian intelligence officer. That was his code name when you recruited him in London about a hundred years ago. It's changed a couple of times since. He defected not long before you left MI6, if you remember. You were brought back into the case to help with the exfiltration.'

Viktor Koslov. The then youthful KGB officer had been Charles's first case, though it was an exaggeration to say that Charles had recruited him. He had recruited himself, more or less, which was often the way; you had to be there to catch the falling apple. 'He can't still be working for us, surely? And cyber security was never his field, was it?'

'No but it was his brother's field. May still be. He had an amateur interest and was beginning to get good stuff from his brother – without the brother realising – at about the time you left the case. You might even have reported some of it. It expanded exponentially afterwards and became his main contribution. It continued after his defection.'

'How? Surely, the Russians—'

'The Russians don't know he's here. Or didn't. They may now. Nor did or does his brother. You remember how the exfiltration went at the time?'

Charles remembered. It was a rush job after the Berlin Wall came down and while the Soviet empire was disintegrating. Fortunately, it was well rehearsed and a new identity including bank accounts, driving licence, passport and employment, built up over years in the UK, was waiting for Viktor to flesh it out.

The first indication of trouble was when Viktor was reassigned within the SVR, as the KGB was by then called. He had been working in a counter-espionage department that looked for spies within the Russian bureaucracy, a priceless position for MI6 and even more so for the CIA, until abruptly moved to processing intelligence reports from the Middle East. This was a post normally occupied by no-hopers, by people without patronage or by those under punishment. Then his father-in-law, an influential apparatchik, fell out with the new ruling clique over the ownership of a bank. He escaped prison only by keeping quiet and retiring to the rented family dacha in Latvia, leaving his wife in Moscow. Finally, Viktor's wife decided she would no longer tolerate his philandering and demanded a divorce.

Viktor used a dead letterbox in a Moscow suburb to trigger the exfiltration, announcing that his current mistress was coming with him. That entailed emergency clearance from a reluctant foreign secretary for the import of an unknown and possibly unreliable woman. At the last minute the mistress – fortunately still under the illusion that Viktor was proposing that they should run away to Latvia – declared that she couldn't leave Moscow, so Viktor travelled to Latvia alone.

His cover was that he was pleading with his father-in-law to help save his marriage. In fact, his father-in-law was interested only in Moscow gossip and having someone to shoot with in the forest and get drunk with in the evenings. The exfiltration was to have happened when Viktor notionally returned to Moscow. He and Charles would have rendezvoused and then crossed the Finnish border, Viktor posing as Charles's Polish business partner. He spoke Polish as a result of a Warsaw posting and the alias passport Charles carried for him was up to date with forged entry and exit stamps.

But the sudden death of his father-in-law – drunk and supine in an armchair, he hiccoughed twice and fell half out of it, dead – delayed everything. For the better, it turned out. Viktor returned to Moscow where, after risky communications with London, he retired from the SVR, putting it about that he and his wife were separating and that he was taking on the dacha. His wife was compensated for the loss of their SVR flat by moving with their two children to her mother's much larger one, content that the major part of Viktor's pension was sent to her monthly from his bank in Latvia. Viktor, so far as his wife and former employers were concerned, simply faded into wooded obscurity. The exfiltration proceeded as planned.

'Any more wives since he got here?' asked Charles.

'Probably but not his own. He's still married, anyway, and neither she nor his former employers know he's here. We think. They're still paying his pension.'

'That's incredible.'

'Incredibly useful, too, as Tim will tell you. His cryptologist brother works for the military bit of their signals outfit. Thinks Viktor's still in Latvia, goes and stays. We reinsert Viktor back for a couple of weeks and they gossip about the brother's work. He doesn't come over with the algorithms, of course, but Viktor's pretty mathematical and a bit of a computer geek with an amateur interest in cryptology, so he picks up a lot about directions of travel and recent access that makes Tim and the NSA happy bunnies. Luckily it's all very tightly held and wasn't betrayed by Snowden, the NSA defector. They play chess with each other on the Internet, Viktor and his brother. That's mainly how they keep in touch.'

'But surely his brother must be able to see from that—'

'We've fixed it so that Viktor's computer is routed through servers in the Baltics,' said Tim. 'Worked very well until the SIA interregnum, shall we call it, when defectors ceased to be looked after. Your old MI6 resettlement section was disbanded. So far as the new management was concerned, defectors had told all they knew, had their pay-offs, got their pensions and were on their own, left to themselves in this rather foreign country. Liberated and self-sustaining, they called it. Abandoned, in other words, with an emergency number to call but no regular point of contact or support. A lot of them need that, as you know.

'Point is, we lost contact with Viktor. His last case officer resigned after a spat with the SIA, lives with a dancer in Bangkok and is no longer vetted. We need someone to re-establish the relationship, get Viktor to see his brother and ferret out any gossip on these cyber attacks. It's not precisely his brother's area but he mixes in those circles and may know whether or not the Russians are doing it. He may even have an idea how. If he knows nothing we'll concentrate resources on the Chinese. At present we're having to look at them and the Russians.'

Operational involvement was not normally expected of a head of service, but to Charles it was the sound of a trumpet, a call to arms, an echo of youth. 'Where is Viktor?'

'He's your neighbour,' said Tim. 'Your about-to-be neighbour, anyway. He lives not far from the cottage you're renting in Sussex. We know all about that, you see.' They all laughed. 'We met your landlord-to-be recently, former colleague of yours, now an MP and serving on the Intelligence Services Committee.'

'No—'

'Jeremy Wheeler. Afraid so, Charles.' They laughed again, except for Angela who smiled.

'I'd no idea. Sarah's been dealing with the agents and I've never seen the contract.' He and Jeremy had joined the old MI6 together. They had never been close and whenever their paths intersected it had been to their mutual dissatisfaction, though they had never actually fallen out over anything. Charles shook his head in disbelief. 'And he's on the ISC already?'

'We had to brief them last week to ask them not to go too public about what's going on and we met him then. Seemed to think he'd got you in his power at last.'

'He doesn't know about Configure?'

'Not as far as we know.'

'Let me have Configure's contact details and I'll see him on Saturday when we go down to take over the cottage. Someone had better brief me on what I can say and what to ask him.'

The meeting broke up, with Angela rushing back to the Foreign Office after a hurried discussion with Tim about *Beowulf*, which Charles only half heard and didn't at all understand. Anglo-Saxon verse seemed a surprising mutual interest, but Whitehall had always been full of people with surprising interests.

Michael Dunton touched his elbow. 'One other surprise for you. News of another old friend of yours. Nothing to do with what we've been talking about. Peter Tew, aka Stoat.'

'Not out already, surely?'

'Freed himself. Walked out of the open prison he was in, a sort of halfway house for those coming up for release. Strange thing was, he hadn't long to go, thanks to the last government's wizard wheeze of releasing everyone early. Must be mad.'

'He was never mad, unless there was method in it. But he was bitter.' He could still picture Peter's face in the dock as he stared across the court at Charles and Frank Heathfield, two of the four who had unmasked him. His grey eyes, so often playful, had rested on Charles's for a long unforgiving moment. They had been friends, not just colleagues, had toured the eastern states of the US together when Peter was in New York and Charles was visiting CIA headquarters at Langley. It later turned out that that was when Peter had begun spying for the Russians. Charles had talked freely about what he'd learned at Langley.

'Trouble is, he must still know stuff,' said Michael. 'And

he never told us all he'd passed, anyway, not once he'd decided to clam up. Presumably he'll try and make a bolt for Russia but would he really want to spend the rest of his life there, like George Blake? Never believed in the cause, anyway, did he? Rather more personal motivation, wasn't it? If they'd have him now.'

'They'd have him, they'd make a great thing of it, show the world they always look after their own. I'm not sure it was purely personal for Peter, anyway. There was a dollop of ideology in the mixture.'

'Maybe escaping was a spur of the moment thing and now he doesn't know what to do with himself.'

Charles shook his head. 'He was a calculator, Peter, it wouldn't have been spontaneous. I don't think most of us realised how much his life had to be calculation in those days, given what he was and the way things were. He should have stayed in banking, with his beloved statistics. He loved numbers.'

'That's what he did before he joined your lot?'

'He thought spying would be more interesting than making a fortune. Which he'd already done, anyway. He was right, it was. Just a bit too interesting. Couldn't stop doing it.'

'Well, life is going to be pretty different for him now, wherever he is. Whatever he calculates.' They were in the corridor leading to the Whitehall entrance. 'Bloody nuisance from our point of view. It's police and probation business really, of course, but we're going to have to go back through all the files for clues as to where he might go or what he might do, who his friends were and all that. Last thing we need, historic espionage investigations taking people away from international terrorism. Not to mention all this cyber business. At least he's not involved in that. Next thing we know there'll be a terrorist bomb somewhere and we'll get blamed. Your identity must have been blown to the Russians by Stoat, of course? Stoat Red, as we used to say.'

Stoat, strictly speaking the code name for the investigation into Peter which had inevitably come to stand for him, had confessed to identifying Charles and many others in MI6 to the Russians. He had also, when on remand, passed names and addresses to imprisoned IRA terrorists. 'As Red as it gets.'

4

The next morning Charles paused before addressing the faces around the boardroom table. His five directors, three men and two women, had all been appointed before him. They were in their forties or fifties and each of the men was bald. He had to stop himself touching his own hair for reassurance.

Simon Aldington was director of operations. Charles remembered him from the old MI6 as a youthful head of station in Cairo who had since risen through the ranks of the SIA, gaining weight and losing hair. Clive Thatcham was director of requirements, moved from the Foreign Office for his last job before retirement with a compensating promotion. Melissa Carron was another SIA survivor, formerly a career MI5 officer and now director of security. He had known her slightly in her MI5 days as pedantic and particular, not overly imaginative or clever, but particularity was a virtue in security. Stephen Avery, director of cyber and technical support and also on his last posting, had been brought in from GCHQ. Michelle Blakeney, director of human resources, was the only one to have contacted Charles before the meeting, emailing him her CV and explaining that she had been brought in from industry in order to professionalise what she called 'the antique and amateur human resources structures and practices that had previously characterised the agency'.

At the end of the table, facing Charles, was Elaine, his private secretary, recently assistant private secretary to Angela Wilson and posted, he suspected, to keep an eye on him and the new MI6. But anyone who survived working for Angela would also be good. She was athletic-looking with quick, intelligent features and an obliging manner.

'Welcome to Croydon,' he said. They smiled. At that moment a power-drill started in a nearby office. They laughed. 'We won't complain if there are gaps in the minutes,' he told Elaine, 'or perhaps no minutes at all.'

Elaine stood. 'I'll just see if I can—' She hurried out.

The boardroom was in the corner of the fourth floor of the 1960s block, which was to have been refurbished before they moved in. The continuing works were described as 'making good' the trunking routes for the IT system. It was running late because of delays in security clearance for the workers and frequent power cuts. The emergency generators were installed but not yet working.

The drilling stopped and Elaine returned. 'They're going to find somewhere else to drill.'

'Well done.' Charles turned to Stephen Avery. 'We may as well start with a progress report on the move here, which I gather you had wished upon you.'

'A cup I prayed would pass from my lips but to no avail.' Stephen smiled. 'Naturally, it's all taking longer and costing more than anticipated. No surprises there. The main thing now is not just when it's going to work but whether. We've had to change the IT specifications more than once in view of all these recent hacking attacks but our internal system works okay, more or less. The problem is we've still got no secure way of communicating with OGDs – other government departments. We're having to rely on the GSN, the government secure network. Which, as everyone knows, is not really secure.'

'So we can't email CX reports to our customers?' asked Charles. 'What about comms with our overseas stations?'

'They're all right because they're on our own system. It's where we link with outsiders that we have problems. We can do it but not securely.'

'How are we getting our reports out?'

'We're not,' said Clive Thatcham, director of requirements. 'Not since the last of the old SIA reports went out the week before last. We're getting them in from the stations but we're sitting on them until we've got secure comms. Not ideal, I agree. Quite appalling, in fact. But par for the course where things technical are concerned.' He sounded almost gratified.

'It's worse than appalling. It's unacceptable.' Charles stared at Clive, aware of the stiffening around the table. Most of what he had achieved in life he had achieved by being pleasant, being reasonable, but he was conscious now that he had to be, if not unpleasant – invariably counterproductive in Whitehall – then at least unreasonable. Unreasonably but justifiably demanding. He had hoped for a board that was keen, collegiate and cooperative. So far, it had the smell of complacency.

'How many reports are we sitting on?'

Clive shrugged, as if it weren't really anything to do with him. 'Well, I couldn't say exactly, of course. We wouldn't have issued them all anyway. Maybe not most of them. So many don't really come up to the mark, if we're honest with ourselves. Fall into the "interesting if true" category. Of the good ones – well, a dozen or so, maybe.'

'Could you find out?'

'Of course.'

'Now, if you please.'

For a moment Clive didn't move. Then he got up and left the room.

Charles turned to Simon Aldington, director of operations. Like the rest now, he looked sombre. 'That doesn't sound very many. How many stations do we have?'

Simon pursed his lips. He had become bloated since his days as an energetic head of station and his complexion had coarsened. 'Well, about – I would say – probably a couple of dozen worldwide.'

'You don't know?'

'I could find out, if you like.'

'Do.'

Simon also left the room. The meeting was beginning to resemble an Agatha Christie novel, thought Charles. The body would be next. Those remaining looked chastened. It was not going as he had intended. He would not backtrack but neither did he want to bully. 'An intelligence service that can't issue reports may as well not exist,' he said. 'If we go for too long without reporting, the government will cease to miss it and conclude it doesn't need us anyway. We must get those reports out this week even if it means taking them round ourselves.'

That was what happened. When the two directors returned with their figures Charles asked them to organise a daily delivery system of paper copies, which had been the norm before Whitehall went over to electronic systems. Granted, there had been more drivers and cars then and MI6 was just over the river in Lambeth, not Croydon; granted, too, there were rules about the numbers of people required for carrying top-secret material in public places and the kinds of security container required. These would all have to be complied with.

'It will be cumbersome, costly and inconvenient and if not enough bodies can be found then we – I mean us, the board – will set an example by taking them ourselves. I was in the Cabinet Office this morning and will have to go to the Foreign Office tomorrow afternoon so if there are any urgent reports overnight, Clive, I could take them with me. Not on the train, of course. I'll need a car and driver.'

'There may be health and safety implications,' said Michelle Blakeney, HR director.

Charles stared. She didn't seem to be joking. 'Let me know if you find any. Meanwhile, we start this afternoon.'

He was about to ask whether there was any other business when a mobile phone rang. 'Sorry,' said Melissa Carron, director of security. She scrabbled in her handbag and silenced the phone, then stared for some seconds at the screen.

'Which reminds me,' said Charles. 'Mobiles. I noticed one

or two people had them on their desks this morning. I thought we weren't supposed to bring them into the building? That we had to lock them in those special cages downstairs?'

'The ones you saw would have been HMG people – higher management group,' said Melissa. 'They're issued with office mobiles, like us. All senior managers in the SIA had them.'

Charles had been hoping to end the meeting on a conciliatory note. 'Why don't junior staff have them?'

Melissa looked at him through her heavy-framed glasses, irritation and puzzlement contending in her enlarged eyes. 'Because of the security threat. Because of how they can be turned into microphones, cameras, tracking devices, quite apart from normal call interception. You must remember from your previous service what we can do with them – identify all the members of a group from one number, travel patterns, contacts, everything. And phones have got more sophisticated since you left the old MI6, and the more sophisticated they are, the more we can do with them. And if we can do it, others can.'

She spoke carefully as if explaining to someone of limited understanding.

'I myself am fully satisfied that there's a strong security case for not allowing mobiles into the office, apart from the

HMG,' she continued. 'It's what we did in the SIA, it's what MI5 do, it's what we should do. I don't think anyone around this table would disagree with that.' She looked at the others.

Charles waited to see if anyone wanted to make the obvious point. No-one did. He too spoke slowly, trying not to sound confrontational. 'So why are we allowed them? Is a phone any less of a threat because someone in HMG or on the board has it? More, surely.'

He wondered whether he was on the verge of provoking a bureaucratic insurrection and becoming the shortest-serving C on record. He wondered too whether Angela Wilson and George Greene would back him up. They wouldn't want a fuss, especially if it became public.

Michelle Blakeney leaned forward, her fingers resting on the closed laptop before her. It was the first time Charles had noticed it. No-one else had one. Laptops, too, he thought. But that could wait.

'Of course, there's no denying that mobiles are a threat,' she said, sounding as if it were an effort to remain polite. 'But in themselves they're neutral. It's the user who determines whether or not they are actually threatening. As with firearms. If we trust the people who have them – and I hope we can trust ourselves and the HMG in general, otherwise we shouldn't be here – then they shouldn't be a threat. In fact, for many people in the outside world, as I well know – people we have to influence and communicate with – it would look very odd indeed if we didn't have them. It would be hard to explain and would make us look corporately quaint and out of touch.'

'Also, from an operational point of view, case officers need them for agent contacts,' said Simon Aldington. 'Especially if they're under natural cover as business people or whatever. It would be frankly incredible – unworkable – for them not to have them.'

'And people do have family responsibilities,' said Melissa. 'Arrangements with children and childminders and so on. Some of us, anyway.'

Charles looked at Clive Thatcham and Stephen Avery. They may as well all have their say now. 'Any other views?'

'Michelle makes a good point,' said Clive. 'If we want to be taken seriously within Whitehall and beyond we have to be like the people we work for. Ministers carry mobiles, everybody does. We can't afford to look like some furry little creature that hides in the undergrowth and has to be dragged blinking into the sunlight of the modern world.'

Stephen was doodling, eyes downcast. 'Everything that's been said so far is true. True – but.' When he looked up his eyes took in everyone. 'More than one but. The first is that the phone itself is the danger. It's not like a gun. Its user may be entirely trustworthy and innocent but the phone itself may have been tampered with or accessed remotely without the user knowing. If it is like a gun it's one that someone else can aim and fire without your having any control over it, or even knowing they've done it.' He put down his pen and clasped his hands. 'The second but is that where I come from, GCHQ, this would not be tolerated for a moment. If it were, the Americans – the NSA – would suspend sharing stuff with us. We know only too well the potential for any electronic device to be turned into something apart from what it's meant for. We know it because we do it. I was frankly astonished when I first went to the old SIA head office and found people with mobiles on their desks. And then here. The third but – last one, I promise – is, where do they come from? Who, physically, supplied these mobiles?'

All except Melissa shrugged or shook their heads. 'I don't know, I'm sure,' she said, as if she had been unreasonably accused. 'Presumably the supplier who supplies our operational phones. They've always been perfectly reliable.'

'Perhaps you could enquire,' said Charles.

'Meanwhile, I'm afraid I have to agree with Charles on this,' said Stephen, who had picked up his pen and was doodling again. 'Mobiles are bad news.'

'I think we'll have to do something about it,' said Charles. 'We'll return to the subject.'

They broke up with a shuffling of chairs and no lightening of the atmosphere. Charles had been conscious throughout of how much he was keeping back from them: the fact that they were penetrated, that GCHQ were secretly monitoring their systems, that he was going to recontact Viktor, the very existence of Viktor, all the concerns of COFE. He had thought he could tell them about Peter Tew, warning that anyone who had known him should report contact, but decided to turn it into a fence-mending exercise by offering it to Melissa to announce to the Office as a whole, to make the issue hers. However, she left the room first, closing her bag with a snap, followed by Michelle with her laptop. He would have to ring her later. Elaine, still finishing her notes at the end of the table, was the last to stand. 'Come and chat about the minutes before you do them,' Charles told her.

His office was occupied by workmen.

'They're just connecting some trunking,' said Elaine. 'They said they'll only be another ten minutes.'

'Let's go to the canteen.'

'There's quite a list of things we need to discuss.'

'Bring it.'

They were early and there were not many people. They

took curries and salads to a table in the far corner. 'I suppose this will have to close when they get round to refurbishing it,' said Charles.

'It's been done. Finished two weeks ago.'

She laughed, which he was glad to see. She had with her a list of impending visits from Dutch, American, French, Danish, South African, Indian and Singaporean heads of liaison services, with a longer list of calls he had to make in Whitehall and of cases into which he had to be indoctrinated. There were also issues arising from his previous service, adjustments to his MI6 pension, and a photograph swipe-card pass to be arranged. Elaine had had to escort him in that morning on a visitor's pass. There were also alias identities, including passports, to be set up for when he visited liaisons overseas. He queried this. 'I was blown decades ago, I've been global Red for years. Anyone who Googles me can see what I was and now that what I am is being publicly announced what's the point in hiding it?'

'Security department ruling.' One of many, I'm afraid. Because of the public announcement, you're an obvious terrorist target if you appear on any flight manifest in your own name.'

He thought he'd left all that behind him when he ceased operational work. 'What if I'm prepared to accept the risk?'

'You'd be accepting it for everyone else on the flight, too.'

He held up his hands. 'Okay, just make sure my new names are easily said and spelt. No Cholmondelys.'

'Believe it or not, the first one they've come up with is Goodenough.'

'But what is it?'

She laughed again. But he still felt she was watchful, as if he might explode. He knew from having been one that you had to have complete trust in your private secretary, even if she were reporting back – ad hoc and informally, of course – to Angela Wilson. 'That was a surprise, that meeting this morning,' he said. 'I hadn't expected it to turn out like that.'

'I don't think they did, either.'

'Was I unreasonable in making them go and get those figures?'

She hesitated. 'You were quite firm. Particular. They were a bit complacent. Now they know not to be.'

If things became difficult she could be a useful intermediary between him and the board. 'When you write up the minutes, just say that the directors produced the relevant figures. Don't say they were asked and didn't know them. On mobile phones, just say that a more restrictive policy is under consideration and that DS – director of security – will announce and implement any changes in due course.'

She looked relieved. 'I think they were all a bit taken aback by that.'

'Not as much as I was to see people with phones all over the place. And laptops – Michelle had hers on the desk and referred to it. Though I suppose that's different if they're just locked into our own system.'

A mobile rang. After a moment's puzzlement he groped in his jacket pocket, switched it off and pushed it across the table. 'Life. One damn thing after another. Don't give it back until I leave the building'.

5

Sarah was awoken early on the Saturday morning by the bleep of a text but couldn't remember where she had left her mobile. She stared at the ceiling while the components of the present reassembled themselves. She had dreamt a kaleidoscope of the Brussels apartment she had shared with Nigel, inhabited in her dream by Miss Sage, the red-faced, white-haired headmistress of her primary school. Miss Sage had lost her wire-haired fox terrier and they were searching a green Morris Minor belonging to the Foreign Secretary, who was about to return and drive away.

The present cohered into the fact of Charles sleeping beside her, her husband after all these years, as strange as any dream. They were in their new house in Westminster, possibly with horrors hidden beneath the new paintwork but nothing that pressingly needed doing. They were properly in now and just needed to make it a home. Books were the problem, boxes and boxes of them stacked in every room. There just wasn't the wall space, no matter how ingenious they were with new shelving. They would have to get someone in for that; it was already apparent that it would be no good relying on Charles.

And it was Saturday, so no work, though she would have to go in for an hour or two on Sunday. Today they were to drive to Sussex to pick up the keys and formally take over the rented cottage. Some of the books would go there, of course. She looked forward to that, but then remembered that there was no silver lining without a cloud. They were to have dinner with the landlord, Jeremy Wheeler. She recalled him from when he worked with Nigel as a big, fat and boastful man with a surprisingly attractive – perhaps necessarily quiet – wife. What was her name? She'd have to ask Charles.

The invitation had come via Katya Chester. Sarah had demurred at first, pleading that the cottage was unfurnished and that they wouldn't want a late-night drive back to London after dinner. But they'd then been invited to stay the night, which would be even worse. The last thing either of them wanted at the moment was to spend the weekend as the guests of virtual strangers, tiptoeing around.

'We can't,' Charles said when she told him. 'No question. He's just wrangled his way onto the parliamentary Intelligence Services Committee. It'll be bad enough appearing before them with him preening himself as former colleague and now our landlord, without having spent cosy weekends with him. Wouldn't look good.'

'Could we not go at all, then? It would be much nicer not to but it's a bit awkward to say no when he knows we're down there and have the time.'

'We could say yes to dinner and spend the night at the cottage.'

'On what? The floor? It's completely unfurnished.' Charles's lack of domestic awareness could still surprise her. Already he seemed to treat the packing cases as permanent, sitting or putting things on them without any apparent thought of unpacking.

'I'll book a hotel, then.'

'That will look rather pointed.'

'It is, with reason. I'll explain to him.'

'And is it still up to me to get back to his Snow Queen secretary?'

'You do that and I'll do the hotel.'

Rather to her surprise, he did it without a reminder while she, gratifyingly, was able to leave a message for Katya without having to speak to her and be told once again that

Mr Mayakovsky was a very wealthy man and keen to meet her.

Sarah got up and found her phone on a packing case beneath a pile of Charles's pullovers. The text was from Katya Chester, confirming the arrangements and contact details for Jeremy and Wendy Wheeler. Wendy, of course, Wendy Wheeler. She must have been in love.

They drove down to Battle later that morning, a journey made leisurely by the A21. The polite young man in the letting agent's had the keys and remaining paperwork ready. 'Your landlord's almost next door. In the memorial hall, holding his monthly surgery. I'm sure he wouldn't mind if you dropped in. He seems anxious to meet you.'

'We'll be seeing him tonight,' said Sarah. 'He's invited us to dinner, which is very nice. We have his address but don't know where it is. It must be very near here, isn't it?'

'The Old Court House. Five minutes' walk. Up the high street and first right. A big house about a hundred and fifty yards on the left.' He grinned. 'Nicest property in the town. It must be – we sold it to him.'

The cottage was in Brightling, a hamlet high in the Weald about five or six miles out of town. It was a pretty stone cottage, about three hundred years old, with a tiled roof in need of attention.

'It's prettier than I remembered,' she said, as they stood

inside the gate. 'But this garden is going to take some work.'

'Not quite the Cotswold stone you're used to.'

'No but it's stone, which is good enough. And you can see the sea from that end bedroom.'

'Smaller than I remembered,' he said, pacing the tiled floor. 'Not much room for guests, which is good. Probably catches the wind in the winter, too, which is also good.'

'You can have it to yourself if you're going to be such a misery.'

Upstairs was cheerful and light. 'I think I could love it,' she said. 'So long as you keep it warm. I suppose that great open hearth downstairs is hideously inefficient?'

'Cosy on a winter's eve with the wind rattling the windows and the draughts whistling round your chilblained feet.'

'Any sign of chilblains and I'm back to London.'

They unpacked cleaning things, kitchen things and toiletries from her car then drove to the nearest pub for lunch. 'Remind me why you have to see this man,' she said.

Charles had exercised his prerogative as Chief to tell her about Viktor, who lived a few miles away.

'If he can help stop these wretched power cuts that would be a really good start for you, wouldn't it?' she said. 'Not that there've been any today, so far as we know. You must be having an effect already.'

75

'It goes wider than that. Whoever's doing it is getting into government systems.'

'Do I have to come? Is he expecting me?'

'Haven't been able to get hold of him. No answer from his phone. I've left messages. If he's not there I'll leave a note. But if he is, I'm sure he'd like to meet you. He likes attractive women.'

'Better not disappoint him, then. I'd sooner get on and clean the cottage.'

Promising he wouldn't be long, would either leave a note or stay just for tea, Charles set off for Bodiam in her car.

It was an easy drive, using her satnav. He didn't really approve of them, feeling he should always know where he was on ground and on map, but it meant he could think on the way. He began well enough, recalling his first meetings with Viktor in London, then the fallow period when Viktor was back in Moscow, then his re-emergence in Africa and confirmation that he was serious about spying for MI6. Finally, their last meeting in a palatial room in the Hotel Sacher, Vienna, while Charles was notionally attending one of those forgettable disarmament conferences. They had met earlier that day, and Charles was about to check out when Viktor triggered the signal for an emergency second meeting.

'I have twenty minutes,' he said, looking unusually pale

and serious. In those days he had a moustache. He was often jokey, usually at Charles's expense, but this time there was no joshing. 'There is a problem. Not a problem with me. With you. MI6 has a problem.'

In intelligence officer parlance this meant only one thing. 'Who?'

'I don't know. It's new, the case has just begun. Could he know about me? You must catch him before he finds out.'

They were standing facing each other. Charles crossed the room and locked the door. Viktor ignored his invitation to sit. Charles sat himself at the desk and tore a sheet from his notebook. The hard surface of the desk would not record the imprint of soft pencil. He pointed at the chair again. 'Sit down and tell me what you've heard.'

Viktor looked for a moment as if he might walk out. He glanced at his watch, then abruptly sat.

'Tell me,' repeated Charles.

Viktor stared at the portrait above the bed of a 1930s or '40s Sacher, a handsome woman wearing Austrian costume. He addressed her. 'There was a meeting two days ago in Prague of heads of services for all the Warsaw Pact. Marcus Wolf, the head of East German foreign intelligence, visited us today on the way back. He is an old friend of Guk, our Resident. They served together somewhere. When they were alone he congratulated Guk on the recent success against the British – those were his words. They were speaking in Guk's office outside the safe speech room. I heard them because I was still inside, collecting papers after our morning briefing, and they didn't know there was anyone there. It was careless of them. Guk should not have allowed Wolf into the Residency and Wolf should not have spoken like that outside the safe speech room. They were going to lunch with the ambassador and I stayed still till they had gone.'

'No names or dates or indications of where or how? Or what sort of success?'

'Of course, all of that. I was forgetting.' He waited for Charles to hold up his hands. 'No, but they continued to talk as they left the room. I didn't hear everything. I heard Guk ask, "He is definitely MI6?" Wolf said, "Yes, now. We know about him. Everything he's said checks out. A pity you've just been posted here, otherwise you could have become his core officer and got the glory." Guk asked, "Can he get over here again or are they running him in London?" I didn't hear Wolf's reply. He said something but they must have been going through the door then.'

Charles went back over it twice in the minutes remaining. Later, in the Vienna MI6 station, he sat at the cipher machine himself and sent a DEYOU – decipher yourself – telegram to C/Sovbloc in London, confirming that the main meeting had been successful and adding that there had been another to discuss possible developments. He would brief C/Sovbloc and DCIS – director of counter-intelligence and security – on return, knowing that the mention of DCIS would indicate that there was something serious. He then committed his notes to memory, shredded and incinerated them.

The investigation ran for months, an invisible stream beneath the thick ice with which Matthew Abrahams, DCIS, covered all his secret work. Charles was occasionally called in to be questioned or to comment, but otherwise never discussed the case with anyone or had any idea how it was progressing until summoned again to Matthew's spacious corner office in Century House.

He arrived to find Frank Heathfield also there, a tubby, florid, genial man with sandy hair going white. He had spent most of his career in security posts and now, on the verge of retirement, he was listed as DCIS/res – research. It was a usefully unspecific title.

Matthew waited for Charles to close the door. 'We've got coffee, knowing your habits.'

Frank smiled. 'Sign of a long meeting.'

Matthew gave a sinuous account of the investigation, illustrating the layered links of each element with movements of his slender hands. He and Charles had worked together more than once and Charles had learned never to expect to know everything that Matthew was involved in. But in this case, it soon became clear, he was being brought into the citadel.

'We started,' said Matthew, 'with the assumption that your friend reportedly accurately and that what he heard was true. It told us that someone from the Office has made contact with the Russians, that he – and it is a he – is now based in London, that he passed information that checked out and that all this happened not long before Guk arrived in Vienna. Guk arrived five months ago, so the contact was probably not long before that. We assume – a bit of a jump, this – that something had made the volunteer known to the Russians before he joined the Office. Or, at least, that they knew what he was doing before he joined. That seemed the most likely explanation for Wolf's saying that he was in MI6 'now'. Of course, meanings change in translation so it will be important, next time you meet your friend, to ask him to write it down in Russian. But meanwhile we'll keep it as a working assumption.'

The two of them, with no-one else informed apart from the Chief and Sonia, Matthew's secretary, had trawled through staff records and recent postings home. Personal files were scoured for indications of resentment or dis-affection. Using the assumption about 'now', they narrowed the search to four men whose previous employment might have brought them to Russian attention. One had transferred from MI5, one from the Army, one from the Foreign Office and one had visited Moscow as an academic.

'We thought they were unlikely to have identified the former MI5 officer because he was not exposed to the Russians,' said Matthew. 'Then we had information from the CIA to the effect that one of the subjects discussed at the Warsaw Pact heads of service meeting in Prague was new intelligence – you don't need to know what – that only a handful of people in this service know about. Of course, rather more than a handful of people in the CIA know about it too but for our purposes we checked all four candidates to see whether any of them were indoctrinated into that particular case. One of them is, the one who had visited Moscow as a student. We're going to interview him and I'd like you to sit on the panel because you know him quite well. If you feel awkward about it we won't include you. But if you are there it will make it trickier for him if he's hiding anything because he'll be fighting on two fronts, as it were.'

'What about MI5?' asked Charles. Security investigations were their responsibility, jealously guarded.

'They have been informed that we are examining the possibility of a suspected leak from within SIS. As soon as we are able to confirm that there really has been such a leak, they will be brought in.' Matthew held up his hand, his smile just detectable. 'Yes, I know. Don't say it. We've got away with it so far because of their usual reluctance to investigate espionage they haven't themselves uncovered. Any investigation threatens trouble for them, either because it's inconclusive and a waste of resources but might still come back to bite them later. Or because a spy is discovered and they get blamed for not having caught him earlier. So they've agreed we can continue to examine all four of those we think might be in the frame and let them know our thoughts soon. We are sending them the paperwork today. It'll be a week at least before they look at it if they work at their usual pace. They don't know we're going to interview anyone. And we – I – will be in serious trouble if it doesn't work.'

'Who is it?'

When Matthew named Peter Tew, Charles was conscious that they were studying him carefully. He had an immediate image of Peter's pale, intelligent features, his grey eyes often on the brink of laughter, his quick smile and ready perception. Trying to match the new image of Peter as traitor with the old of Peter as friend was like having a tracing that didn't fit the map. Yet, somehow, he was not surprised. There was much that was unknown about Peter, an uncharted interior. That was true of many people, of course, but with most there were myriad casual indications that the interior existed, suggesting what kind of country it was. In Peter's case, he realised as Matthew talked, there were none. The beach was all you saw, sunlit, entertaining, attractive, intended perhaps to forestall curiosity about the interior. Content with the superficiality of daily intercourse, Charles had never sought to explore.

'The interview is arranged. He believes it will be a routine personnel interview to discuss his next posting,' Matthew was saying. 'Meanwhile, we have discovered he is homosexual.'

Quite unexpectedly, that was a tracing that did fit the map. The Office was known for its attractive and talented women and Peter was popular with the girls, charming them, but he had no girlfriends. Unless you counted the one he used to mention – what was her name – Jane? Jenny? – who died of leukaemia. That was a long-standing relationship which had broken his heart, he implied, leaving you to conclude that it was difficult or impossible for him to consider another, yet. But no-one had ever met Jane, or Jenny. No-one had ever seen Peter's Marylebone flat. Now, as Matthew described how the FBI in New York, where Peter was serving, had come across him visiting clubs in drag and that since his return on leave in the last few days surveillance had seen him picking up young men in a noto-rious pub in Vauxhall, the tracing drew itself.

Charles recalled various minor incidents, remarks, tones, inflexions he never realised he had noticed. Peter's almost maternal solicitude when Charles went down with flu, the follow-up telephone calls, Peter's silences when people mentioned girls or sex, his abrupt and uncharacteristically brutal condemnation of someone who had been dismissed, allegedly on health grounds, as 'a flaming poofter'. And that lunch in another Vauxhall pub which they drifted into simply because neither knew it and which turned out to feature a striptease in the bar. A young black girl cavorted to loud music on a raised dais, thrusting herself into the faces of the men nearest her. The performance was more vigorous than seductive and Charles watched, he told himself, more through cultural curiosity than interest, let alone arousal, but Peter was disgusted. He backed away, muttering, 'Revolting. How can they?'

Afterwards the girl resumed her white bra and knickers and red shoes and walked amongst the crowd in the bar holding out a man's tweed cap for contributions. Every man put in something, including Charles, but Peter withdrew as if from contagion.

As they walked back to the office Charles remarked on the contrast between the girl as symbol and presumed object of desire while on the dais, and the same girl, minutes later and still provocatively clad, walking unmolested amongst the drinkers who threw their change into her cap and treated her with indifference or familial affection.

Peter wasn't interested. 'I can't – the proximity. It makes me almost physically sick,' he said, his eyes on the pavement. 'So vulgar, very vulgar.' He repeated the phrase softly to himself.

Like many of his generation, Charles had grown up unaware he knew any homosexuals. He never looked for it in anyone nor had any idea what to look for beyond theatrical camp. A couple of girlfriends had told him about affairs they had had with women but that, though erotically interesting, somehow didn't seem to count. Until quite late in his career homosexuality had been a bar to joining the Office because it disqualified anyone from being PV'd – positively vetted. The reason given was that it was a criminal offence in many countries and disapproved of in many more, rendering practitioners vulnerable to blackmail. There was also, no doubt, an unexamined assumption that homosexuals led more promiscuous lives and were less trustworthy; Burgess and Blunt cast long shadows. You could be a promiscuous and adulterous heterosexual so long as you didn't lie about it in vetting interviews and kept clear of women from communist countries; NATO and other

Western states were preferred. That was not too difficult – there were after all well over twenty NATO countries – though Charles mildly regretted having never been the target of a KGB honey-trap. He might have enjoyed being the object of seduction, watching the game being played before him.

'It means he lied in his vetting,' Matthew continued, 'which means his PV certificate can be withdrawn, possession of which is a condition of working here. So we can dismiss him immediately if we want, whether or not we can prove he is our man. But if he is a spy – and we believe he is – we want him in prison, not free to be debriefed by the Russians whenever they choose.'

'How strong is the evidence?'

'Nothing that would stand up in court. We need a confession.'

The interview was planned for the following week. It was essential that no-one suspected there was anything unusual going on, so Charles was to continue his current job but spend as much time out of hours as he wanted reading the papers in Matthew's or Frank Heathfield's office. It was then that he began to know Peter Tew in a way he never had before.

6

Tea with Viktor, without either tea or Viktor, took over three hours. Charles had to wait at the house and tell his story several times.

He paused now, before doing so again. He had already described his arrival twice, once to the young policeman who was first on the scene, then to the inspector, the woman in plain clothes who was interviewing him now. But that was in the garden where he had waited because it felt inappropriate to wait in the house. A house not his and where Viktor – assuming it was him – lay dead on the polished hall floor with no face and bits of his brain and skull splattered over the first few steps of the stairs. His hair had gone grey, it appeared from some of the larger bits.

Charles paused because he wanted to get it right, if this was to be a more formal statement. He was trying to be helpful although the inspector's manner made him feel more like a suspect than the witness who had found the body. The inspector was in her thirties, pale, thin-faced, with a beaky nose and an officious manner. Her short bleached-blonde hair was darkening at the roots. She looked tired. It was hard to feel she had much going for her; perhaps she liked her job, perhaps she was good at it. Her plain-clothes assistant was a younger man with dandruff and a plump pasty face that looked as if it needed washing. Long hours, late nights and shift work did no favours for either, Charles thought.

They were sitting at Viktor's dining table with notebooks open and no visible recording equipment.

'So,' continued the inspector, 'you say you were calling on Dr Viktor Klein, the owner, who was an old friend of yours but he didn't know you were coming. When did you last see him?'

'I'm not sure – over ten years ago.'

'Not a close friend, then?'

'Not in recent years.'

'And you say you were calling on him to tell him you are moving into the area?'

'Renting a cottage in Brightling, yes.'

'Can anyone vouch for that?'

'The landlord.'

'Who is?'

'The MP, Jeremy Wheeler. I'm not sure whether this is part of his constituency but he lives in Battle.'

They noted that, their expressions giving nothing away. 'What did Dr Klein do, exactly? He was foreign, wasn't he?'

'By origin, yes, but he was naturalised British many years ago. He was a scientist, not a medical doctor.' He knew only the outline of Viktor's post-defection identity and his new name, Klein. The police would have to be told the full story but it might leak less, or at least more slowly, if it came to them down their own chain of command, from their chief constable.

'Where did he work?' asked the man.

'I'm not sure he did. I think he was retired.'

A white van drew up on the pebble drive, joining the police cars. Two men got out and put on white overalls. A uniformed policeman, the alert young one who had been the first to arrive and who had turned pale at what Charles had shown him, walked towards the end of the drive with a reel of white-and-blue tape.

'And you say the door was ajar when you got here?' continued the woman.

He was fed up with having what he'd said played back to him as if implying disbelief, but didn't want to upset them.

He wanted them to succeed, more than they could know. 'Yes, I noticed straight away but I knocked a couple of times first, then I called out. When there was no answer I pushed the door open. Then I saw the body.'

'But you couldn't know for certain it was Dr Klein if you hadn't seen him for over ten years, could you?' said the younger one.

'I still don't, without a face to go by. It's an assumption we've all made.'

There were footsteps and voices in the hall and the sounds of equipment being set up. The mantel clock above the fireplace struck five. Accurate, according to Charles's watch. Typical of Viktor. It had struck the half-hour while he waited for the police. The longcase clock in the hall had stopped.

'And then you entered the house, you say?' continued the policeman. 'Despite the fact that you'd seen there was a body there. Why did you do that?'

'I entered because I'd seen the body, not despite it. Firstly, to see whether there was anything I could do—'

'But then you went all over the house. Why?'

'– and secondly to see if the killer was still here.'

'What would you have done if he had been?'

'Disarmed and arrested him.'

'We're not being funny, sir,' said the woman.

'Neither am I.'

He was but he stared back, as unsmiling as they were. For a moment he had thought it might be suicide. Seeing no weapon, he had tiptoed throughout the house, looking into each room. It was a good house, generous proportions, high ceilings, well but sparingly furnished, a bachelor's home, solid and comfortable, no frills.

'That was very dangerous,' said the inspector. 'You should have waited for us. It's our job to do that sort of thing.'

Yes, he thought, after a few hours, with a convoy of armed response vehicles, helicopters, dogs and a stand-off ending with the shooting of a gardener who turned up carrying a fork. Charles had seen enough of police overkill. Anyway, he'd been pretty sure the killer would not have hung around waiting to be caught. It looked too much like a contract killing for that.

'You might also have contaminated or destroyed forensic evidence,' continued the inspector. 'We'll have to ask you to show us exactly where you went and we'll need to take your fingerprints, DNA and samples of clothing. In order to eliminate you from our inquiries.'

Or include me if you possibly can and it looks like an easy conviction, he thought.

'Did you see anything suspicious?' asked the younger one. 'Anything strike you?'

This was more like it. 'Nothing at all except that the door was open. There were tyre tracks on the drive but I guess there always are on beach pebbles. I didn't see anyone driving away. There were vehicles in Bodiam, a bit of movement around the castle car park and the pub, but I don't remember passing any on this lane.' Especially not motorbikes, he nearly added. The contract killings he'd known of had been two-wheel jobs. But they'd all used pistols rather than sawn-off shotguns which, judging by the upper-body devastation, was the case here. 'No doubt you'll work out time of death from the body, but the grandfather clock in the hall might give you a rough idea. It's stopped at twenty past one.'

'You mean it was caught in the blast?'

'I don't think so, I didn't notice any damage. It's probably a thirty-hour clock and he would probably have wound it yesterday morning, but not today. Assuming he wound it in the mornings, that is. So as it's stopped at twenty past one that might suggest that he was killed between winding it first thing yesterday morning and failing to wind it first thing this morning. But your forensics will be more precise than that.'

'Unless it wasn't going at all.'

'Possibly, but he used to be meticulous about that sort of thing. His clocks would have worked. He liked mechanical things.' And gadgets of all sorts, he thought, recalling Viktor's mingled delight and frustration with the ingenious but far from faultless concealed cameras and recording devices Charles occasionally issued him with. The electronic revolution had been a particular pleasure and he used to enjoy taunting Charles for his ignorance.

'D'you know anything about Dr Klein's lifestyle?' asked the inspector. 'What he did with his time, what sort of reputation he had with neighbours or in the village?'

'I don't. Judging by the books and magazines in the office upstairs, he maintained his scientific interests. Three expensive-looking computers, too. He used to be keen on chess.' He did not add that one computer was still on and that he had touched it to see what was on screen, finding a chess game. Possibly with his brother. They could discover that for themselves.

'Spent some time up there, did you?' asked the man.

'Enough to make sure there were no assassins behind the curtains. Blinds, actually, in that room.' He paused as they scribbled. Their mingled interest and resentment were palpable. 'No photographs, though. No indications of family.' He couldn't remember how many children had resulted from Viktor's marriage and liaisons. Plainly, he hadn't wanted to advertise them in his new life. 'But it's clear he continued to enjoy classical music, particularly choral. Also flora and fauna, especially birds. Apart from those, the few paintings are copies of landscapes and seascapes. No portraits. Smoked cigarettes and cigars, as you can see.' He nodded at the ashtrays on the table and mantelpiece. 'A bit of a loner, perhaps, but not a hermit.'

The inspector stopped taking notes. 'Kind of you to give us your impressions, Mr Thoroughgood, but we have to judge by the evidence.'

He smiled, which he could see irritated her. 'My inferences – which is what I call them – are evidence-based. But you're right: I shouldn't romanticise or incorporate what I knew of him from years ago. You must draw your own conclusions.'

Her pale blue eyes were flat, lacking depth or expression. 'We will need to speak to you again. We'll want a more formal statement. We might also need to speak to your wife, who you say is at the cottage you're renting.'

'Who is at the cottage we're renting.'

'We'd also like to walk you round the house so you can show us where you went, if we can fix that with the forensics team.'

'Just to eliminate you from our inquiries,' added the man, with an attempt at menace.

It took time to fix. Charles stood in the doorway and was reprimanded by a man in white overalls when he put a foot into the hall. There were more police and vehicles now, including a senior uniformed officer who stared disapprovingly at him while listening to the inspector. Eventually the officer nodded, more white overalls were unloaded from the van and the younger detective brought some over to Charles.

'We can tour the house if we all wear these. Trouble is, we'll have to wait till they've finished with the first few steps of the stairs. Covered in bits.'

'There are other stairs off the kitchen.'

'Two lots of stairs?'

'Servants' stairs.'

They put on their thin but voluminous white suits in silence. Charles led them around the tangle of lights and wires in the hall. Three more white suits were kneeling over the corpse, concealing all but Viktor's splayed legs and hands. He remembered those hands from long ago, deftly disarming the booby-trapped Russian arms cache by the Suffolk coast. Viktor's slippers were leather-soled, probably Church's. Neither the young student he had first known nor, later, the young KGB officer, had such tastes. Viktor must have changed as he had prospered, firstly under communism, then under the cronyism that replaced it. But not everything about him had changed, judging by what Michael Dunton had said. His appetite for women was what had first brought him and Charles into professional association, when Viktor's rule-breaking made him a target for recruitment. His appetite had lasted, apparently. Neither had any conception of where that first dance would lead; certainly not to this.

Charles showed them how far he went into each room, indicating anything he might have touched, including the computer. 'No sign of theft. No hasty searching or ransacking.'

'We don't know nothing's missing,' said the inspector.

'True, but if anything is missing the murderer must have known exactly where to find it. He didn't need to search.'

The younger one made a note, the inspector said nothing. Only in the study room did their expressions betray interest. 'Jesus,' said the man, gazing at the bank of screens and computers.

A smaller room opening off was panelled with oak and furnished with bookshelves, a leather-topped desk and a wooden swivel chair, in contrast to the high-tech study.

'Lot of computer analysis for us here,' said the man, after glancing without interest at the scientific journals and well-worn leather address book on the desk.

Charles pointed at the address book. 'Worth looking at that, isn't it?' It might include Viktor's Office contact number, unless he kept that on his phone. That would lead them to the truth about him, if they weren't briefed first.

'We'll bag everything up,' said the inspector. 'Examine everything.' They went back to the study, staring at the screens and keyboards.

Charles unzipped the front of his suit. They looked at him as if he were about to pull a gun. 'Just ringing my wife again.' There was still a pleasing novelty about the phrase. He dangled the phone between his thumb and forefinger. 'Letting her know how things are going, how long I'm likely to be, find out when we're due out for dinner. Okay?' Sarah already knew what had happened because he'd rung her immediately after ringing the police.

'We may need to examine that phone,' the inspector said when he'd finished. 'And your car before you go.'

He proffered the phone. 'Take it.'

'Just give us the number for the time being.'

'Not much of a call history. It's my work phone. I haven't had it long.'

'What is your work?'

'I'm the head of the secret service. Chief of MI6.'

She stared. 'Perhaps you'd like to show us which other rooms you went in, sir.'

When they had finished the tour, his white suit was bagged and numbered and they followed him out to Sarah's car. He held out the keys. 'D'you want to search it?'

'Just open up, sir, if you don't mind.'

'Sawn-off shotguns in the boot?'

This time the inspector almost smiled but her assistant cocked his head on one side. 'If you don't mind my asking, sir, what makes you think it was a sawn-off shotgun that did it?'

Obliteration of face, disintegration of head, wide-open throat and ravaged shoulders suggest a close-range blast of lead or metal rather than bullets, he could have said. No pistol would do that sort of damage, nor an AK47 unless held and squirted like a hose for some time. A full-length shotgun would have produced a more concentrated blast.

'I watch too many films.'

They conducted a cursory search of the Golf and spent rather more time examining its tyres. 'Nearside front's a bit worn,' said the man.

'Thank you. I'll tell her.'

There was further delay while they moved the police vehicles blocking him in. The inspector repeated that they would want to talk to him again, adding, 'I must ask you not to discuss this incident with anyone else including your wife who we might want to interview later.'

'Of course not,' he lied.

He waved goodbye to the young constable in charge of the blue-and-white tape and drove back through Bodiam, past the castle and over the restored steam-train line to Tenterden. He drove slowly through the clear evening with a fading blue sky and high white puffy clouds. The car park by the castle was emptying, except for a couple of families lingering by the moat. He was trying to recall Auden's poem about Icarus plunging earthwards while a ship sails by, someone opens a window, someone else eats. Whatever happens, the lives of others go on. But without Viktor now. How could they have got to him? Someone must have access to Office systems, or access to someone who did. And the only people with an interest in killing Viktor were surely his former employers. They would have done it if they could – Putin had enacted a law during his first presidency legitimising the assassination of any who had offended the state – but they didn't know Viktor was here. They couldn't, surely. Nor did anyone else in MI6 now, apart from him. Only the members of COFE had access to that address, and perhaps one or two who worked for them. Meanwhile, Viktor, like Icarus, was falling and falling inside Charles's head, while the lives of others went on.

7

They were late for the Wheelers' dinner. Sarah's car was low on fuel and there wasn't time to fill up. Charles wasn't sure there'd be enough fuel to get back to the hotel and to a filling station in the morning. He had suggested they refill before leaving London but she hadn't stopped. She sensed he was suppressing criticism, which was almost as irritating as if he had kept on about it. Neither felt like going to a dinner party, each sensed they were unreasonable, neither wanted to say anything about it. They walked up the path to the Old Court House in silence.

'Not carrying, are you?' Jeremy Wheeler asked in a whisper, keeping Charles in the hall while Wendy showed Sarah in.

Charles hadn't heard the old euphemism for years.

Before he could reply, Jeremy slapped him on the shoulder and grinned.

'Just wondered whether your new status involved self-protection in these hazardous times. Didn't really think you were likely to be armed. How's it going? Feet under the desk yet?'

'One of them. Enjoying your new status?'

'Should've done it years ago. So refreshing to be able to do something for people instead of messing around playing spy games. Something grown-up at last. Glad I've left all that behind.' Jeremy's gift for gratuitous offence had not lessened with the years. Nor was it inhibited by any recollection of how hard he had striven to stay in the Office. He had put himself forward as chief before becoming a casualty of the reorganisation, failed, then resigned to stand for a safe seat in a by-election. 'Not sure the way government's going is to my taste. Never was one for compromise, as you know. Main task for now is to stop them cutting more than they have already. Unless of course I'm invited onto the ministerial ladder. Getting on the ISC to keep you lot in order is a start. Could happen, could well happen.' He nodded as if agreeing with something Charles had said. 'Frank Heathfield had political ambitions, too, did you know that? Somewhat to the right of Genghis Khan, of course. Never got a seat, so never got to the first rung. Too late now. You'd heard, had you?'

'Heard what?'

'Dead, found dead, at his home in Hampshire. Heart attack, I suppose. Not surprised. Did well to last as long as he did. Heavy smoker, of course.'

Charles remembered that Jeremy was always uncomfortable about death until he found a way to blame the victim. 'How did you hear?'

'One of the perks of being on the ISC. Plenty to read. You'd know too if you'd checked your office computer recently.' He patted Charles's shoulder again. 'Come and be introduced.'

Being late, they felt obliged to be effusive. They were introduced to a couple who turned out not to be a couple, the headmistress of a local private school and the widowed chairman of Jeremy's constituency party. Charles took to the headmistress, who had a round, good-natured face and seemed anxious to put people at their ease by taking an interest in anything that interested them. The constituency chairman, a short square man, began telling Sarah about his achievements as a county councillor. The others, who were a couple, comprised a tall man with a paunch who turned out to be the senior partner of the estate agency dealing with Jeremy's cottage, and his wife, a thin and anxious-looking woman who seemed content to say nothing. Wendy Wheeler appeared between intervals in the kitchen, managing a couple of sentences each time before disappearing without waiting for the answer. She had darkened her hair since Charles had last met her and this, with bright red lipstick and her taut, tanned face, made her look slightly overdone. But she was attractive and every time he met her he had to remind himself that there was no reason why Jeremy should not have an attractive wife.

Through long habit of not talking about what he did, he found himself asking the headmistress about the charitable status of private schools. His thoughts, though, were on Frank Heathfield. Frank had been on his mind because of the connection with Peter Tew and his interrogation. He had always liked him for his cheerful and unpretentious practicality. There was little of Genghis Khan about him, despite what Jeremy said. Matthew Abrahams had died over a year ago, and now Frank. That left Charles as the sole survivor of the Tew investigation, apart from Peter himself. Even Viktor, whose information had provoked it, was gone. Charles was becoming history.

He felt he ought to rescue Sarah but the headmistress was asking about their new house. He could guess from the angle of Sarah's head the feigned attentiveness that overlaid her exasperation and boredom as she endured the monologue. He caught a phrase about the old rate support grant compared with the iniquities of the new system. It was the other couple, Rodney and Elspeth, who came to the rescue by describing to Jeremy and – intermittently – Wendy the adventures of their journey.

'We would have come along the lane through Bodiam but it was closed by the police so we had to go all the way back and come down the A229 where there was an accident which held us up for ages. Police everywhere tonight.'

Everyone agreed that everyone drove too fast on the A229. It crossed the county border and the constituency chairman described the difficulty he had had in negotiating a speed limit on part of it. Charles said nothing about why the lane to Bodiam might be closed. Police would now be 'combing' – as the press would inevitably put it – the area for clues. They wouldn't find anything, if the killing was what he thought.

'Maybe it's because of the body they've found,' said Elspeth, her small tinkling voice cutting across the chairman in a rush of words as if released under pressure.

Jeremy's eyebrows arched. 'A body in Bodiam?'

'Yes, at the house at the Sandhurst end of the lane. You can't really see it from the road, the old rectory I think it was, at least it looked like it on the South East news.' Wide-eyed, she darted looks at everyone as if fearing attack.

'The house of the mad scientist,' said Rodney. 'German or Polish or whatever. No idea whether he's actually mad or not but he's definitely foreign. We handled the sale a few years ago. Polite man, very polite. Lives on his own.'

Wendy paused in the act of handing round nibbles. Jeremy's eyebrows arched again. 'Dr Klein? We know him.' He looked at his wife. 'We know him well. It really is him, is it?'

'I don't know,' said Elspeth. 'They just said a body—'

'Murder or suicide?'

'– with gunshot wounds.'

Jeremy turned to Charles. 'Never a dull moment in this constituency, you see. Well, he wasn't quite in it but not far out. Would have been under the old boundaries.'

The chairman described the redrawing of the boundaries. Rodney talked about a farmer who had shot himself the year before. Wendy disappeared again into the kitchen. Charles was aware of Sarah looking at him. If he said nothing and it later came out not only that he had known the man they called Dr Klein but that he had found the body, it would look as if he was hiding something. Which he was, of course. But if he said something it might provoke awkward questions. Better that than more awkward questions later.

'I knew him too,' he said. 'In fact, I called on him this afternoon. I found the body and rang the police.'

Wendy reappeared from the kitchen. 'You found him? You actually saw him?'

'I saw a body. I couldn't confirm whose it was. It was years since I'd seen Viktor Klein.'

'Wasn't one of ours, was he?' asked Jeremy, in a lowered voice everyone could hear.

Jeremy had never known about the case. It used to be one of his complaints that he was never indoctrinated into any Sovbloc cases and the obvious answer – that he had never been involved with any – failed to satisfy him. He should have known better than to ask but Charles had anticipated he would. 'We'd known each other since Oxford,' he went on, ignoring Jeremy's question and working on the principle of adhering to the truth where possible. 'Then we lost contact, then met up again later. I had his address so thought I'd call to let him know we were moving into the area.'

'Do the police think the body was his?' asked Wendy.

'I think they do, yes.'

'But why – who – was it a robbery?'

'I don't know. I guess they'll have to search the house, see what's missing.'

'There was a contract killing at Cripps Corner a few years ago,' said Jeremy. 'Chap on a motorbike shot the driver of a Mercedes on his way to work. Drugs killing, they thought. Not sure it's ever been cleared up.'

'Bound to be someone who knew him,' said the constituency chairman. 'Murders are usually committed by
family members or by someone the victim knows well.
Probably find an ex-wife or something is behind it. Would
be if mine was anything to go by.' He laughed.

'Are there any ex-wives?' asked Jeremy.

No-one answered. Wendy disappeared again into the
kitchen.

The subject would not have lasted through dinner but for
Jeremy's intermittent resumptions. 'Can't say I took to him
myself,' he said, with his mouth full of stroganoff. 'Klein, I
mean. Arrogant, bit too pleased with himself. I got on with
him, of course. You have to in my job. Wasn't difficult.' He
swallowed. 'Wendy had more time for him than I did,
didn't you, darling?'

Wendy, seated between Charles and Rodney, replied
without looking up from her plate. 'I liked him.'

Jeremy turned to Charles. 'What was he, exactly –
German or Polish or what? And what did he do, who did
he work for, what kind of scientist was he?'

'Bit of a mixture, born in one country, parents from
another, brought up in a third, can't remember precisely.
He wasn't a practising scientist though he had a doctorate
in physics. I think he was more concerned with the admin-
istration of science, that sort of thing.'

'Cern in Switzerland,' said Wendy. 'He told me he worked at Cern on that atomic particle thing.'

'I think he did, yes.' So that was the local version of Viktor's cover story. He had probably visited Cern and could describe it. 'More as a science bureaucrat than an actual scientist.'

'But really nothing to do with the Office, then?' continued Jeremy, adding, proprietorially and for the benefit of all, 'Charles is the new head of my old service.'

'No, not one of us.' The lie direct was better than public equivocation. As a member of the ISC, Jeremy would have to be told later, and told to shut up.

Dinner was the ritual three courses plus cheese. There were long intervals as Wendy lingered, listening to talk of house prices and school and university fees but contributing as little as she ate. Jeremy held forth on what the country needed, the inexplicable inability of all previous governments to take necessary measures and his hopes for this one now that he and a few like-minded souls were there to hold the prime ministerial nose to the grindstone.

'It's our only hope for a truly compassionate society, a society that's both caring and creditworthy. There's nothing incompatible about those three Cs. Indeed, it's our task to render them compatible.' A year in Parliament and he was already sounding like something he'd written, thought

Charles, addressing people as if they were a public meeting. Though perhaps he always had. It did at least prompt Wendy to get up and offer tea and coffee.

It was after midnight and as they balanced cups and saucers in the drawing room, trying not to look anxious to hurry away, Jeremy caught Charles's eye and lugubriously inclined his head towards the door. Charles followed him into the hall as the former constituency chairman pulled his chair closer to Sarah's.

'Other thing that popped up on my screen,' said Jeremy in his theatrical undertone, 'is the news about your old friend Peter Tew.'

'Has he made the news, then?'

'Not the news, our news. Come and see.'

His white-panelled study was on the other side of the hall. On the sparse and tidy desk – Jeremy had always been meticulously and somehow incongruously tidy – was an open laptop. Jeremy tapped a key and a chess game came up. 'Just get rid of this. My opponent's move. Probably won't make it till tomorrow now. Very relaxed games, I usually have with this one.'

'Who is it?'

'Calls himself Mintoff. Probably Maltese. Remember Dom Mintoff, the troublesome Maltese premier? I've about a dozen anonymous chess friends. Most of us use names with some personal connection.' The chessboard disappeared as he tapped the keys.

'I'd forgotten you played. Viktor Klein played computer chess. Couldn't be him, could it?'

Jeremy shook his head. 'Could be anyone anywhere. You don't know unless they tell you.'

Jeremy had been good at chess, Charles now remembered, a solid county player and untypically quiet about it. Perhaps he thought chess wasn't smart or perhaps he was one of those who took whatever they were good at for granted and boasted only about what they wanted to be good at but weren't. Espionage, in Jeremy's case. 'What name do you use?'

'Isaac Newton.'

'Of course.'

A familiar-looking script and format came up on the screen. Headed 'Intcom News in Brief', it comprised a dozen or so items of non-sensitive news that concerned or originated from the intelligence community. The brief report of Peter Tew's escape was item four, preceded by recruitment figures for women and ethnic minorities across the three agencies and succeeded by the announcement of a football competition.

'This isn't an Office computer, is it? You're not still on the system?'

'No, no, don't worry. I'm not privy to all your secrets. Not that I'd want to be. They're mostly in the news two days later anyway.' He patted Charles's shoulder again. 'Although, yes, it is actually an Office laptop. Everyone on the ISC has one now for accessing privileged but not really secret stuff about all three agencies – staffing, structures, obituaries, honours and awards, numbers of submissions put up, that sort of thing. This is my old one, actually, I just hung on to it when I left but all the other members have been issued with one. One of your predecessor's ideas, part of the open government agenda – though I may say I had no small part in getting him to do it. We can't get into your operational or reporting systems, of course. Absolute fire-wall. Just as there is between my personal stuff and access to Intcom on this. Says here, look, he escaped from an open prison. You knew him quite well, didn't you?'

'Not as well as I thought, it turned out.'

Further down the list was the announcement of the death of Frank Heathfield, obituary to follow. 'Seems everyone you knew goes missing, dies or gets killed,' continued Jeremy. 'Not to mention your marital predecessor, of course. Odd to see Sarah with you. At least she's survived – so far.' He laughed.

'And you,' said Charles.

There were prolonged and exaggerated farewells, then

relieved silence in the car. He didn't allow himself to worry about the fuel. It was too late, anyway. They'd either make it or they wouldn't. Sarah had offered to drive but he'd drunk little and wanted distraction from a small but ominous stream of thought.

Eventually she sighed. 'I suppose we'll have to have them back.'

'Sure it's too late to rent somewhere else?'

'Jeremy will still be on your committee. Did you hear what he said about your friend just before we left? You'd gone to the loo, I think. He said Dr Klein wouldn't be a social loss because he wasn't very sociable, didn't repay hospitality, but it would be good news for Rodney because he'd presumably end up selling the house again unless there were heirs no-one knew about. Then he looked at Wendy and said, "No little Kleins running around. There won't be now, anyway. Something to be grateful for." She didn't say anything but she looked upset.'

'Wouldn't put it past Viktor to have something going with Wendy.'

'I don't know what he meant but it jarred. Struck me as odd. She's not that attractive, is she?'

'Not bad. Wouldn't need to be for Viktor, anyway. She's a woman.'

'D'you really think so, with that funny little mouth?

Makes her face look squashed. Perhaps Jeremy murdered him. Crime of passion.'

Not for the first time, Charles was struck by the knack women had of making other women less attractive. He would never now be able to look at Wendy without thinking of her face as squashed from the sides. 'But Jeremy – I can't get over what's happened to him. A lesson in how prats may prosper. Pratishness doesn't seem to be any bar to progress.'

'I thought you were past puzzling at the progress of prats.' She yawned. 'How many more Ps can you get into a sentence?'

'Pissed prats.'

'I meant to ask Jeremy about his glamorous Russian-American assistant who wants me to handle her conveyancing but with all this Dr Klein business I clean forgot.'

'I think that was the turning to our hotel.'

While Sarah was in the bathroom Charles rang the duty officer whom he knew would be spending the night in two scruffy top-floor rooms in Croydon. The question he asked did not need answering urgently and was probably – almost certainly, he thought – a red herring. 'Tomorrow will do,' he told him. 'Or Monday. Whenever's convenient.'

But he slept better for having asked it.

8

The doorman at Sarah's office seemed pleased to have something to relieve the Sunday tedium.

'Your clients rang earlier to see whether you would be in, Ms Bourne.' Everyone in her working world knew her by her maiden name. 'I said you were expected and they said they would be along in about – let me see' – he looked at his record-book – 'about ten minutes.'

'Clients? Which clients?'

'A Ms Katya Chester and a Mr Mayakovsky. American, by the sound of it. The lady.'

Sarah dumped her bag on her desk hard enough to shake the computer screen. With the sudden demand for billing and a long-running commercial property deal at London Bridge going critical, as her managing partner put it, she had more than enough to catch up on without the Snow

Queen and her Russian sugar-daddy. She had no mobile or home number for Katya Chester and her House of Commons office number was, unsurprisingly, unanswered. She felt like telling the doorman to say she was in a meeting all morning but she'd then have to see them another time and if Katya complained to Jeremy it might make things difficult in Sussex or for Charles at work. So she would see them, but they'd pay through the nose for every minute.

This time Katya Chester was even taller in platform shoes, with tight jeans and a tight white T-shirt. She towered above Mr Mayakovsky who was shorter than Sarah and stocky, wearing a blue suit, shirt and tie. His round face was tanned and his thinning brown hair was brushed straight back from his forehead. He had pale blue eyes, three large gold rings on his fingers and a handshake that was disconcertingly limp and passive, as if what his hand did was nothing to do with him. Or as if he was indifferent to whomever he met.

'It is so very kind of you to see us,' said Katya, with a fusillade of smiles. 'Especially during your weekend when you are so busy, I know. We shall be very brief but it is very important that we progress certain transactions this week as Mr Mayakovsky will be happy to explain. I understand you had a very nice dinner yesterday. Mr Wheeler was very pleased to meet you again.'

'You've spoken to him already?'

'Someone he knew has unfortunately been murdered and it may be in the papers. The victim was a scientist and lived alone and Mr Wheeler asked me to prepare statements for the press.'

'You must let me have your telephone numbers. I have only your office one.'

'Yes, and I must give you Mr Mayakovsky's too?' She glanced at Mr Mayakovsky, who nodded.

Mr Mayakovsky either didn't know his number or didn't care to be seen as someone who had to bother about that sort of thing. He seemed content for Katya to act as his secretary. Katya then repeated everything that had been said before about her house purchase. Sarah interrupted to say that there was nothing more to be done pending responses from the Land Agency. She strove at first not to let her irritation show, then decided she didn't care.

'Thank you, I think we've said all that can be said now. Is there anything else?' She looked at Mr Mayakovsky, who was staring past her out of the window.

He turned to Sarah, without alacrity. 'I should like you kindly to transact my property business.' His English was slow and heavily accented.

'What is your property business?'

Katya opened her handbag and handed Sarah a sheet of

Ritz notepaper with a handwritten list of about a dozen properties, all in Knightsbridge or Belgravia.

'I wish to buy them,' said Mr Mayakovsky.

Most meant nothing to Sarah but there were three or four in Eaton and Belgrave squares, probably flats. 'Are these residential properties or offices?' She addressed Mr Mayakovsky but he ignored her and left Katya to speak for him.

'They are both,' said Katya. 'Mr Mayakovsky owns many properties in London and in other cities. He wishes to increase his property empire by buying these.'

Total value would be into the high double figures of millions, if not more. 'Are they all for sale or are you intending to approach the owners and make offers?'

'Some are and some are not. Mr Mayakovsky would like you to approach all the owners on his behalf.'

Sarah looked at Mr Mayakovsky, saying nothing until eventually he condescended to nod. 'May I ask where the finance for this investment comes from, Mr Mayakovsky?'

'From my business.'

'Mr Mayakovsky owns many properties throughout the world and in Russia he has interests in oil and gas and industry and banks,' said Katya. 'This is just part of his business.'

Sarah handed her back the list. 'If you would send me a

printed version indicating those advertised for sale and the identities of the owners of those that are not, along with indications of what Mr Mayakovsky is willing to pay in each case, we would then approach them on his behalf. This would of course mean an enhanced fee.' It was gratifying to see a flicker of irritation cross Katya's beautiful features. Perhaps work was uncongenial to her. They parted politely.

She left the office just before four, reckoning that Charles would be heading back from Croydon by then. He hadn't intended to go in but felt he had to because of the murder. There was so much to sort out in the house which, despite her efforts so far, still felt like a sorting office. Perhaps after an hour or two of that they could relax and do nothing for the rest of the evening. Since their marriage a few months ago it seemed there had never been time to talk.

As it was Sunday she had left the car on Blackfriars Road rather than go in and ask the doorman to open the firm's underground car park. This was normally reserved for partners and important clients, on the grounds that partners often worked late and couldn't trust public transport to get them home. None was in that day.

She had almost reached her car when she became aware of someone very close to her left shoulder.

'I am sorry to surprise you, Mrs Thoroughgood,' said Mr

Mayakovsky, 'but there is another subject I should like to discuss with you, if you please.'

He spoke more fluently than before. She stood looking down at him. Most Russians she had met were tall but Mr Mayakovsky's very compactness was threatening, as if he had been compressed by great forces into a thick square block that could be compressed no further. The indifference he displayed in her office had been replaced by an unsettling concentration. Sarah looked around for Katya. She had never thought she would miss her.

'It would be convenient if we talk in my car.' He nodded at a black Rolls-Royce parked not far from hers. She could make out a driver wearing a cap.

'I'm afraid I'm in a hurry. Could it wait until we meet again? You could make an appointment.'

'We can talk in your car if you prefer.'

'No, I'd rather not.' It came out too quickly, before she'd thought what to say next.

'Very well, we can talk here.' His pale eyes were unblinking. A bus passed, then two Lycra-clad cyclists, talking loudly. A taxi pulled in for a fare on the other side of the road. 'I have some information which concerns your husband. It is important for his career.'

She waited for him but he seemed to be waiting for her. Let him, she thought. He can say it himself, whatever it is.

The taxi pulled away but still he said nothing. They looked at each other. It was becoming ridiculous. She sighed. 'Well, you'd better tell me quickly or better still tell him. I'm in a hurry.' She edged towards her car, putting an extra yard between them.

Mr Mayakovsky did not move. 'Your previous husband was also chief of the Single Intelligence Agency,' he said slowly, as if she needed reminding. 'In his youth, when he was diplomat, he became a spy for French special services. He gave them English secrets. You know this and your new husband, Mr Thoroughgood, he knows it. But it has never been acknowledged by the British government. If this knowledge is published in the English newspapers it would be very harmful for your husband and for you. He would have to resign.'

A droopy young man with hair over his shoulders slouched unseeing between them. Sarah heard everything, understood everything, was aware of everything going on around her, but somehow couldn't engage. Afterwards she thought that was what it must be like to have a stroke.

Mr Mayakovsky continued, still without moving any closer. 'In Moscow, Russian special services also have this knowledge for a long time. But they have not used it. Now they are thinking they will use it. Perhaps the world should know about this thing. But it is possible to stop them. Perhaps.'

An artery throbbed in the side of Sarah's head. Mr Mayakovsky was moving towards her now. She found herself moving too, alongside him, towards his car. He was speaking again but this time she was taking nothing in. There was a thickening fog between her and what was happening. Mr Mayakovsky touched her elbow, his car door opened and she stepped in, almost without stooping. It felt and smelt luxurious, the seat was huge. They sat beside each other facing the back of the driver's head but the car didn't move. It was as if she was struggling against anaesthetic. Concentrate, she told herself, concentrate. But the threatened resurrection of all that she and Charles had gone through swept through her like a numbing and nauseous wave. It would be the end of Charles; the end of them, perhaps.

'If it can be arranged sensibly for both parties,' Mr Mayakovsky was saying, 'if they believe they will learn things, special things, they will do nothing.'

The fog was lifting. 'What things?' Her voice felt normal. 'What do they want to learn? How do they think they will learn it?'

Mr Mayakovsky's eyes rested on the fat immobile neck of his chauffeur. 'State secrets. If they learn state secrets from you, they will be silent.'

'State secrets? I don't know any state secrets. How do they think they could learn them from me?'

'From your husband. He will tell you things.'

'He doesn't, he talks very little about his work – past or present.' It was true; she knew the kind of issues Charles would deal with but he would say little about the detail. Neither would she of her work, come to that. His telling her about the late Dr Klein that weekend, giving her the history of the Configure case, was an exception. But that was history now and was going to come out anyway. 'What's more,' she said, her confidence growing with her indignation, 'if you think there's the remotest chance that I'm going to run along to the KGB or whatever they now call themselves and prattle about our pillow-talk, you'd better think again. And if you don't mind I'd like to go.'

'It would not be necessary for you to meet Russian special services. It is better you never meet them. You can talk to me.'

His disregard of normal social responses and his unnerving persistence were intimidating. But she felt offended, which helped. 'So you're their spy, are you? Is that what you are, Mr Mayakovsky – a spy?'

'I do not work for special services but I know them and they have told to me about you and your husband and how

I can tell you how you can save yourself from this difficulty. You do not have to tell them very much, nothing at all yet. It will be sufficient for them to know that we are friends.'

'Friends? You and me friends, Mr Mayakovsky?'

'So long as they believe that, it will be sufficient. It is necessary only that we meet and talk sometimes. My properties can be the reason for that.'

'Of course, your properties. Your would-be properties. You mean you're really going to buy them? That all this portfolio business is real and not just a camouflage?'

'Of course it is real.' For the first time there was evidence of a reaction. His skin colour changed slightly, as if after a slap. 'I buy what I want. If I want something, I buy it. Why else have money? I will buy these properties.'

Sarah was beginning to feel thoroughly herself again. She sat upright on the edge of the deep seat, her handbag on her knees. 'Then I'm sorry to disappoint you but you're not buying me. I am not going to spy on my husband. In fact, I shall go home and tell him exactly what has happened. He will know what to do with people like you.' She thought she must sound ridiculously prim and proper, but that was the way it came.

'There is one other question I must ask.' He waited for a reaction. 'Mr Peter Tew. He was friend of your husband until he was sent to prison. Now he is out of prison. Is he friend of your husband again? Has your husband seen him?'

The name meant nothing. 'I've no idea. I don't know who you're talking about.'

'I would like to meet this man.'

'Then you'd better ask my husband.'

'He has computer which we—'

'Then you can ask him yourself. Goodbye, Mr Maya-kovsky.'

Her exit was marred by the few seconds it took to find the door handle. Mr Mayakovsky did not help. His gaze had returned to his chauffeur's neck. 'Think carefully before you tell your husband, Mrs Thoroughgood.'

9

'We'll have to think very carefully about what we say,' said Melissa Carron.

That much they could agree on. They were in Charles's office. Melissa, who lived in Richmond and had a child's birthday party to host, had been reluctant to come in but Charles had insisted. Her journey had been slow and vexatious. Power was off throughout south London and the office generators were still not working, thus there were no lifts, no computers and no lights. Only the phones worked.

'Since it's possible that his work for us was what got Configure murdered,' said Charles, 'we've no alternative but to tell the police everything. But can we trust them not to plaster it all over the press or the blogosphere or whatever it's called?'

'Would that matter? If it was the Russians who killed

him they already know what he did and where he was. And if it wasn't them it's too late for them to do anything about it anyway. So there's nothing left for us to protect. Also, it's an old case, it's not as if we remained involved after he was resettled, we didn't have anything to do with him, so it's really nothing to do with us any more. And it would all come out in the inquest, anyway.'

He couldn't tell Melissa the nature of Viktor's continuing work via his unsuspecting brother. Nor could he show her the handwritten note from the duty officer, shielded by his empty coffee mug. He would have given a lot to fill the mug but there was no power for the kettle.

'All you say is true,' he said, 'but we mustn't simply assume it was the Russians and not look anywhere else. It's one possibility among others. Perhaps the most likely – certainly the most obvious, it looks like their sort of job. But' – he chose his words – 'Configure continued to be consulted after his debriefing was over. He was almost more a current case than a resettled defector. We can't keep that back from the police but at the same time we don't want to let the Russians know. Or open their eyes to what we were doing with him if it wasn't them that killed him.'

'But who else could it have been? Robbery wasn't a motive, from what you say.'

'No.' He glanced again at the note. He was tempted to

tell her all but the COFE meeting had been unequivocal: someone within MI6 was permitting the Russians or Chinese access to its systems and he could tell no-one. Melissa was one of the last people he would have suspected of treachery but the sight of her unopened laptop on the desk before her was another reminder. He said the next thing that came into his head. 'A jealous husband, perhaps. He had form in that area.'

'Why not get MI5 to brief the police? They work with them more than we do and have a better feel for who to trust and how to manage things. And they both come under the Home Secretary.'

He remembered that she was ex-MI5. 'Good idea. Brief your opposite number and give them my numbers. Tell them not to hesitate if I'm needed.'

She picked up her bag and laptop. 'You knew him well, Configure?'

'We go – went – back a long way. I was his first case officer.'

'Must be upsetting for you.'

'Yes.' It sounded a cold and inadequate response but he was thinking again of the note. 'His is not the only recent death. Did you know Frank Heathfield?'

'Only by name, from long ago. Headed your counter-intelligence section, didn't he? Used to work closely with our CE – counter-espionage – people. I saw he'd died in the e-newsletter.' She tapped her laptop. As she did so her mobile rang. She scrabbled in her bag to quell it. 'Sorry. Security breach for the director of security?'

They both smiled. 'Not on Sundays between consenting adults. Good luck with the party.'

He rang the duty officer. They had reverted to the rota system of using a pool of retired officers but this one, Derek, sounded younger than most and was unknown to Charles.

'Any news on this power cut?'

'No, sir, except that it's more extensive than first thought. Seems to be most of south London. Whitehall's okay. I've just been on to the MI5 duty officer. They've been fine all morning. Still problems with our own generators, apparently. We're waiting for parts.'

'It's MI5 I want to talk to. Could you get me the DG? And find out whether he has a secure phone at home.'

'He does. I'll call you back on yours when I've got him, sir, and put you through.'

'Thanks, Derek. And let me know if you hear anything more about Frank Heathfield.' Charles waited. He was still getting used to being called 'sir' again, the first time since he had left the Army many years ago. His predecessor had abolished the practice, insisting that everyone should call him Nigel but Charles had reverted to the old MI6 tradition under which everyone was on first-name terms with every-one else except when addressing the Chief, who was called 'sir' or CSS. Charles favoured it not because it enhanced his importance but because it emphasised his difference. As Chief he could be friendly but no-one's friend; it was part of his job to sack or censure people.

'This is a bit keen, isn't it? In the office on a Sunday? What can I do for you?'

The secure phone made Michael Dunton sound as if he were shouting in Charles's ear. 'You can tell me whether I'm being a paranoid fantasist,' said Charles. He described Viktor's death.

'Oh Christ.'

'And now there's Frank Heathfield, too. Have you heard about that? Our duty officer has it from your duty officer who had it from the police that Frank was murdered in pretty much the same way but with his wife in the house and at night. Knock on the door, he answered, a single shot – shotgun again – then the sound of a disappearing motorbike. She didn't see anything.'

Michael said nothing for a moment. 'I knew Frank from when I was in CE. Nice man, kind man, very shrewd. You think there's a connection? Hard to believe there isn't, but what?'

'Peter Tew.'

'Go on.'

'Four people were responsible for unmasking Peter: Matthew Abrahams, who died while Peter was in prison, Configure, murdered since Peter's escape, Frank, ditto. And me.'

'Jesus. I'd better come in.'

'No need. Nothing to be done just now, apart from check on the police hunt for him.'

'I'll do that and make sure you're kept informed. The police need to know about this. We'll raise it at the emergency COFE this afternoon. You know about that, don't you?'

'No.'

'I did hear they were having trouble getting hold of you. Your mobile was off and no-one seems to know where you live. The meeting's not about this but there may be a connection. It was you he confessed to, wasn't it? Tew, I mean.'

'Me plus the other two. It was my question that provoked his confession but that was by chance. I wasn't the main inquisitor. Then we spent the weekend together, he and I, walking and talking. He told the whole story. Then we handed him in.'

'Wouldn't happen like that now. Better watch your step.'

Charles sat for a while, gazing out of the window at the Sunday morning traffic that seemed to manage perfectly without traffic lights. With the computer system down he couldn't check whether Peter's file had been preserved in paper form or whether it had been digitised or, worse, microfilmed.

Not that he needed it to recall Peter's interrogation, boldly coloured in his memory. A Thursday and Friday were set aside for it in a panelled room in the Carlton Gardens house the Office then used as a front office, overlooking the Mall and St James's Park. There was an ancient polished table with three leather-padded captain's chairs on one side and one on the other. On the table were a water jug and four glasses, a heavy circular glass ashtray, three white blotting pads with plain notepaper and pencils and several fat, buff, red-striped files. There were no telephones or screens. On a smaller table to the side, near the stone fireplace, were cups and saucers with a milk jug, tea, coffee, kettle and a plate of custard creams. Embedded in the walls and ceiling were concealed microphones operated by a button on the underside of the desk. Downstairs, in one of the green brick basement offices which recalled wartime austerity, were two large tape recorders, two black telephones and a built-in cupboard of radio communications kit. There were four grey metal desks, two with microphones, manned by a man and a woman. They too had tea and coffee, but plain biscuits.

When Matthew Abrahams, Frank Heathfield and Charles reassembled in the panelled room on the Friday morning the air was still stale with cigarette and pipe smoke from the day before. Smoking, already discouraged in the office, was not actually banned and Peter Tew was a regular smoker. For most of Thursday he had not smoked but towards the end of the day, when Matthew handed him a paper from the top red-striped file, he opened the packet of Gauloises he had put on the desk before him not long after they began. The paper was a four-page top-secret report with a distinctive blue border.

'Do you remember this report?' Matthew asked as he pushed it across the desk. 'And could you explain how the Russians came to have it?'

Peter read quickly and smoked slowly. When he finished he laid the paper on the desk, flicked his ash, sat back and stared at Matthew. 'What am I supposed to say? Of course I remember it. I wrote it. It's one of P24029's early reports from New York, one of his best. He's always good on Security Council machinations. I was his case officer at the time. But I've no idea how the Russians got hold of it. Nor how you can be sure they have?' He raised his eyebrows.

Matthew ignored the question, speaking slowly. 'What puzzles us, Peter, is how they come to have that copy and not another. Because that is the telegraphic version you sent from New York station back to the Requirements officer in London. She made one or two stylistic alterations to your text and added a paragraph of R desk comment. It was her version that was circulated to customers, including the Americans and your own ambassador and other CX readers in New York. But the first version – your own unedited version – was seen by very few people: you, your head of station, your secretary and the R desk here. And that's the version the Russians have.' He paused. Peter said nothing. 'If you were in our shoes, Peter, confronted by this problem, where do you think you might start?'

Peter shrugged. 'I think I would start where you have, with the New York station.'

'I'm glad you agree.' Matthew laid one hand on the file. 'Especially as this is not the only New York station paper that found its way to the Russians.'

'Although there's always the R desk. The leak could be from there.'

'We considered that. But the R desk gets reports from all Western hemisphere stations, none of which is known to have leaked. And the leaks from New York began, we now know, not long after your arrival and stopped about when you left.'

The only sounds were the traffic on the Mall and the ticking of the oval clock on the mantelpiece. Peter stubbed out his cigarette, staring at Matthew, ignoring Frank and Charles. 'I do see you have a problem.'

'Think, Peter, about what you would do in our position.' Matthew paused again, then surprised everyone by saying, 'Meanwhile, I think we should call it a day.'

The Thursday morning had started quite differently. Peter arrived in Carlton Gardens having been told by Personnel in Head Office that some interviews were temporarily relocated due to building alterations. When he saw who his interviewers were and it was explained that this was an informal board of inquiry seeking his help, he was at first puzzled, then irritated. As they shook hands he said to Charles, 'Didn't know you had security interests. Career move or here for the fun?'

'I was asked to help out.'

'Kind of you.'

He faced them with his legs crossed and an expression of polite scepticism. Matthew explained that this was a general inquiry into a leak of information. It was not necessarily related to him but they hoped he might be able to cast light on the context and on other individuals who might in due course be interviewed. It was not part of any legal proceedings. They then took him through his career, post by post, seeking his opinions on those he had worked with and issues he had dealt with. Matthew concentrated on subjects he had reported on, Frank Heathfield, with his Cornish burr, on how he felt the Service treated staff and agents and on his own professional relationships. Charles said nothing.

Peter relaxed as the morning went on, perhaps because he was talking about others rather than himself. They adjourned for lunch on an almost jocular note, with Peter saying, 'I suppose it wouldn't do for me to invite you to join me in the Savile?' His eyes danced across all three, resting very briefly on Charles. 'No, I see it wouldn't. You might be accused of frivolity. Important to maintain seriousness of purpose.' He put on an exaggerated frown.

Followed up to Brook Street and the Savile Club, he gave no indication of suspecting surveillance. 'Perhaps he assumes it,' said the woman in the basement ops room who was in radio contact with the team on the ground. 'They can't follow him into the club so we've got no idea who he might be talking to or ringing from there.'

In the afternoon session Matthew and Frank moved on to Peter's time in New York, without at that stage referring to the leak from New York station. They did not focus on Peter himself but sought his opinion on why anyone in MI6 – assuming it was a human source, not technical – might in the post-Cold War era wish to spy for the Russians.

'It puzzles me,' said Matthew. 'The old ideology, the

communist ideal that motivated the likes of Philby and co., and George Blake, is busted. The Russians themselves don't believe it – never did, really, it was always primarily a Western illusion. The press seems to have taken its place – MI5 had Shayler going public, we had Tomlinson, the Americans of course Wikileaks and Snowden. But what, in your opinion, could possibly motivate someone to spy for the RIS now?'

Peter twiddled the then unopened Gauloises packet on the desk before him. 'Anti-Westernism, anti-Americanism in particular, the fact that the Russians still provide an alternative for the protest vote. Money – they still pay, I imagine? Then there's admiration for the people, their stoical endurance of suffering and all that sentimental wartime legacy stuff. Then love of their literature – still a Dostoevsky fan, Charles?'

Charles nodded.

'But that's not enough to make Charles spy,' said Frank.

'No, but it might help set him on the road. It's a gradual process, I suppose. I have some sympathy with it.'

'You do?'

'Imaginatively speaking.'

'Then there's MICE, of course,' said Matthew. 'Beloved by the Americans. Money, ideology, compromise, ego. Not bad but something of an oversimplification, I've always thought. What do you think, Peter?' His tone was gentle and he paused for what seemed a long time but Peter did not respond. 'What puzzles me, Peter, is what would make someone in the New York station start spying at that time?'

There was another pause. 'If they did.'

'If they did.'

They continued in hypothetical mode for most of the afternoon. Peter agreed that anyone in MI6 who spied for the Russians would know that the consequences for Russian agents he betrayed would be lengthy imprisonment at best, possibly death. He agreed too that this might weigh heavily on his conscience, that conceivably he might even welcome discovery or the chance to confess, especially if he had been pressured into spying. But such a person should still be punished, he thought. He should not be excused punishment because he had been put under pressure or because he had confessed. Questioned several times on this, Peter insisted: however understandable, or for whatever motives, betrayal was wrong. There were always alternatives. The session seemed to Charles more a seminar on agent motivation that an investigation but that, he realised as Matthew and Frank circled ever lower like leisurely red kites above his native Chiltern hills, was what they wanted.

It was only when Matthew showed him the leaked report

that Peter showed signs of tension, not only by taking up his cigarettes at last but in slower, more studied and precise articulation. He also moved less, as if each movement had to be thought about in advance.

Surveillance covered him to his flat in Marylebone that evening. He stopped only to buy milk and provisions and stayed in all night, receiving two telephone calls and making none. Matthew, however, rang Charles at home.

'Tomorrow. Tomorrow we deploy you. We stay in hypothetical mode with me suggesting he was blackmailed into doing it and you suggesting that that would be forgivable reason. He won't want your sympathy, he's too proud, but it might provoke him. We will also imply the possibility of immunity from prosecution in return for a full confession.'

'Can we offer that?'

'Of course not. It's only ever been done with the blessing of the DPP once everybody's sure there's no hope of evidence for conviction. So we won't be offering it. We'll be talking about a hypothetical individual and whether it would be right that he should escape prosecution. Our friend has a strongly developed, if somewhat distorted, moral sense. This, allied with his pride, may tempt him to confess by asserting his superiority of motive.'

'If he's got any sense at all he'll just stonewall. He could walk out and there's nothing we could do, nothing that would hold up in court.'

'If he had sense he'd never have done it in the first place. He'd have simply resigned. Then he could have done and said what he wanted, lived as he wanted.'

'You're sure he did do it?'

'Of course I'm sure. There's no doubt. What we know from your source of what Guk and Wolf said in Vienna, from the FBI about his cottaging in New York and from the CIA that the Russians have copies of reports he sent is more than enough to nail him in reality, if not in law. We can also now see the pattern in the carpet of his time in New York – initially open about his dealings with the Russians, all fully reported, then an abrupt stop. Apparent stop. That was when he was recruited. I suspect they discovered his sexual predisposition when he was a student in Moscow and when he appeared on their radar in New York the SVR residency traced him with Moscow and came up with that useful little nugget. So they exploited it. Not having doubts, are you, Charles?'

Charles was not so much doubtful as reluctant. The pile of files from which Matthew had produced the leaked report may contain more unanswerable stuff, but he almost didn't want Peter to be guilty. That day, for the first time, he had sensed beneath the apparent insouciance of Peter's act an almost lifelong struggle to keep up the much bigger act of pretending to be normal, to be like those he lived and worked among, to be one of them. As he became more brittle at the end of the afternoon Charles had sensed something alive and squirming beneath the ice of his act. He felt for him. But those red-striped files brooked no sentiment.

Friday began with coffee, Peter balancing two biscuits in his saucer and placing his cigarettes and silver lighter on the desk before him.

'What I'd like to do this morning, Peter,' said Matthew, 'is to carry on from where we were yesterday. By which I mean that we should continue to discuss this case hypothetically, leaving aside your personal position in the matter.'

Peter's cup was halfway to his lips. 'Forget my personal position, did you say?'

'That's right. Whatever it may be. And give us the benefit of your opinion and advice unrelated to yourself.'

'In what respect?'

'Whether, if someone had done what we think, it would be reasonable to suggest to him that there might be circumstances which would excuse him from prosecution.'

'Leave him with a gun, a bottle of whisky and an empty room, you mean?'

'Nothing quite so melodramatic. We were thinking more in terms of his having been coerced into spying. Blackmailed through compromise. Whether you think it would be reasonable under such circumstances for someone to be excused prosecution in return for a full confession.'

'I – I don't know whether that would be reasonable.' He sipped his coffee, lowering his eyes. 'It's been done before, hasn't it, long ago, with Anthony Blunt? But I'd find it difficult to believe that now, under modern circumstances, it would be permitted. After all, if someone had done' – he glanced at the stone fireplace – 'what you say has been done, he presumably might have caused the imprisonment or deaths of agents within Russia. And I'm not sure that the authorities would be prepared to overlook such – such actions.'

Matthew nodded. 'How do you think someone might feel, knowing his actions had such consequences?'

'I think it would be on his conscience.' There was a harsher note to Peter's tone. 'I think it would get to him.'

'And there are various ways, I suppose, in which he might justify it to himself?'

The rest of the morning was taken up by another extended discussion of hypothetical justifications for treachery, with Peter again arguing against leniency. They broke early for lunch, considering over sandwiches upstairs whether they could continue into the weekend. Matthew thought not, for the same reasons that they could not risk a more hostile interrogation. Peter's attendance was voluntary, this was not part of a legal process and anything he said, short of a full confession to which he adhered subsequently, would be inadmissible in court. Continuing into the weekend would also make it more difficult to claim to MI5 that this was merely an exploratory interview with unexpected results.

'So we've only got this afternoon,' Matthew concluded. 'I'll bring you in, Charles, as Mr Nice Guy. Of course, we're all Mr Nice Guy in this but you must be Mr Super Nice Guy. Make it appear that you're looking for excuses for him. He refused the possible lifelines we threw him this morning but if you persist it might provoke him, put him on his moral high horse, as it were.'

Frank was called away to the ops room, returning ten minutes later. 'Surveillance report that he's eaten no lunch and went into St James's Piccadilly and prayed. Or seemed to pray. I'm not sure they really know what praying looks like, they've never had one do that before, but they had a couple in with him and said he went to the quiet bit and knelt at a pew with his head bowed and hands clasped for twenty-three minutes. They had to do the same, complained that their knees hurt afterwards. Then he went for a walk in the park. He's on his way back now.'

Matthew turned to Charles. 'Not normally religious, is he?'

'Not now but he was. He nearly became a Methodist minister before he went to university. Then he was a Christian Socialist, then a banker.'

'Nothing about a religious vocation on his file.'

'Probably because he didn't do it. Files tend to record what we did, not what we didn't. He told me when we were travelling in the States.'

When they reconvened after lunch Matthew opened the top red-striped file again, unhurriedly selecting three or four papers from the bottom half and placing them on the desk before him. They were covered in dense type. Frank made a note. The clock on the stone mantelpiece struck the quarter.

'Before we continue,' Matthew said, looking at the papers rather than Peter, 'I want to introduce a personal note, in parenthesis, as it were. Your homosexuality.' He pronounced the word carefully, syllable by syllable, looked up and placed his elbows on the table, his hands palm to palm. 'We haven't mentioned it before and I'm not going to dwell on it, unless you choose to deny it – which I hope you won't?'

Peter stared.

'Good. I mention it now only so that we're all clear that it's in the open. You are of course aware that lying about it in your positive vetting interviews, declaring that you weren't, means that your PV certificate can be withdrawn which in turn would mean that you could no longer be employed by the Service?'

'I was always aware of the possible consequences of my actions.' Peter's tone was as deliberate as Matthew's.

'Charles has a question arising from this.'

Charles couldn't read Peter's eyes – was he imagining the slight widening, was it a hint of playfulness, or appeal, or was it preparedness, acceptance of whatever was to come? 'Peter, I want to return to the hypothetical, to consider whether there are circumstances in which someone might feel he has no choice but to spy for the Russian intelligence service. If, for example, he were put under pressure through imprisonment or torture or the vulnerability of family members or—'

'Blackmail as a result of compromise?'

'Yes.'

'Of course there are such circumstances. We all know that.' Peter reached for his cigarettes.

'And if he genuinely felt that he had no choice—'

'But he would have a choice. Whatever he felt about it, he would have a choice and would be making one.'

'Can you imagine a situation where any member of this service could be in a position where he had no option but to cooperate?'

'No.'

'You can't? You really can't?'

'No.' Peter lit his cigarette and sat back, exhaling vigorously before continuing in the harsher tone he had used before. 'I shall tell you – the truth. I do not however want to benefit from any suggestions that I had no choice about what I did and that it should go unpunished. It is true that I have cooperated with the RIS. But you should know that it was not the RIS who approached me, but I who approached them.'

Matthew picked up his pen. 'Thank you, Peter,' he said quietly. 'When was this?'

Peter spoke for the rest of the afternoon, a trickle that became a torrent of relief and justification. He insisted that he had not been blackmailed into spying for the Russians, that the process of what he called his self-recruitment had been brewing for years, that it had been a principled and considered decision arising from the loss of his Christian faith – 'I could no longer accept that it was founded on reality' – and his growing appreciation of the Russian soul. They had always been a profound and religious people and although their great experiment with communism had gone wrong they had at least struggled to achieve a more just and equal society, one that espoused the values of the Christian Gospels minus the superstition. Their nationalism and their aggressive self-interest were understandable in view of Napoleon's and Hitler's invasions and American and Western hostility. The corruption of their current polity was the contagious effect of American materialist culture. The Americans were the world's villains.

'Disliking Americans is fine if that's how you feel,' said Matthew. 'But why spy for the Russians against your own country?'

'More tea?' asked Frank.

Peter nodded to Frank. 'I was a foot soldier in this war. I knew the Cold War was technically over but there's still a war, a permanent struggle for values, justice and equality. I came to the conclusion that right was on the other side. The logical thing if I wanted to do good, therefore, was to change sides, not to run away from the war.'

'Whom did you approach?' asked Charles.

'Grigory Orlov, second secretary in the Russian mission to the UN. We had him down as a straight diplomat, MFA rather than RIS. As did the Americans. I had legitimate cover reasons for dealing with him and I figured he'd be under less scrutiny than any of the identified or suspect intelligence officers.'

'How did you convince him you were genuine?'

Peter paused while Frank handed him his tea. 'I gave them some names, names of one or two cases I knew about. So that they could check them out and see I was genuine.' He spoke into his tea.

Matthew held up his pen. 'Peter.' Peter looked up. 'Which names?'

'I'm not sure I can remember now. Firefly, Bookend, one or two cases like that, fairly old ones.'

Matthew noted them. 'Restless?'

'Yes, I think so, Restless was one of them. I think you're right. I'm not sure he's still going, is he?'

'He's dead. They shot him. Wife and family imprisoned.'

Peter stared. 'They told me they wouldn't do that.'

'Of course. They always say that. Then they do it. And the other names?'

Peter shook his head. 'Come on, you can't expect me to remember them all. It was a while ago now and I didn't exactly do any homework for this.'

'Tell us what you can remember.'

He named agent cases and technical operations, agreeing some that were suggested to him, denying others. They all three noted them, though they'd be on tape anyway. Most meant nothing to Charles. Asked which documents he'd photographed and handed over, Peter shrugged.

'Anything, anything I could, whatever I thought might be of interest.'

'The whole caboodle, then,' said Matthew.

'Yes, the whole caboodle,' he asked defiantly of Matthew. 'Am I permitted to go to the loo?'

'You know where it is. You might ask in the secretaries' room if there's any chance of another pot of tea.'

'Was that wise?' asked Frank when the door closed. 'Might he not scarper?'

'He might, he could at any time and there's nothing we can do about it. He could simply deny everything he's said and we wouldn't be allowed to produce it as evidence, tape or no tape. What we have to do is keep him sweet and get him to make a formal statement to the police. We've got to set that up with Five. There's more to come, he's keeping something back, something personal. We want him to walk and talk, walk and talk. Walking is conducive to confidences. You can help, Charles.'

'Take him for a walk?'

'As far as necessary. And talk, talk in pubs, by firesides, on footpaths, everywhere. Your mother still lives near Henley? Take him down for the weekend, as your friend, if your mother's up to it. Be very nice, don't argue with him, just seek to understand. Get him to open up about his personal life on rambles through those beechwoods. I don't believe that this ideological self-recruitment, this love of Mother Russia, this I-did-it-all-myself is the whole story. That is, I do believe he believes it – now – but there's something else. There always is. We need to know everything. Meanwhile, we'll set up Five and the police at this end and I'll ring and tell you when to bring him in.'

'But what if he decides to make a bolt for it, as Frank says? The RIS will have agreed an exfiltration plan with him, won't they? We'll look pretty silly if he just disappears. It'll be us getting Gordievsky out of Moscow in reverse. Can't he just be held?'

'We've no usable evidence. We need his written confession and he won't confess if he feels coerced. We have to hold his hand. That means you, Charles. You were his friend. You must become so again. Hold his hand all weekend.'

10

Looking back on that weekend was like recalling an old film in parts. They ate and drank and walked and talked, as Matthew had ordered. Charles's mother was pleased and flustered to hear her son was coming down for the weekend with a friend she'd never heard of. She got food from the freezer despite Charles's insistence that they would eat before they arrived – 'In case you couldn't find anywhere open, dear.'

In fact, they had a curry after picking up Peter's travelling bag from his flat, allowing the Friday evening rush out of London to ease. It was during that meal that Peter first indicated the nature of his relationship with Grigory Orlov, the Russian second secretary in New York.

It began with Charles asking how he came to make his offer of service, the initial approach when the volunteer offers up his future, possibly his life, with no guarantee of security. 'We always see it the other way round,' said Charles. 'We're the hunters looking for offers. Or provoking them. We'd be pretty good on the mechanics of how to offer ourselves but psychologically we wouldn't—'

'Psychologically, it's like declaring yourself to someone you're trying to recruit, confessing what you really are when you're asking him to spy for you. It's the moment of truth. Only it matters more. The other difference is trust. You only do it when you feel you can trust him.'

Peter spoke and ate rapidly, having had only prayer for lunch. Charles put that episode aside for later. 'How did you know you could trust Orlov?'

'Firstly, he's a loyal Russian patriot. They are very patriotic, you know, it's one of the most striking things about all the Russian officials I've met. Most evident in the Second World War, of course. Admirable.'

Unlike you, Charles thought, but he merely nodded. Keeping him talking was what mattered.

'And then there are people – some people, not many, certainly not in my life – whom you just know, know you can trust and – and be close to. It's as if you've always known them, like an electrical charge, positive and negative, instant recognition. You must have had the same in your life? At least, I hope you have. I don't mean I did it straight away, that I just came out with it. I – we – felt our way with each other over a series of meetings.' He spooned yogurt onto his curry. 'God, this is the real thing. I'm out of practice with vindaloo. D'you think they do curry in prison?'

'Bound to.'

As the weekend went on, talking by the fire after Charles's mother had gone to bed, walking through the woods to Hambleden to get a Saturday *Guardian* from the shop – Charles's mother's *Telegraph* wouldn't do for Peter – or browsing bookshops in Marlow and Henley, Peter spoke increasingly of himself and Grigory as if they were lovers. Charles didn't at first ask him outright, sensing a protective wall around Grigory that, so far, would resist probing.

'You're sure he's MFA and not RIS?' he ventured after Peter described Grigory's reaction to his offer. 'His questions sound like an intelligence officer's questions.'

Peter bridled. 'Of course I'm sure, I asked him straight out and he told me. Anyway, the questions are bound to resemble those any intelligence officer would ask because they're the obvious ones. How d'you think you can help, why would you like to help, is it true that you're really MI6, what do you know that would most help us—'

'He said "us"?'

'What else could he say? He was talking of the Russians in general, couldn't very well say "them", could he?'

'But he didn't hand you over to the SVR? That would've been the normal thing.'

'It was a personal relationship, I told you. It would have continued if he'd got cross-posted here. He tried but he couldn't.'

'So who's your case officer here?'

'I don't know yet, as I said in the interview yesterday. They're waiting for me to initiate third country contact, when I'm sure all is well here. The first meeting is to be in The Hague, then I'm to be run here. I didn't do it before because I was having doubts anyway, as I intimated yesterday. Not about the cause, why I did it, but the actual doing of it. It's tiring. Quite a strain.'

'Hell of a strain.'

Peter looked grateful. 'Until you do it, you've no idea how stressful it is, living a big lie. Even when you're used to it, like me. Two big lies in my case.'

They were on a bench at the top of the hill above Fingest, with church, pub, farm and brick-and-flint cottages laid out like a toy hamlet below. The footpath wound on up through the beech trees. Off to their right was a badger sett that Charles had known from childhood. The wooded hills and green valleys were England as it was supposed to be and mostly wasn't. But here – just here – it was, and for Charles this alone, apart from myriad considerations of

principle and association, would have been enough to prevent him betraying his country. But he was a romantic, he
supposed, and Peter wasn't.

'It's always been all right for you,' continued Peter. 'You
belong. You always have. You belong so completely that
you're probably not even aware of belonging. I never felt
I did. Even before I knew I was gay I felt different, apart.
And lonely, so very lonely. I wanted to belong, you see,
I wanted desperately to be a part of what you and Matthew
and Frank and the others take for granted. So I pushed
it – myself, that is – aside. And I pretended. Most of the
time I coped, I was all right. Of course, it wasn't all right
really but it was manageable, sort of, until I went to New
York. Something happened there, I just went with the
flow. I put myself about, you might say. Then I met
Grigory and for the first time in my life I felt I belonged,
really belonged. I knew it was impossible, of course, but
I feel that even if he and I never meet again – I hope we
will, you know, in future, after all this' – he waved his
arm – 'it was worthwhile. It was something. I have
been there, wherever "there" is. My life is not completely
unfulfilled.'

Unlike Restless, Charles thought, our agent in the Soviet
rocket troops whom you got killed.

Peter put his hand on Charles's shoulder. 'Sorry, Charles,

this is very self-indulgent. Must be the view. I'm a hopeless romantic. You're the opposite.'

'I'm not so sure.' Charles scoured the turf with the black-thorn stick his father used to use. 'How did it come about, you and Grigory?'

Peter smiled. 'It embarrasses you, doesn't it? How did we meet, do you mean, or how did we come to find each other?'

'Both.'

'Through work. We had dealings at the UN, sat on two committees, got to know each other. Then we had lunch one day in the UN building – my suggestion, I think, maybe his – no, he joined me at the table. Then at the end of lunch I said it would be nice to do it again and he rang me a couple of days later and we went to an Italian restaurant a couple of blocks away.'

'He rang you?'

'Not over-pushy, was it? Let's have lunch? Not like let's have a dirty weekend in the Appalachians – though we did have one of those later. Took a lot of fixing on both sides.'

Charles's experience of getting Russian officials to lunch or dine alone was that they didn't come easily unless sanctioned and almost never took the initiative, unless they were SVR and scented a prey. 'But when – how – did you—'

'Get it together? Had to be in my flat, of course. Couldn't

be his because of his wife. He was quite nervous, mainly at visiting my flat without approval. I remember he said, "You don't know what I'm risking, coming here." It was a big step.'

'I meant your offer of service. How did—'

'Oh, that just sort of emerged in discussion. I mean, I knew I was going to do it, it had been coming for some time as I said yesterday in Carlton Gardens. But I didn't have a formula, it just sort of happened one day. Part of a continuum, not a separate or new thing. It was a time when I was pretty disgusted by American interventions abroad, treating the world as if it was their backyard. We both were.'

I bet he was, thought Charles. He had felt it so often, the anti-American pulse pumping through most of the spies, terrorists and extremists he'd met. The Americans didn't always help themselves, of course, but it was a common enough theme for him to wonder what their haters would do without them. Something against their own, presumably, because that's what haters did, whoever their own were. 'So you were disgusted by America but loved New York.'

'I know. Couldn't help it, either way.'

He was a perfect guest, helping with the clearing up, refusing to smoke in the house, sympathising with Mrs

Thoroughgood's gardening quandaries, advising on new curtains, appreciating the food and gently tutoring her on the unused laptop Charles and his sister had given her for Christmas. He also bought her a smart leather-bound address book in Henley to replace the tattered cloth-bound one she had kept by the phone for forty years. Charmed, she told Peter when they were alone in the kitchen that she wished Charles would find a nice girl and settle down. When alone with Charles she said she couldn't understand why he hadn't mentioned Peter before. Matthew Abrahams rang once, fortunately while she and Peter were in the garden discussing roses.

'Bring him in to Carlton Gardens on Monday morning at ten,' Matthew said. 'After the rush-hour. The arresting officers will be waiting. Better there than in Head Office or a police station, more discreet. Tell him what's going to happen. We don't want any nasty surprises that make him uncooperative. Now, quickly, tell me everything.'

On the Sunday evening, during a dramatic sunset after a day of broken cloud, they walked down the lane to the pub while Charles's mother roasted the chicken. 'They want us in Carlton Gardens at ten tomorrow,' said Charles, deliberately using the plural. 'The police will be there.'

'Face the music, eh?' Peter took out his cigarettes. Charles accepted one, to keep him company. 'At least no innocent person's going to be hounded. It's all me. D'you think I'll be treated leniently for having coughed up?'

'The court is bound to take it into account, I'd have thought.'

As it did, up to a point.

11

The court also took into account what Peter did after the FBI's New York field office had leaked his story to the press.

Staring still at Croydon's Sunday traffic, Charles struggled to remember the details. Even at the time he caught up with them only belatedly and piecemeal. Once Peter had become an MI5 investigation and a police case Charles was – with one exception – no longer involved, not needed even as a witness since Peter pleaded guilty and made a full confession.

The exception was when Peter requested through his solicitor that Charles visit him in prison. He wanted to thank Charles in person for his 'hospitality and understanding during the wonderful weekend we spent together'. He was still on remand in Belmarsh which meant that MI5 and the police had to suspend their interviews until after conviction and sentence. Even so, the request was weeks old before Charles knew of it. Eventually it was agreed on condition that Charles did not discuss the case, and that he reported back. During this time more had happened to Grigory Orlov than Charles knew.

Getting into Belmarsh seemed almost as difficult as getting out might be. The checks, the searches, the waiting with other visitors, mainly female, the overheating, the constant locking and unlocking of doors, the contrast between the often overweight, slow-moving staff with their bunches of keys and ponderous helpfulness and the young, aggressively indifferent, fit-looking prisoners glimpsed through bars or at the ends of corridors, the non-stop shouts and zoo noises from the wings, the cages and high wire fences dividing the open ground, the sinister, two-storey, windowless and segregated high security wing were sufficient to convince him that no crime was worth it. The unceasing noise and proximity of others would be hell for Peter, he thought, his only hope being separation in the high security wing.

But Peter managed better than he thought. They met in a room with half a dozen prisoner and visitor tables, divided by mesh screens and overseen by two prison officers. Tables and chairs were screwed to the floor. Peter,

wearing jeans and a T-shirt, was already seated when
Charles was shown in. Unable to shake hands, they smiled
and nodded awkwardly.

'How is it?' asked Charles.

'What is it the army officer is supposed to have said on
escaping from Dunkirk or the Somme or somewhere –
"But, my dear, the *noise* and the *people*"? But no complaints.
It's prison, full of ordinary blokes who got caught. I'm sharing a cell with a rather nice chartered accountant, quite
inoffensive but pretends he's not guilty of embezzlement,
silly man. I think they're being kind to me.'

Charles, curious about daily practicalities for the recently
imprisoned – whether Peter's post was sent on from his
flat, whether he could pay bills, how he managed for clothing and washing and shaving kit, whether there were
books – thought a show of concern might encourage further talk. But Peter held up his hand. "Cut the social work
crap. Grigory. What's happened to him? What do you
know?'

'I've no idea. If anything.' It was almost true. The Office
had briefed the FBI on the withdrawal of the officer they
had liaised with in New York until they discovered his
cottaging activities and suspected they were not getting the
full story on his relationship with the Russian diplomat.
Confirmation that they weren't had led them to look again

at Orlov, whom they now assessed to be an intelligence officer after all. As did the Office. The FBI also suspected
Orlov might not have admitted to his own people the full
extent of his relationship with the English spy. His people
would not approve of one of their own officers being a
closet gay, even if he had been deployed against Peter to
charm him.

'I haven't heard from him, you see. I'm worried he might
be in trouble.'

'But you weren't meant to hear, were you, until you activated your contact arrangements in The Hague?'

Peter smiled. 'Not officially, no, not as far as his people
were concerned, anyway. That was when it was supposed
to become a truly professional relationship, when I'd have
been handed over to the SVR to be run instead of passing
on stuff through him. That's partly what I – didn't like.
Why I decided to – you know, come clean. But also he and
I had a personal communication arrangement. Let's call it
a PCA, shall we, in honour of the Office's love of acronyms?
I activated it but he hasn't replied.'

'How? From here? What is it?'

'Ask no questions and you'll get no lies. I suppose you'll
report this, will you?'

Charles nodded.

'Good old Charles, ever loyal. But I want to know – has

anything happened to him? Do you know anything at all? Has the Office told the Americans about me yet?'

'I'm not supposed to discuss the case but—'

'Come off it, what else do they think there is to talk about?'

'– but I think you should assume they have. You told the Russians what you knew about FBI coverage of them in New York, so they'd have felt obliged to.'

'That bloody Bureau field office had better not target him. It would get the SVR looking at him and end his career. If I find they've done that, Charles, all bets are off. You can take that back with you. Tell them that.'

Peter's grey eyes were hard and flat. Charles wondered how he would react to learning that Orlov was an SVR intelligence officer after all, that their relationship had not simply blossomed in the way he fondly thought but had been a calculated seduction, an intelligence seduction. Admittedly, the other bit, the physical bit, almost certainly went beyond what Orlov was supposed to have done. It was a technique the Russians had used before, albeit with agents they had compromised, not one of their own officers. 'I'll tell them,' he said.

'All bets are off,' Peter repeated. 'If I find they've done anything that threatens Grigory.'

What did you expect? Charles wanted to say to the tense

pale face behind the mesh screen. That your betrayal of trust, your betrayal of friends and colleagues, your giving our secrets to a corrupt and brutal regime that means us harm, would be accepted in silence? That we wouldn't tell our closest ally, some of whose secrets you betrayed and who helped us catch you? It was surely that same dissociation from reality, the same failure of consequential imagination, that had tempted Peter down this path in the first place. His wishes continued to father his thoughts. It was a fatal disjunction.

There was movement around them and a change in the voices, with some people standing.

'Thank your mother,' said Peter. 'She's a very nice lady. Tell her I understand that she'll be disappointed when she hears what I've done but that I hope one day to see her again and explain all. And tell the Office that if Grigory suffers anything through anything they've done, I'll bring the whole house of cards down. I mean that, Charles.'

It would have been easy, at that moment, to torpedo his assumptions about Grigory, to leave him with only the consequences of his actions to brood on and no consoling imaginary cause. You were set up, Charles could have said. They saw you coming and they tasked Grigory to recruit you by pretending to be your friend. The oldest trick in the book and you fell for it. If Grigory went further than he should that's his problem – and yours. Whatever happens to him now is the fault of the SVR and you, not the FBI. But he left without saying anything. They had not spoken since.

Grigory Orlov's house of cards came down soon afterwards, very publicly. It first broke in the American papers as the story of an un-named predatory Russian official at the UN whose frequent advances to junior UN staff were upsetting diplomatic protocol. Next it came out that the official was gay, then that he was an undercover SVR officer who seduced young men into spying for him, despite the fact that gays were disapproved of within Russia and the SVR. Finally, Orlov was named and it was announced that he was being withdrawn to Moscow. The *New York Times* quoted security sources as saying that the SVR was believed not to have realised that their officer had sexual relations with a British diplomat, since withdrawn, and that it was possible that this was also an intelligence relationship. The story was picked up in the British press and the link soon made to charges under the Official Secrets Act against an unnamed official. When Peter came up for trial it was relaunched as a leading news story, with much comment on gay rights. Orlov's fate, and that of his family, was unknown.

There was also much comment on the severity of the

sentence. With the ending of the Cold War espionage began to be seen as a not very serious offence, with trivial consequences. A sentence of twenty-three years, taking into account Peter's guilty plea, was condemned as excessive.

Also taken into account by the judge, but unknown to the wider public, was what Peter was discovered to have done during his time on remand. As the Orlov story percolated into the British press he became uncooperative and increasingly insistent upon his rights, real and perceived. He also began attending Catholic mass as well as Friday prayers with the Muslim imam. The prison authorities had seen this as what it was for many prisoners: a break from routine, the assertion of a right and time out of the cells. It was MI5 that discovered that Peter was using his association at mass with a couple of Irish terrorists, and at Friday prayers with Islamist terrorists, to pass on the identities and addresses of MI6 agents and staff, Charles's among them. MI5 first learned of it from an agent within the prison, then had confirmation from sources outside who were in touch with inmates.

Surprisingly, Peter didn't change his guilty plea, calculating perhaps that it would benefit him in the long run not to do so. He was sentenced and moved to a high security prison in Yorkshire. After some years there he was assessed as no longer a high-risk threat and moved to a more relaxed category B prison in Surrey. Good behaviour and pressure on prison places qualified him for release after less than half his sentence. The puzzle was why he had chosen to escape now, with only a year or two left to serve. Charles, though lacking any evidence, thought he knew.

12

S arah was relieved to be alone when she reached home
that afternoon. It was late but there was still time to
collect herself before telling Charles about the attempted
blackmail. Not that there was any question of wrong-
doing or cover-up by either of them but as head of MI6 he
was reputationally vulnerable if the story was spun in the
right, or wrong, way. Dredging up all that business again
was the last thing they wanted. She felt responsible because
it was baggage she brought with her. Talking to Mr
Mayakovsky made her feel dirty. She showered and
washed her hair.

The phone rang just as she put the hairdryer down and
heard Charles's key in the latch. She picked up the bedroom
extension. It was the MI5 duty officer. She called to Charles
from the top of the stairs and could see from his face how

much he welcomed it the moment he got in. He took it on the kitchen extension.

Later, hair done and wearing comfortable old jeans and jersey, she went downstairs. He was still on the phone. She offered tea in sign language and he nodded. He continued listening, asked a couple of questions, then gave directions to the house. When she turned on the kettle he took the cordless phone into the drawing room. She waited until he had finished, then took the teas in, looking at him questioningly. He took the tea as if he wasn't seeing her.

'The police liaison officer from MI5 wants to bring the police round to talk about Viktor. Then there's an emergency meeting of that committee I was telling you about in the Cabinet Office.'

Clearly not the best time to tell him, unless it was really a police matter. She wasn't sure. 'They're coming here, now?'

'They're on their way.'

'Everything's such a mess. They'll think we live like this all the time.' She tried a smile. 'There's something we need to talk about.'

He nodded but still looked preoccupied. 'When's that wedding, your nephew's?'

'Danny's? The 16th, two weeks, just under. He should be back now. I can't remember when his ship – boat, he calls it, his submarine – was due in. They never seem to have a date but he told everyone he'd be back in good time. I must ring my sister.' A car drew up outside and three men got out. 'That was quick. I suppose they're only just round the corner, aren't they? I'll leave you to it.' This time her smile elicited a brief response. She went upstairs to unpack boxes in what was to be her study.

Charles sat them round the kitchen table. They all said yes to tea. They were from SO15, part of the counter-terrorist command formerly known as Special Branch. He knew one of them as DI Steggles, whom he had privately nicknamed Corduroy. 'We know each other of old,' he told the others as they shook hands. 'He arrested and inter-viewed me in the bad old days of the SIA. Did it very well.'

They all laughed, a little uneasily. The outline of his story was known within Whitehall in versions of varying vivid-ness and reliability, and Steggles would no doubt have mentioned it in the car. Charles had always been open about it but now, it seemed – because of his new position – no-one would mention it in front of him. It was therefore better he did, and made light of it.

He described what had happened to Viktor, giving them the background to the case but not Viktor's contacts with his cyber expert brother. 'We need to ensure that the local police have all they need for a proper investigation while also trying to ensure that the details of his work for us aren't leaked,' he concluded.

'Best brief from the top down,' said Steggles. 'If you give me the name of the investigating officer you dealt with we'll brief the assistant chief constable. May I say you'll be available to help at any time, sir?'

Discussion turned to the Russians, whom everyone assumed to be behind the murder. The MI5 liaison officer said they would have used an illegal, someone unconnected with the embassy who would have been sent to Britain from a third country for that operation only. He would probably have been abroad again within hours. The police thought that nevertheless an alert should be sent to ports, albeit it was useless without a description. MI5 surveillance on the Russian Embassy, abandoned during the optimism of the immediate post-Cold War years and reintroduced only with the break-up of the SIA, would be briefed to report any unusual comings and goings or signs of heightened community activity.

Charles did not argue. It was possible, all of it – perhaps even likely – and there was no evidence for his alternative theory. But the more he thought about it, the more he believed in it. 'Nice to be back in harness again,' he remarked to Steggles, as they stood to go.

'Very much so, sir. Nice to see you back.'

'Are they keeping you busy?'

'Here and there. Nothing as interesting as this, though.'

'There's Peter Tew.'

'The old spy from your lot? Done a runner, hasn't he? Won't be having him back, will you?' He laughed.

'We want him found. Also, there are a couple of things we'd like to know about. How he spent his time in prison, any contacts outside, particular friends inside, hobbies, attitudes, anything he said that's at all unusual. If you can get that sort of thing out of the prison service.'

Steggles took out his notebook again. 'A big if with that lot. They see any question as an attack. But we'll have a go.'

Sarah came downstairs when she heard the car pull away. It was remarkable to be in the heart of London yet in a street so quiet that you could listen for individual cars and footsteps. Charles was putting on his jacket.

'You've got that other meeting now?' she asked.

He nodded.

'You'll be back for dinner?'

'Hope so. Our first dinner here. Shall I bring a take-away?'

His bachelor assumptions had long roots. 'It's all right, I've got some bits and pieces.'

'You're a genius.'

The COFE meeting this time included Mary Cox and

Desmond Bowen, permanent secretaries at the Home Office and MOD. Mary was a distinguished-looking woman nearing retirement, with hair in a bun and a reputation for calmness and acuity. Desmond was a new appointment, looking improbably youthful, his thick brown hair just edged with grey.

The mood of the meeting was sombre. Tim Corke explained that there had been a *Beowulf* development of which ministers would have to be informed. A decision was needed. He turned to Charles. '*Beowulf* is one of our nuclear subs, one of the four missile boats, and she's gone missing. Overdue and off air and we don't know what's happened. Off air's not unusual. They patrol for about three months at a time somewhere in the North Atlantic. No-one, not even in the Admiralty, knows where they are. We transmit to them but they don't transmit to us unless there's real need, in which case they use a delay system, very low frequency burst transmissions from where they were, not where they are. A boat that's overdue would normally let us know why. We've sent messages asking but answer came there none. Now there's been this latest development.' He looked at Desmond.

Desmond Bowen was the only one without a notepad. He spoke rapidly. 'Being overdue is not so very unusual. In fact, it was quite convenient for a while because *Beowulf*'s successor on patrol, *Beauty,* had a technical problem, *Bellerophon* is undergoing maintenance and *Battle's* crew are all on leave. That's why we need a minimum of four boats for twenty-four-hour coverage. But overdue without explanation is exceptional and no response to requests for one is unprecedented. Now we have what looks like a mass deployment of Russian hunter-killer submarines.' He looked at the faces around the table. 'Naturally, the Russians are always trying to locate our missile boats, to learn their sonar characteristics so they can identify them in future. As do we with theirs, of course. They send their hunter-killers out after our boats and we deploy ours to monitor them and to protect the boats by distracting them. During the Falklands War, when they knew we'd sent all available hunter-killers to the South Atlantic, they deployed nineteen to locate our patrolling missile boat. They failed, I'm glad to say, but a similar situation seems to be developing now. Up to a dozen, the Americans reckon. And we don't know why. Or why now.'

'Coincidence?' said Angela. 'A major exercise? They must have them. How do we know they're looking for *Beowulf*?'

'We don't. And that's the other thing, of course. No more Crown Jewels.'

Tim looked at Charles. 'Crown Jewels is the name of the

cryptographic product that Configure helped us achieve via his brother. Very tightly held, as you might imagine. Basically, it means we can recognise – not read, recognise – Russian nuclear release procedures. It's a three-stage process, culminating with the President. There's no indication they intend Armageddon despite their more aggressive patrolling, the resumption of daily provocations in our air space and so on, but it means that if ever they did we'd get enough notice for the US President to activate the hot line. It also means that we can recognise – again, not actually read – exercise signals, concentration and dispersal orders and whatever. Very, very useful.'

'But now we can't. They've recently changed their procedures and we can't even find the signals, let alone interpret them. They may be smuggling them out under something else or somebody else, as the Israelis used to conceal their signals beneath Arab diplomatic traffic. Satellites picked up the launch of this shoal of hunter-killers but we're blank on where they are now, where they're going or what they're doing.'

Angela, who had been doodling, shook her head impatiently. 'Of course this is all very serious and unfortunate and there's no doubt we've got to find out what's happened to *Beowulf*. But we mustn't get carried away by hypothetical possibilities which, however serious, remain extremely hypothetical. There is no reason at all to think that the post-Cold War Russian state is remotely near even thinking about a nuclear strike on us or anyone else. Indeed, there's evidence – including some from Charles's predecessor – to suggest the opposite, that they're sufficiently confident now of their relations with the Americans to rule it out. So the context is benign, even though the events themselves – what's happened to *Beowulf* and so on – are undoubtedly serious. As I understood it, the decision we have to reach today is whether to ask ministers to ask the Russians if they know anything about our missing submarine and whether they'll help us find it. For what it's worth, my feeling is that the Foreign Secretary would be decidedly against, although' – she shrugged – 'he never ceases to surprise.'

'What could have happened to *Beowulf*?' asked Mary Cox. 'What are the options?'

'Chances are she has a technical fault, is on her way home and keeping quiet because she's detected Russian submarines in unusual numbers,' said Desmond. 'The worst and least likely case is that she's suffered some catastrophe and sunk. But it would have to be unprecedentedly rapid for her not to break radio silence and get some sort of signal off. It would have to be something drastic like collision with a Russian sub that was looking for her. Which might account for what the Russians are doing – looking for their own missing sub. The other possibility is that our signals are not getting through and she's waiting to find out what's happened. She can sit around on the seabed for as long as she wants, pretty well. If she goes on hearing nothing from us, of course, the captain might open his letter of last resort.'

He was looking questioningly at everybody. Most nodded but not Charles and Graham Wood from Civil Contingencies. Desmond explained that the letter of last resort was a sealed letter carried by missile submarine commanders containing the Prime Minister's wishes for what they were to do if a major nuclear strike destroyed all functioning government in Britain. Handwritten by each prime minister on taking office, alone and without sight of his or her predecessor's letters, they were to be opened only in the event that no signals could be raised from Britain and that no BBC radio broadcasts – particularly Radio 4's *Today* programme – were detectable. The letter would express the late Prime Minister's wish as to whether the commander should retaliate with his own nuclear missiles. Either after retaliation or without it he was then to choose between sailing to Australia and placing himself under command of the Australian government, or sailing to America and placing himself under command of the US government.

'So, serious stuff,' said Desmond with a smile. 'Actually, the Russians know all about it. We told them years ago during the Cold War. It means they can never know whether a successful first strike would prevent retaliation.'

'But surely,' said Mary, 'even assuming a complete radio blackout from Britain the commander could simply tune into radio broadcasts from other countries to find out what's happening. I know we don't count for what we did in the world but I'd have thought a nuclear strike on London might make it onto most news bulletins.' She smiled. 'I'm rather with Angela on this. I don't think we should assume disaster without more evidence.'

Desmond nodded. 'Of course. Even if they had a technical fault that meant they couldn't pick up broadcasts from anywhere, you'd expect them to realise it was their own malfunction. I mention it only as part of the worst case scenario. But we still need to decide whether we're going to recommend to ministers that we seek Russian assistance. It might help us find a stricken *Beowulf* but risks exposing a possibly healthy *Beowulf* to Russian analysis and identification.'

'My vote is that we should not,' said Angela. 'We should warn ministers that we may bring such a proposal to them and will have it in preparation but that – subject to their views – we should give *Beowulf* more time.'

'Meanwhile doing all we can to follow this Russian submarine deployment,' said Desmond.

Nobody dissented. Tim Corke turned to Charles. 'There is another aspect to this with which your old friend Configure may be able to help. Have you seen him yet?'

Charles glanced at Michael Dunton, who nodded. 'I have seen him, yes. But only his corpse. He's been murdered.'

They listened in silence, save for the hum of a generator somewhere. When he had finished Charles glanced again at Michael. 'There's been another murder, too. Possibly related.' He told them about Frank Heathfield. Michael then told them about Peter Tew.

'Of course, it's only Charles's speculation,' he concluded. 'Tew may or may not have launched a one-man campaign of revenge. To my mind, it's much more likely that the Russians did Configure. They have form in that area. But they don't generally go around knocking off retired intelligence officers, so Frank Heathfield does complicate the picture, I admit. But Tew didn't show signs of bitterness in prison, had one or two friends but otherwise kept himself pretty much to himself, we're told. Apart from organising inter-prison chess championships, which he persisted with despite less than overwhelming demand.'

'No chance of getting Configure's brother to help regain Crown Jewels?' asked Desmond. 'Get us back into their signals?'

Michael Dunton shook his head. 'He's not even remotely conscious of his brother's relationship with us. And we've no way of contacting him unless we pretended to be Configure. And that would unravel pretty quickly.'

'Okay.' Tim put both hands on the table, edge-on again as if holding a ruler between his palms. 'We brief ministers on *Beowulf* and on the possibility of approaching the Russians, but we don't recommend it yet. We also tell them we are reserving judgement on whether the silence of *Beowulf* is connected with the multiple attacks on our CNI and with the loss of Crown Jewels, but that it's possible. Not all of them know we even had Crown Jewels, incidentally, so some might be upset that the Prime Minister kept them in the dark about that. I don't suppose that will worry him unduly. I think we should also mention the two murders, stressing however that we have no evidence of a connection either between them or with anything else. Finally, we should tell them that the fact that the cyber attacks are confined to Britain and their frequency and duration has led us to conclude that their route in is via an MI6 computer, which means MI6 has a serious insider problem. Which we are investigating urgently.

'As for ourselves, we need to decide whether we're looking for what physicists sometimes call a unified field explanation which would account for all the above. Or whether we think that is an alarmist fantasy. Whichever line of investigation we take, ministers will be most concerned about the CNI failures because they're slap bang in the public domain and the whole nation notices when the lights go out. They want action on it and we'll have to report some.' He turned to Graham Wood. 'Graham, update us on CNI.'

Graham pushed back his black hair, as he usually did before speaking. 'We can't do more than we're doing already, which is to maintain intermittent services across the whole range of government systems but without guaranteeing any of them. The latest to go down is the mainframe social security system in Newcastle, but with luck no-one will know about it because I had a text on the way here saying it was down for minutes only and it's now back up. But if it did go down for any time millions of people would see their pensions and welfare payments drying up. There is a back-up, of course, but we don't want to bring that on stream while the main one's infected in case it somehow gets infected, too. Luckily, most of these infections are short-lived, leaving everything perfectly normal afterwards. It's like malaria – when it gets into the bloodstream you've got it, when it's lying dormant in your liver or wherever you haven't. Except that you have really.'

'I still don't understand how it gets from the MI6 system

into the social security system,' said Mary. 'They're not linked, are they?'

Everyone looked at Charles, who had no idea how the MI6 or any other system worked. He could understand the infection analogy but that was about all. He was saved by Tim.

'They're not linked but there are links. A kind of reverse engineering by some of our twelve-year-olds at Cheltenham has established that someone with internal access to the MI6 system who knew what they were doing – a contractor, for example, a British Snowden – could exploit the few links there are not only to communicate with other government systems but actually get inside them. On most MI6 terminals you couldn't because it's a sealed system, as Charles knows, but on some terminals you could. At one time it was literally no more than a handful but under Charles's predecessor the number increased, including some laptops. So we're looking at every MI6 user with access to those terminals. But it takes time because it has of course to be done in absolute secrecy and access lists are woefully incomplete or even unavailable. It's essentially a cyber access problem, that's the key to it.'

Everyone nodded, including Charles, although he was unconvinced. Of course it was a cyber access problem but if the two murders were admitted as part of it, it became something else as well. The existence of Viktor, let alone his address and cover identity, was probably unknown to anyone within the contemporary MI6. Viktor's details might possibly be recovered from computerised files but only by someone who knew what to look for. Frank Heathfield's address would be easier to find but the link between him and Viktor would be known to – whom? He could think of no-one apart from himself and Peter Tew.

He would need more than that to convince those around him, but he had to say something. 'The first question,' he said, 'is whether we adopt the unified field theory by seeking a single explanation uniting everything that's going wrong. Or whether we take each aspect on its own and seek separate solutions. My own hunch—'

Michael Dunton intervened. 'They fall naturally into two groups – the murders and the escape of Peter Tew on the one hand, the cyber, Crown Jewels and communications issues on the other. With the latter it's easy to see how one might flow from the other through clever cyber exploitation but there's no indication of any link between them and the murders and Tew. In the absence of any evidence we'd be chasing a red herring to search for a unified field explanation or whatever we want to call it. That said, Charles's theory that the murders are linked to each other through Tew is plausible enough to offer it to the police as a possible line of inquiry. But any suggestion that Tew could also be somehow hacking into the MI6 system from outside and getting from there into the CNI and beyond is stretching belief. I mean, I know that while in prison he acquired a reputation as a bit of a computer geek but bringing down the CNI is a step or two up from geekery. Is it not, Tim?'

Tim and Graham nodded. Charles held up his hand as if in capitulation. 'Michael is right, of course. There's a clear distinction between the two elements and we mustn't confuse them.' Matthew Abrahams had long ago taught him one of the secrets of success in Whitehall meetings. You had to start with an agenda, a clear idea of what you wanted to come away with, then occupy the middle ground by presenting yourself as objective and reasonable, conceding arguments on both sides. In a culture that placed a high value on collective responsibility this ensured you a hearing, since it was not done to attack the demonstrably reasonable man or woman. But by occupying that middle ground you had in fact advanced your own front line to your enemy's, unopposed, while conceding nothing.

Charles had entered this meeting without an agenda but now he had one: to leave with his freedom of action unimpaired. He would use that freedom to establish the link between Michael's two groups which he was now convinced must exist because, while Michael was speaking, he had remembered something else from the investigation of Peter Tew.

After Peter's Carlton Gardens confession Charles was sent to interview members of the New York station to find out what opportunities Peter might have had to stray beyond his official access. The head secretary asked to see him privately after the formal interviews were over.

She came to his hotel room. 'There's something else you should know, something I suppose I should confess. I didn't want to say it in the station with everyone else around. I don't know whether it amounts to much anyway.'

'Have a drink.'

Over a gin and tonic she described how while Peter was still on station a telegram had come in addressed to the head of the Washington station, who was visiting New York. It was an early Configure report but the name meant nothing to her and the security classification was no higher than usual. That was a mistake by the sender, someone on the Requirements desk in London who should normally have sent Configure traffic as DEYOU – decipher yourself – which meant that H/Washington would have had to take it from the cipher machine without even the cipher clerk being allowed to see it.

'It came in with a whole load of other stuff and I put it in the tray for H/Washington to see. Meanwhile Peter, who'd been in the UN all morning, came back and hung around gossiping. I picked up the telegram again to see where it should be filed after H/Washington had seen it and he said, "You look puzzled, what is it?" I was puzzled because the file reference wasn't one I recognised and there seemed to be a lot of technical stuff about signal transmissions. I had a feeling it shouldn't go on one of the ordinary liaison files that anyone can see.

'Anyway, at that moment the phone rang and I put the telegram down to answer it. Peter picked it up and looked at the distribution list and file number, then he put it down. But the phone call went on a bit and he stood looking at the first page. He could see only the first page, I'm sure of that, but I do remember noticing he was reading it. As soon as I put the phone down he turned away as if he'd lost interest.

'"Don't bother to file it," he said. "Just shred it when he's seen it. It'll be filed in Head Office and Washington and it's nothing to do with us. So much crud gets copied to us just for the sake of it. I'd chuck it if I were you."'

She thought nothing of this at the time and didn't realise she'd remembered it until Charles arrived with his questions.

'I feel awful; I should have thought. I knew Peter wasn't on the distribution, of course, but he didn't try to read it all, didn't seem that interested. And I just thought it was something technical that was nothing to do with us, the name Configure didn't mean anything and there were other things going on, you know how it is. I'm sorry, I'm so very sorry.'

'Not your fault but thank you for telling me. He almost certainly didn't pass it on because he was back in London shortly after and he had no more meetings with his friend. It was the head office's fault, not yours.'

The telegram, it later transpired, was the first Configure report indicating the possibility of Crown Jewels. Charles had written it, unaware of its full technical implications. But Peter Tew was scientifically more literate and probably did. He may not have been able to pass it at the time but now that he was out of prison he could have put it to use, if he had a mind to. And he probably had.

Tim was talking by the time Charles gave the meeting his full attention again. 'Michael's right that we must keep the police fully informed of anything relevant in the backgrounds of Frank Heathfield and Configure, which means explaining the possible link with Peter Tew. Meanwhile it would help if Charles could get us a more complete list of who in MI6 has access to computers which link to the outside world and whether it is possible for anyone other than the staff member concerned to access them. It would also help if we could have a staged shut-down, allegedly for maintenance, of MI6 servers. If we could identify a server which, whenever it's down, means that no other systems are accessed, that would narrow the search.' He looked at Charles. 'It might, of course, mean that you would have to indoctrinate someone else in MI6 into what's happening.'

'Unless I simply say it's a process all government systems have to go through during the present crisis.'

They discussed technicalities. All was going well from Charles's point of view until Michael, trying to be helpful, said, 'If we're assuming Tew as the link between the murders, then we're also assuming he's revenging himself on those responsible for putting him away. Of whom there's only one left alive – and he's sitting here.'

Everyone laughed. Angela mentioned Agatha Christie. Michael said that had struck him too. Everyone laughed again. 'But there is a serious point here,' said Michael. 'Protection. Should Charles have police protection?'

It was the last thing he wanted. Smiling with the others, he rushed to reoccupy the middle ground. 'Reluctant as I am to be a further charge on the public purse, I agree it's something we should seek police advice on. I'll raise it with them myself. Fortunately, we've just moved house and I think I've neglected to let anyone know the new address—'

'Why does that not surprise me?' interjected Angela, to further laughter.

'– but I'll discuss it with the police, I promise.'

13

Sarah prepared a prawn stir-fry for supper and opened a bottle of claret, which Charles would drink with anything, including fish and chips, if he could. Most of the unpacking remained but their bedroom and her study were more or less done. She dared not start on his study because that would mean arranging his precious books and whatever she did would doubtless be wrong. There'd be no more unpacking this evening, anyway, just a cosy dinner during which he could tell her about his meetings and she could confess her approach from Mr Mayakovsky. She still felt as if, merely by being approached, she'd done something wrong.

Again, the telephone rang as she heard his key in the door. This time it was Jeremy Wheeler, exclaiming how wonderful it had been to see them both, how they must get together more often and how delighted he and Wendy were to have them in the area. She mouthed his name to Charles who gritted his teeth and turned his eyes to the ceiling. She mouthed, 'Are you here?' while saying how much she was looking forward to writing to Wendy that very evening. Charles shook his head too late because by then she'd had to say he'd just got in. He made a strangulated grimace as she passed him the receiver. She closed the door and left them to it.

Dinner and the claret were restorative and Charles's irritation with Jeremy found relief in expression. 'Bloody fool wanted a line to take with the press over Viktor's murder. When I said he didn't need one, it was nothing to do with him, no-one was going to ask him about it, he said he thought they would because they had known each other socially and what was he to say if they asked whether Viktor had been bumped off because he'd worked for us? Then when I said there was no reason for anyone to suspect that Viktor had worked for us and so the question wouldn't arise, he confessed he'd already put out a press statement saying he much regretted Viktor's death but had no knowledge of his past. Can you believe it? After we'd all gone last night Wendy told him that Viktor told her he had been a British spy. Wendy saw more of him than Jeremy did, apparently.'

'How much more?'

'No idea but between them, for good reasons or bad, they've hit upon the right answer and Jeremy, true to form, has done the one thing guaranteed to bring about the very thing we want to avoid. Needs to protect his own public reputation, he says. Pompous twat. He didn't have one before but he might be on the way to one now. Publicity is the last thing we want at the moment, publicity about anything.'

Again she put off telling him, asking instead how the meeting had gone. By the time he'd finished that, the claret was also finished. She emptied the remains of her glass into his. 'Your unified field theory, or whatever you call it, your desire for a single explanation for everything—'

'Maybe impossible, I admit, but I'm sure it's more likely than Michael Dunton's two groups theory. For one thing—'

'You haven't heard what I'm going to say yet—'

'– there is already a link between the two groups: misuse of the Service's system. Someone is using it to wreak cyber havoc and someone must have used it to it to get Viktor's name and address. Assuming, as I do, that there's a professional explanation for his murder—'

She put her hand over his glass as he was about to drink. '– because you won't let me finish—'

'– and that explanation is Peter Tew—' He struggled not

to smile as he tried to take his glass with the other hand and she leaned across the table and grabbed his wrist.

'The point about your unified field theory is that it doesn't have to account for everything at once,' she said, as they contested the glass. 'It just has to account for enough for you to run with it and see whether the rest falls in later. The missing submarine, for instance—'

He stopped struggling. 'Your nephew who's about to get married – what did you say was the name of his ship? Boat, I mean. The Navy calls submarines boats.'

Her grip slackened. 'I didn't, I don't know—'

'*Beowulf*?'

She let go. 'Oh God, it might be. I must ring Susan, I meant to earlier. Does she know?'

'Don't ring yet.' He emptied his glass.

'I think we might need another bottle,' she said. 'There's something else I have to tell you.'

He heard her in silence, all the while holding the new bottle. When she finished he poured for them both and questioned her on detail, gently and precisely going over exactly what was said and in which order. At the end she smiled in relief and sipped the wine she didn't want. 'Doesn't do much for your unified field,' she said.

'It does, it reinforces it. The fact that they want to know whether I'm in touch with Peter Tew and that odd reference to his computer suggests they don't know where he is but would like to. They may be in some sort of contact but not as close as they want. Well done.'

'I didn't do anything. I was done to rather than doing. It was horrible. Will they really try and ruin us, d'you think?'

'Maybe, maybe not. Certainly not yet. They'll want to see if it works first. It's a very crude approach. I'd have thought better of them.'

'But I said no, absolutely clearly. And I said I'd tell you. They can't be under any illusion that it's going to work.'

'If they're crude enough to have done it in the first place, they're crude enough to hope for second thoughts and have another go. Puts us in a good position.'

'What do you mean?' He was talking about it as if it were happening to someone else. Professional detachment was all very well but this was personal, personal for them both. And she had felt so wretchedly guilty, as if she had brought trouble upon him herself.

'There's some advantage in playing them along for a while, if you could bear it. Getting them to expose more of themselves – whom they're using, what they need to know, how they would run you if you agreed. Give them enough rope to hang themselves, then prosecute or expel them. Michael Dunton would enjoy a good expulsion case.'

She put down her glass. 'You mean I should pretend to agree?'

'Not if you don't want to.'

'He's a horrible man, I hate him.'

'Just once and only if they approach you again. Just so that you can find out what they would ask you. Useful to know what they want to know. We might even wire you up, stick something on you. So you can bug the conversation. Miss Moneypenny stuff.' He smiled. 'Could be fun.'

'I don't think that's fun at all. What if they do what they threaten? Go to the press and make a great fuss about you and me and Nigel? It would be so easy to spin all that to make it sound sleazy and disgusting. And mud sticks, you know. For the rest of our lives.'

'They wouldn't if they knew that we would roll up their cosy little network here and expose it, complete with *News at Ten* recordings of clumsy attempts to debrief you.'

She was horrified. 'You'd put me on the news?'

He laid his hand on hers. 'It won't come to that. This is a little game for them, a tiny part of the Big Game. Nice if it works easily but drop it if it doesn't, that's what they'd do. Mayakovsky and his Snow Queen are just walk-on players, trying to face both ways. Keen to stay here, anxious to keep in with Moscow and show they're nice, patriotic, rich, capitalist, modern Russians. Moscow wouldn't expose them like this if they weren't expendable.'

'But don't you think Katya Chester might be spying on Jeremy Wheeler? I mean, he must come across things – political gossip or more serious things to do with this committee he's on – that they can use in some way.'

'Almost certainly. That's another reason for not letting it run on too long. Michael Dunton will want her out, provided the Home Secretary agrees and our ECHR judges don't say we're depriving her of a happy family life.'

'With Jeremy perhaps?'

'That would make expulsion a kindness.'

Monday for Sarah was wall-to-wall meetings. The two London Bridge project meetings were lengthy but fine – that at least was what the job was supposed to be. But the two career appraisals, her own and the one she was obliged to give her temporary trainee, were the waste of time all three participants privately knew they would be. No-one should need formal sessions with people they worked alongside everyday. On top of that there was a tele-conference with the New York office at which she had to stand in for her managing partner. It took an hour and they never got to her agenda item because there was so much grandstanding by two of the litigation partners. Then there

ALAN JUDD

was the quarterly meeting of the business flow committee, a body supposed to determine who did what but which merely recorded everything and determined nothing.

The day was also punctuated by calls from Katya Chester, who had the irritating knack of leaving a message nearly every time Sarah was away from her phone. When Sarah eventually rang back she had to endure waves of apologies for bothering her and tender concern for how she was feeling, her weekend, the dinner party at Jeremy's and whether Charles had enjoyed it. Eventually she cut Katya short with, for her, unusual brusqueness.

'Katya, I'm fine, we're both fine, everything's fine and I'm very busy. What is it you want?'

'Of course, I understand. I am sorry. I shall be quick for you. First, the conveyancing on my house. Is everything all right and is there anything else I can do?'

'Until you send me the details I asked you for the other day there's nothing I can do. You just need to get on with it.'

'Of course, yes, thank you for reminding me. I will do that immediately.' There was a very slight pause. 'The second thing is a message from Mr Mayakovsky. He wishes to know whether you are able to act for him concerning the properties he wishes to buy.'

There was a brief struggle between conscience and desire. Her desire was never to see Mr Mayakovsky again but she still felt, irrationally, as if she were potentially a cause of trouble to Charles and that she should therefore do what he wanted. She knew he didn't see it like that but nevertheless she felt responsible. 'Yes,' she said, 'please tell Mr Mayakovsky I am content in principle to act for him.'

'He will be very pleased.' Katya giggled, an irritating tinkle. 'He told me that if you agree to act for him he would like me to make an appointment for him to see you. May we do so?'

She wasn't having that. If he wanted her to play ball he could make some effort himself. 'Tell him to ring and make an appointment with me or my secretary. If you've nothing else, I'm afraid I have to go now.'

She put the phone down and sat for a few seconds wondering if she had got that wrong; perhaps he wanted to make an appointment via Katya not because he couldn't be bothered but in order to edge their relationship towards a clandestine footing. Charles would want her to encourage that. But he might also want time to prepare her for the next meeting, to wire her up, as he had inelegantly put it. In which case, the more notice the better.

The phone rang again. She answered mechanically, noting a Sussex number. Something to do with the cottage, presumably.

'Sarah, hello, sorry to bother you at work.' A woman's

voice, clear and confident. 'It's Wendy Wheeler. I'm sure you're very busy but I'd like to consult you in a professional capacity about a personal matter. I want to divorce Jeremy.'

Until the last sentence Sarah was gathering breath to enthuse about the dinner party and promise that the thank-you card would be on its way that evening. Unless Charles had sent one, which was highly unlikely. She then had to suppress her second reaction, which was to say she wasn't surprised. She said she was, and was sorry to hear it. 'But I'm afraid I'm not a divorce lawyer—'

'That doesn't matter, I'd just like some advice even if it's only to tell me where to go. You're the only lawyer I know who's not in some way involved with Jeremy. I'll pay you properly, course.'

'Don't worry about that if you're not formally engaging me. We can meet for a drink or coffee or something when you're next in London—'

'I'm coming up today. We've a flat in Pimlico. I could meet you anywhere any time.'

She sounded determined but not emotional. Sarah sighed inwardly. She had been hoping to get home at a reasonable time and do some more unpacking. 'All right, let's arrange something. I am sometimes peripherally involved in divorce cases because I do a lot of property work but I should say first of all that you don't need a lawyer if it's by mutual consent. If it's contested or if there's a lot of money involved you'd best engage a specialist. What does Jeremy—'

'He doesn't know yet. Have you time for a drink after work? I could come to you.'

Sarah suggested the restaurant in the crypt of St John's, Smith Square, convenient for the new house in Cowley Street. She would be home within minutes afterwards. Wendy rang off before she had a chance to thank her for the dinner. She didn't sound as if she were about to burst into tears or want a lengthy heart-to-heart, which was just as well. Sarah returned to her screen. There were a further six emails from a wealthy Hong Kong property speculator who had failed to get his son into Eton and wanted to sue the college. The firm's proposed new Hong Kong office couldn't open soon enough so far as she was concerned. Meanwhile, she forwarded them to the litigation department; they were welcome to him. But all the time, between her and the screen, was the image of Wendy's face when Charles announced the death of Viktor. It was Wendy's stillness that had struck her then, and that stayed with her now.

14

Despite his experience of bureaucracies, Charles had assumed that being Chief of MI6 would mean being at the pinnacle of operational endeavour and decision-making. The reality, he realised as he spent most of the day on the phone or in meetings, was that operational decisions were taken lower down and that his role was more the overseeing of a production line, an unending process of reports, meetings, agreements, liaisons and procedures which, he felt, would function as effectively with a virtual chief as with a flesh-and-blood one. It was clear that significant change would call for determination and constant vigilance to see that what was agreed was enacted. There was surely some law of thermodynamics expressive not of chaos theory but of continuous reversion to comfortable stasis. Chief Nag was the title he privately awarded himself.

However, there were two telephone calls concerning his real task, as he saw it. The first was from DI Steggles with some not very useful answers about Peter Tew's time in prison; the prison service was proving ponderous and reluctant, as usual, and Steggles had no contacts in that particular prison. The second was from DI Whitely who wanted to travel up from Hastings to take his formal statement. Aware that this would be difficult to explain to his staff without saying more than he wanted, and tempted by the excuse to get down to Sussex again, he insisted he would come to her later in the day. Her disappointment was palpable.

The Bristol was in the basement garage where there was a store of camp-beds for people who had to stay overnight. From long habit, he kept travel kit and spare clothes in the boot of his car. He would take a camp-bed to the cottage, a chance to withdraw and think. Both Sarah's numbers were on voicemail, so he left messages, told Elaine he was helping MI5 with a spot of police liaison and pointed the long nose of the car towards the M25 just before the rush-hour. It would do the ancient V8 good to fill its 5 litre lungs on motorway and dual carriageway.

Driving gave time to think and he made good progress. He would be early and so, seeing Bodiam signposted, he swung off the A21, towards Viktor's house. It was the nearest he would get to saying farewell, a final handshake with the past. The place would no doubt be taped off, boarded up, maybe even guarded against press intrusion – he had seen from his phone that the brutal murder of what they called the leading Cern scientist had made national news – but just looking at it for a few minutes would be enough.

It was neither taped nor boarded and there were no cameras, but nor was he alone. A light blue Ford Fiesta was parked in the drive. He placed the 410 carefully alongside it, taking his time as he thought how to explain himself. The front door was opened by DI Whitely, wearing jeans and a dark jumper that emphasised her pallor.

Charles spoke first. 'Hope this isn't illegal but I thought I'd drop in on my way to you as a kind of farewell. I thought there'd be a guard on it. I wasn't going to come in.'

'You may, sir. Forensics have finished with it now. The lawyers are running round trying to find out who owns it. No-one's found a will yet.' They shook hands. Her manner had changed. The official's resentment of outsiders was replaced by the simulacrum of respect and openness. Someone had spoken to her. 'There's no family that anyone knows of?' It was a question rather than a statement. She knew enough now to know that he would know.

'There's a former wife abroad but I doubt they've had

contact for many years.' The old MI6 would have insisted on a will when they bought Viktor a house as part of his resettlement package, in which case there should be a copy on file. He would get someone to check, assuming the file was recoverable. Presumably they were still paying his pension, too, just like the SVR. He'd opened his mouth to speak again but a thought stopped him, a thought so obvious he couldn't believe it had only just occurred. The SVR was a bureaucracy like his own, a wounded one at that; if the Russians had discovered where Viktor was, they wouldn't have gone on paying his pension. Even if they kept it going to conceal their discovery they certainly wouldn't go on paying after they'd killed him. Bureaucracies were like that. If Viktor's pension was still being paid, it was unlikely to be the Russians who had killed him.

DI Whitely was waiting for him to speak. 'Okay to look round?' he asked.

The bloodstains had been cleared from the hall. The part of the floor where Viktor's body had landed was conspicuously clean. 'Forensics did a good job clearing up after themselves,' he said.

'They didn't. They don't. It's usually left to the family or the owners. Pretty awful for them.'

'Who did it this time, then?'

'Me.' She was staring at the floor.

'Why?'

She looked up with a half-smile and turned away. It was the first time he had seen her smile. 'Silly, really, kind of superstition. I just felt it might somehow bring me closer to what's happened, being here, you know. It's my first murder, you see. Well, it was, before the ACC got on to my superintendent and told me to, you know, soft-pedal because the Met and SO15 are involved. Taking over, he meant.' She looked at him. 'I understand you – er – you know something about all that, sir?'

'I was professionally involved with Dr Klein a long time ago. But I share your superstition, as you call it. That's really why I dropped in today.'

She looked relieved. 'I got the impression from the ACC that the investigation's not likely to go anywhere, not here anyway, because the perpetrators are – er – overseas where we can't get at them.'

'That's what most people think. We don't have a very happy extradition history with the country concerned. Even when we do have names of suspects, which we don't here. Okay to walk round?'

They went from room to room, looking at everything and nothing. There was an impression now of unloved functionality, a common characteristic of solitary male occupancy. The house was used, organised, probably appreciated, but unadorned and not obviously cherished. Charles wondered whether his Chelsea flat had felt like this to visitors. His Scottish house almost certainly did.

'Houses need to be lived in, don't they?' she said, lingering by the leather-topped desk in the smaller study.

There were a few sheets of A4 printing paper on the desk, some with scrappily pencilled equations or algorithms, one with what looked like notes for chess moves. Viktor's several computers had been removed for analysis and those mathematical jottings, Charles thought, should probably have gone with them. On the other hand, they could just as well have been abstruse calculations relating to Viktor's betting. He had been a daily gambler, not only with horses. Perhaps you had to be a gambler to do what he did.

'His phone records haven't yielded anything?'

'Nothing yet. Just local contacts. One or two we're following up.'

'Computers?'

'They're still working on those. Takes time, going through the hard drives. Especially with the backlog of terrorist cases.'

They went back down to the hall. 'Why don't we do the statement here? Saves me going down to Hastings and you can presumably go straight home.'

She hesitated, looking at the floor. 'S'pose we could.'

They sat at the dining-room table. Like all the police he'd met, she preferred to write the statement at his dictation rather than have him write it, as was his right. He let her do it; it was short enough anyway and he found himself feeling sorry for her. They soon finished but she was in no hurry to go. Her handbag was open on the table and he noticed a packet of cigarettes.

'Smoke if you like,' he said.

'Doesn't feel right, somebody else's house. Also, it's a crime scene, therefore a work place, therefore illegal.'

'Dr Klein did. You'd have been on your fourth or fifth by now if he'd been here.'

She took out her cigarettes. 'Smoked Turkish ones, didn't he? I saw that. Like James Bond.'

He fetched the ashtray from the mantelpiece. 'Is it troubling you, this case?'

'Not really, no.' She exhaled, then added assertively, 'No, it doesn't at all, not personally. No reason why it should. It's just that – I don't know what it's like in your business – but here you don't often get much of a go at the good cases. This would have been my first murder. Probably my only murder – most police officers never get anywhere near a murder. I was so pleased when the super said I could do it. Perhaps he already knew it would be taken out of our hands. Should've known.'

'He didn't. I'm sure of that.'

'What d'you think will happen?'

'Well, the investigation will go on – including you but not with you in charge – and there'll be an inquest. Bound to be a big story because there's already been publicity, hasn't there?'

'It's gone viral. All over South East news.'

'The verdict will have to be unlawful killing by a person or persons unknown. We may get names through intelligence channels but we'll never get usable evidence or an extradition. That's if it is the kind of case most people think it is.'

'You think it isn't? Sorry.' She proffered the cigarettes.

He shook his head. 'I have a private theory that it isn't. But we need to know more than we do before anyone else would take it seriously. Above all, I'd need to know how.'

She looked at him, waiting. He was debating whether to involve her. 'Perhaps I shall have one.' She smiled and pushed the packet towards him. Smiling emphasised her tiredness.

Accepting a cigarette in Viktor's house was a kind of homage to Viktor. In hotel rooms and safe flats across three continents he had smoked cigarettes he didn't want, to be companionable, to keep Viktor talking, to help him feel he wasn't alone. It might help now.

'There are one or two things you might be able to help with,' he said. 'Provided it's not against your own rules. Don't want to get you into trouble.'

'Tell me and I'll tell you.'

'The main thing is to find an escaped prisoner called Peter Tew.'

'No problem with that. We're always looking for them.'

'Let me tell you about him.' He included the little he had learned from DI Steggles. 'I've noted a few names here, prisoners he got to know who might hide him.'

'I'll run them through the system and make sure Tew's description is circulated.'

Afterwards he took the cross-country route through single-track lanes that for long stretches became hidden leafy tunnels. Two fallow deer leapt across the road thirty yards ahead of him, gliding like ghosts into the chestnut coppice. The sun was setting when he reached Brightling, touching the church tower and the tip on the stone pyramid in the churchyard. Their cottage, local sandstone like the pyramid, looked asleep in the evening shadow. It was a pleasure to behold.

It was less of a pleasure to see Jeremy Wheeler's Range Rover parked across the road and the bulky figure of its owner turning away from the cottage door. Seeing Charles draw up, he raised his hand as if in exculpation.

'Didn't know you were a Bristol owner,' he called, before Charles was properly out of the car. 'Are you a member of the owners' club?'

'No.'

'You should be.' The church clock struck seven. Two cars took the double bend in front of it too fast. Jeremy, red-faced and wide-eyed, stared at Charles as if lost for words for once. Charles resigned himself to inviting him in.

'Passing by, just dropped in to see if you were around. Fancy an early supper at the Swan?'

Despair at the thought prevented Charles from coming up with an immediate excuse. Jeremy, like the law, construed silence as assent.

'Splendid. Just a quick one. Wendy's out this evening, didn't fancy cooking. I'll get up there now and grab a table. Join me as soon as you can.'

The Range Rover's suspension took the strain as Jeremy got in; what Jeremy considered a quickie meal was unlikely to be light. Irritated with himself and resentful of Jeremy, Charles rang Sarah, really for no better reason than to complain to someone. But she was still switched off and he didn't leave a message.

The Swan was not crowded and Jeremy had a window table at the back overlooking the patchwork fields and woods between there and the sea. When Charles arrived he was clasping his near-empty pint glass in both hands and staring not at the view but at the chair opposite, morose and heavy-featured. As Charles approached, his expression transformed itself into manufactured delight.

'Well done. What are you having? I recommend the Harveys. Very good and very local.' He lowered his voice. 'Good thing about coming all the way out here is that it's on the edge of the constituency and I don't run into too many of my constituents. At least, not that recognise me. Always getting caught out over their bloody names. I know politicians are supposed to be good on names but I'm not. The venison's good, so's the pheasant. Both poached, probably. Lot of that round here. You really should join the Bristol club, makes it easier to sell when the time comes. 410, isn't it? Pity. 411s were a better car.'

Jeremy had venison, Charles shepherd's pie. For a while they talked of the plentiful tedium and few pleasures of constituency work, of how immigration lawyers were getting round the system, how important it was to keep in with the party whips, how Jeremy couldn't bear people whose only interest was to climb the greasy pole rather than create a better and more equal society, how gratified he was to be on the Intelligence Services Committee and how he would never want to be foreign secretary anyway.

'Dreadful job, being a minister. At everybody's beck and

call the whole time, never a moment to yourself, one head-
ache after another, almost as bad as being prime minister. I
wouldn't thank you for it, I really wouldn't. Would you?'

'They seem to enjoy it. Rarely give it up unless they have
to. Perhaps they think they're there to do something.'

'Of course, you're a mate of George Greene, aren't you?
Handy, having the foreign secretary in your pocket when
you want to be chief.'

'His idea, not mine.' Given Jeremy's resentment at not
having got the job, it seemed once again best to occupy no-
man's-land. 'But I doubt I'd have been offered it if we
hadn't known each other.'

'Jobs for the boys, eh? Nothing changes.'

Charles let him have that one, as it was demonstrably
true, and Jeremy, contented, dropped the subject.

'How's Sarah?' Jeremy asked.

'Well, thanks. Busier than she'd like to be at the moment,
with the house move and all that, but okay.' Busier partly
thanks to your secretary who does favours for the Russian
intelligence service and doubtless finds a home for copies of
all your ISC papers, he would have added. But there would
be time for that later; Michael Dunton would be pleased to
throw a scrap to his diminishing counter-espionage section,
who were constantly being plundered for counter-terrorism
work. 'And Wendy?' he asked.

'She's fine.' Jeremy took a swig of his beer. 'In fact, I'm thinking we might get divorced.' He emptied his glass. 'Well, you know what it's like, one thing and another. Except that you don't, of course, you've only been married five minutes. The life went out of our marriage years ago and now that the children are off our hands, more or less, there's not much point carrying on for the sake of it. May as well live our own lives.'

'Sorry to hear that. Does each of you have an own life?'

'Well, there's the rub, there's the rub.' He nodded. 'Thing is, I – er – Katya, my secretary – don't think you've met her but Sarah has, she's doing some work for her. Anyway, Katya and I thought we might get together – not marry, we can't, she's still married to a vegetable in America. Very rich vegetable, she's got power of attorney, so that's all right.' He grinned. 'She's buying a house here now. Sarah knows about it.'

'Does Wendy?'

'Thing is, what I was going to say is, Katya's half Russian – well, Russian but with a US passport – and what I wanted to ask – what I want to know is – whether if she and I, you know, got together – if that would compromise my position on the ISC and possibly any future advancement in government, if you see what I mean. No reason why it should, of course – Cold War's long gone and all that – and under the last government and the NIA it certainly wouldn't have. But things seem to have changed since I left the NIA, what with the reinstatement of the three separate services and now George Greene and his ilk in high office, and I wondered if you've got any feel for what attitudes are likely to be. I mean, given that you know George better than I do, I wondered if you'd be able to put out feelers—'

'Questions for the boys, eh?' Charles softened it with a smile. 'But really, I've no idea, I haven't enquired about current attitudes.' Literal, but limited, truth was preferable to honesty. It ought to be a problem and certainly would be once Katya's allegiances were known. But he couldn't tell Jeremy that yet. 'If I were you I wouldn't do anything in a hurry, don't commit yourself. Take time to test the water a bit. How did you come across her and how long's it been going on?'

Jeremy gave a rambling account of how allegations arising from a misunderstanding with a previous secretary had resulted in a series of temps who proved very temporary and how finally an advert on the parliamentary website – most people's first resort but his last because he preferred to work through people he knew – had produced Katya's application as an American graduate student and researcher who wanted some practical, hands-on experience of the British political system. They had become close, they understood each other, it had been a revelation. Jeremy spoke as a man obsessed, from which it was easy to guess that she manipulated him with ease. 'It's not just a physical thing, you see, it's intellectual. She has the finest mind I've ever met.'

Charles's own mind was focused less on Katya's intellectual pre-eminence than on Jeremy's iPad. It had rested unattended on the table throughout dinner until, while Jeremy described the unsatisfactory secretary who was responsible for the allegations and misunderstandings, it came to life with a message. Jeremy raised his eyebrows at it and said, 'Ah – Toast thinks he has me in check. I'll let him wait till I get home before showing him his error.' He grinned. 'His fatal error so far as this game is concerned.'

'Who is Toast?'

'One of my chess opponents, the most regular and the best. Toast is his game name. A good player but not quite as good as he thinks. I'll let him stew, then finish him off later.'

'The game is live now?'

'Resumed just before I came out this evening. He's taken a couple of hours over that move.'

Later, installed at last in the cottage with the Office camp-bed – a clumsy apparatus marked 'War Department', complete with the government arrow – Charles went through his phone. There were numerous messages from Elaine, some of which he could deal with, others which he put off by saying he would discuss tomorrow. There were also two from DI Steggles and one each from Tim Corke and Michael Dunton. He had hoped for news of *Beowulf* to give Sarah but there was nothing. He still found it hard to believe it was as serious as it had the potential to be; if something had gone badly wrong it would surely be evident by now. He rang Sarah but there was no answer on her mobile or the house phone. He rang her office and got the night-guard who said she had gone home early evening, then returned and gone again. He left a long and sympathetic message on her mobile, made tea, put his radio on the floor by the camp-bed so that the *Today* programme would be within reach, and prepared to read for an hour before sleep. He kept the phone beside him in case she rang.

15

Sarah's experience of women considering divorce was that they damned it up for a long time then poured it out in an emotional Niagara of resentment, regret, anger and – quite often – self-recrimination. But Wendy Wheeler was as cool and precise as the smartly tailored suit she wore.

'I want to divorce Jeremy because I can't bear to live with him any more. The mere sight of him makes me sick with distaste and contempt. It doesn't help that I also think he's mad.'

The crypt was busy with the pre-concert crowd. They sat at a small table crammed up against a pillar, each with a glass of Sauvignon. Wendy's dark fringe was neatly trimmed and her cheeks, with their prominent bones, were almost wrinkle-free. Sarah would have assumed a face-lift but her complexion had none of the unsmiling frigidity that usually gave the game away. 'Why mad?'

'He doesn't see the world as other people do. He lives in a world of his own – I know we all do to an extent but his doesn't so much overlap with other people's as collide with them. I don't think he understands other people at all. Nor himself. Something happens and it sparks off fantasies. He never judges by what he sees or hears at all, only by what he already thinks or wants.'

She didn't want a messy divorce, just a quiet and complete separation that left her and the boys adequately provided for. She didn't want to sabotage his career or milk him of every penny. The boys were at university now, one in his first and the other his third year. They would be 'all right' about it.

'But will Jeremy be all right about it? It's bound to be messy if he isn't.'

'He could be. I just never know which way he's going to bounce. It could suit him quite well if he's sensible about it. On the other hand, we all know what hurt pride can do.'

'Is there anyone else involved?'

'Not directly.' She smiled. 'There was but he's dead.'

Sarah waited.

'Dr Klein, Viktor Klein. The man everyone was talking about the other night.' Her lips were still formed in a smile.

'Does Jeremy know?'

'No, not properly. But he's come to suspect.' She looked around. 'I wish one could smoke in these places.'

'We could go outside.'

'It's all right.'

'So why—' Sarah hesitated. She wasn't going to take on the case, didn't need to know the ins and outs of it all and had a couple of good names to recommend to Wendy. But she was puzzled and Charles would be interested. 'So why – if you don't mind my asking – why didn't you get divorced while Dr Klein was alive? Why now, when he's dead?'

'You never met Viktor, did you? He was a lover, not a husband. He'd been married, of course, but he could never have stayed married. It would be a nightmare to be his wife. He'd lose interest the moment the knot was tied and you'd be forever looking over your shoulder at every woman he met. It was all I could do to – to keep him, as it was.'

'But why bother now he's dead? Divorce is costly, you'll both be the poorer for it for evermore. Couldn't you just rub along, leading separate lives? Wouldn't Jeremy accept that?'

'Would he notice?' She shrugged. 'We could, yes, of course we could, like many people. In some ways it would suit him, he could spend more time with his floozie, that Russian tart who works for him.'

'Katya? He's having an affair with Katya?'

'I don't know whether it's an affair or quite what it is and frankly I don't much care. He's certainly having an obsession. She's got him so twisted round her little finger she doesn't have to jump into bed with him. Unless she wants to, of course, which is hard to imagine. No, but I think he might have killed Viktor, you see, that's the thing. And I can't bring myself to stay with him as long as I think that.'

Sarah put down her glass. 'Why do you think that?'

'I just do. I look at him sometimes, I look at the back of his head and his fat neck and I can tell, I can just tell. He's hiding something. I do see things sometimes, not all the time but sometimes I can tell things about people. I'm a bit psychic.'

'So you've no actual evidence? He hasn't got a gun hidden away or anything like that?'

'No evidence and he doesn't have a gun but I know, I just know. Just as I knew he was becoming suspicious from the way he kept mentioning Viktor and started wanting to know where I was every afternoon. Then I found he'd been checking my car mileage. Now he's suddenly much more cheerful. That's why I can't bear the idea of spending the rest of my life with him.'

'You haven't thought of going to the police with your suspicions?'

'Oh no, I don't want to get him into trouble. Anyway, there's no evidence, is there?' Her eyes widened.

Sarah stared back, unsure of which of the Wheelers was madder.

'There's also this.' Wendy took a folded paper from her handbag.

It was a will, the sort downloaded from the Internet, not drawn up by a solicitor. Dated almost a year ago, it was signed by Viktor Klein and witnessed by Jean Goodsell. He had bequeathed all his worldly goods to Wendy Wheeler.

'That's his housekeeper, Mrs Goodsell. There's another copy with his solicitors here in London, but I don't know who they are.'

'And Jeremy knows nothing of this?'

'Of course not.' She took the will and clipped her handbag shut. 'Nor shall he until after the divorce.'

'You should talk to the police.'

They parted after the crowd left for the concert in the church upstairs, Sarah checking her phone as she walked round the corner to their house. There was no message from Charles – a bit early, perhaps, he might still be giving his statement to the police – but there was, exasperatingly, one from Katya Chester. With her usual breathless urgency and faux intimacy, she said that Mr Mayakovsky wished to have further discussion and would call on her at her office as he was in the area that evening. Swearing under her breath and irritated with herself for letting Katya have her mobile number, Sarah called her back but there was no answer. Then she rang the office porter who said yes, a gentleman had called in, hadn't left a name, said he would call back later.

She really didn't want to return to the office and it really wasn't acceptable for clients, even would-be blackmailers, to call without appointments. But Charles wanted her to play him along and this was a good opportunity to talk to him without her secretary or anyone else being aware, even though she wouldn't be able to record it. Maybe she could get him to say enough for her not to have to see him again. Then she could feel her debt was paid, the debt Charles assured her she didn't have. And while she waited there were the London Bridge development lease amendments to be getting on with in the office. She hesitated over whether to take a taxi but decided on her car. Having it with her might make her feel more in control.

The office porter nodded towards the waiting area. 'He's over there, round the corner,' he said with lowered voice. 'On his mobile. Shall I call him over?'

'No, thanks, I'll go up to my office and ring you when I'm ready for him. Make it look as if I've been here a while but was too busy to see him.'

She used the stairs as they were out of sight of the waiting area, switched everything on in her office – gratifyingly
it all worked – and settled herself. She felt better about
dealing with him when she was in charge of the environ-
ment; certainly better than being imprisoned in the back of
his Rolls-Royce.

He was still studying his phone when he was shown in
and barely had the grace to glance up for long enough to
shake hands. They both sat. He resumed his study of the
phone. Perhaps he intended to record her, though he wasn't
being very secretive about it. She said nothing. Eventually
he noticed her silence and looked up. She stared at his
phone, still saying nothing. After a few seconds he put it in
his pocket.

'Thank you, Mr Mayakovsky. Now that we have each
other's undivided attention, perhaps you'd like to tell me
what I can do for you?'

'You can give me answer, please.'

Despite her promise to Charles it was an effort to suppress the answer she wanted to give. It was important, she
reminded herself, it would help Charles, it was in the
national interest that she should play along just this once, to
find out what they wanted to know. But it was hard not to
respond to his morose truculence.

'Perhaps you could remind me of the question.'

'Have you told your husband about our conversation?'

'No.'

'So – you will cooperate?'

'That depends on what you ask. Also, on your giving your word that nothing of what you know of my previous husband will be published or made known.'

She doubted that pleasure was part of Mr Mayakovsky's facial repertoire but the intensified stoniness of his gaze – if that was possible – may have indicated satisfaction. 'You have my word and the word of Moscow.' He took out a gold pen and small black notebook. 'Now, please, what can you tell me?'

That was easy. 'I'm afraid I don't know. Perhaps you'd better tell me what you'd like me to ask my husband about?'

He stared as if the question came as a surprise, then took out his phone and studied it again. It struck her that he might be one of those comically incompetent men whose menace would evaporate the moment she saw him like that. Perhaps he was simply not very good at his job. Charles had been rather dismissive of him. But then Charles hadn't met him.

He looked up from his phone. 'Mr Peter Tew, this man. We want to find this man.'

'I told you before, I don't know him. I don't know where he is.'

'You must ask your husband. He can discover him.'

'I'll try.' She made a needless note, thinking it might impress him. 'But why do you want to know? Why are you so interested in him? Is he still in MI6?"

'Please.' He held up his hand. 'In Moscow they are suspicious of people who ask questions.'

'All right.' She put down her pen. 'Tell me what else you would like to know.'

'Moscow will tell me and I will tell Katya and she will tell you when you talk with her about houses.'

'That's a good idea, it's always nice to talk to Katya. And very useful for you to have her working for you. She doesn't attract suspicion.'

'But sometimes you see me.'

'Even better.'

'She will ring you.'

'Yes. She does that quite often, anyway.'

'When she ring you it might also be message from me.'

'I understand.'

'But also I wish to buy houses. I have money for many houses. I am rich man. Really.'

'I understand that too.'

After consulting his phone again, he put away his pen and notebook and stood, holding out his hand. 'I am pleased we work together, Mrs Thoroughgood.'

'So am I.'

'It is pleasure for me.' His smile – the first she had seen – was almost, quite unexpectedly, charming.

There was no need to make conversation in the lift as he was engrossed by his phone. Only when they reached the revolving glass doors did he look at her once more. 'He uses a computer, another computer, not his.'

'Who?'

'Mr Tew. He uses the computer of Mr Jeremy Wheeler who is the master of Katya. She works for him.'

'Jeremy Wheeler, yes, I know him. Well, Katya could ask him where Mr Tew is, couldn't she?'

'They do not meet, Mr Wheeler does not know, we are sure of this. Katya study him. It is only his computer that is used. Mr Tew has his own computer which can use Mr Wheeler's. We want to know where are Mr Tew and his computer. If your husband can discover where is his computer or the numbers to identify it, you can tell me. Moscow would be very pleased with this information.'

'I'll do my best, Mr Mayakovsky.' That was important, Charles would be pleased. It made it almost easy to tell Mr Mayakovsky that she looked forward to seeing him again.

The porter grinned as she walked back past his desk. 'You unglued his eyes from his phone, then, Ms Bourne?'

'But not his brain, I suspect.'

She rang Charles but his phone was off. His statement must be taking a long time. She worked for an hour until she found she was reading every sentence twice, then switched off and left.

'Gentleman just called for you, Ms Bourne,' said the porter. 'Not the same one, different one. Asked for you as Mrs Thoroughgood. I said you were in and offered to ring but he said not to disturb you but would see you later.'

It was presumably Charles, returned unexpectedly. Odd of him not to have rung.

'Two gentlemen in one evening,' said the porter. 'Must be good for business.'

'I'm not sure about that.'

The rain which had started as she parked was steady now, forming puddles in the gutters She stood in the entrance, putting up her umbrella, then walked quickly round the corner towards her car. It was the umbrella that made her unaware of the man approaching from behind her right shoulder until his hand slipped under her arm and gripped her wrist with sudden painful tightness. Almost at the same time something hard jabbed her ribcage.

'This is a gun, Mrs Thoroughgood. It's cocked and ready to fire. Just keep walking and don't say anything and you'll be all right. We're going to your car.'

He was taller than her and lifted her half off her feet so

that she was propelled along almost on her toes, much faster than usual. For the few seconds it took to round the corner she was too shocked to speak and didn't even turn her head to look properly at him. It was difficult anyway with the umbrella. She thought afterwards she should have dropped it and struggled – he might have tripped over it – but he held her tightly and the pain in her ribs prevented her from thinking.

They were standing by her car. 'Give me the car keys.' He was well-spoken and deliberate.

'I can't, they're in my bag.' She heard herself as if from outside. He still gripped her right wrist. She couldn't open her handbag and search it with one hand.

'Put it on the bonnet.'

She managed it, with some fumbling. Her hair kept falling in front of her face and she couldn't brush it back. 'You're hurting my wrist.'

'Leave the key on the bonnet.' She did that, struggling to close her bag with her left hand. 'Now get in the driver's seat.' He walked her round to the driver's door, took the umbrella from her and held it as she got in. Then he pocketed the gun, which she still hadn't seen, and walked swiftly round to the other side, scooping the key from the bonnet.

He was quickly beside her, the dripping umbrella folded between his legs. Again, she thought afterwards, she could have done something then, she should have got out and run. But she was shaking and still not fully able to believe what was happening.

He took the gun from his pocket and held it in his left hand, resting it on his lap and pointing it at her. 'Just follow my directions and you'll come to no harm, you'll be all right.'

His voice was gentler now but she could still feel where he had pressed the gun in her ribs. There'd be a bruise. And her wrist hurt where he had gripped it. 'What are you doing this for? What do you want?'

'I'm taking you hostage. Just for a while. Start the car and head for Waterloo Bridge.'

'Hostage for what? What for?' She looked at him properly for the first time. He was thin-faced and pale, clean-shaven, with greying dark hair. He looked intelligent and alert. Almost distractingly good-looking, in fact. But the way he looked at her made her feel like the umbrella or the car, an object to be used, of no interest in herself.

'For your husband. Do as I said. Get going.'

16

Charles got up to go to the loo in the early hours. Parting from the camp-bed involved a degree of leverage and calculation he didn't recall from his army days, another sign of youth's silent desertion. His phone showed no text from Sarah. Odd, because even if she finished very late she would surely have sent something in response to his message. But it was too late to ring her now. Perhaps her battery was flat and she feared to wake him by ringing from a landline.

He reinstalled himself in the camp-bed and lay waiting for the feathers of sleep to fall again. There was no wind, no street noise, no background hum of traffic as in London. Once, distantly, the sound of a motorbike penetrated the mothy silence, fading like a very long, very thin tail. Then, quite suddenly, the word 'toast' lit up his mind, the word itself, unencumbered by Proustian associations of taste or smell or occasion. Toast was the nickname Jeremy's chess opponent had chosen for himself. Toast was also an anagram of stoat and stoat was the code name for the investigation of Peter Tew, which Peter had discovered through papers disclosed to his leaky lawyers. He had always had a fondness for inventing simple nicknames for colleagues, often concealed beneath harmless anagrams but sometimes cruelly apt. Charles levered himself out of bed again.

The Head Office duty officer had been asleep, as was permitted provided he could be summoned immediately. So, judging by his initial incomprehension, was the GCHQ duty officer. Torn between wanting to do what Charles asked and fearing to act outside the usual channels with GCHQ authority, he hesitated. 'Not sure of the best way to do this, sir –'

'You can either ring your Director at home and ask him or give me his home number and I'll ring him. It's important. He won't mind being woken.'

'Can it really not wait until the morning, sir? It really requires a warrant from the Secretary of State, you see—'

'That's fine. I'll ring George Greene myself and get him to ring your Director. They'll both agree, I'm quite sure of that.'

Alarmed now, the duty officer struggled to help while wanting the cup of responsibility taken from him.

'I'm sure we can find a way through this,' said Charles, trying to sound considerate and sympathetic. 'I'm asking for two things. One concerns a target you're monitoring already. I just need to know when a particular communication stream within that target started, and when it finished. The other, because it means live interception of an individual's laptop, requires a warrant. If you're prepared to get interception going now, I'll seek retrospective authorisation from the Foreign Secretary first thing in the morning as one of our operations, not one of yours. Thus, you'll be responding to a tasking request on the understanding that it is being authorised. I'll get our duty officer to email you on his channels, confirming it in writing and saying that I take full responsibility. Will that help?'

It helped. Next it was the MI6 duty officer's turn to become uneasy. 'Sorry, sir, but may I – may I just check I've got this right? The laptop whose traffic you wish to read belongs to a member of parliament who is also a member of the ISC and used to be a senior officer here. The reason for urgency is that the laptop may be transmitting from his home now. Also, you believe we should have a record of which laptop it is because we supplied the individual concerned with it while he was with us and it might therefore not be on the list of ISC laptops?'

'Correct.'

There was a pause. 'I – don't want to be awkward, sir – but I believe operations or investigations involving members of parliament require prime ministerial authorisation, don't they? And that a case like this would fall more properly to MI5—'

'You're absolutely right and if necessary I shall seek authorisation from the Prime Minister. But it needs to be done very quickly while the thing might be live. We may not get another chance. If we're doing wrong, on my head be it. Now, would you like me to dictate the Cheltenham email for you?'

It was insecure to do it over the phone but needs must. By the time he finished it was ten to four and not yet light. He made a cup of tea, washed, dressed, ate toast with Marmite and packed the Bristol. His phone rang as he was walking back down the garden path to lock up. The sky was lightening to the east but overhead there was still a great bomb-burst of stars. He looked up as he answered, wondering as always how astronomers could ever heed merely human considerations.

This time it was Joyce, the GCHQ operational night shift manager. They had details of Jeremy Wheeler's laptop from the MI6 duty officer but it would help to know roughly where it was. Charles gave her Jeremy's Battle postcode. She said they should be able to pick it up if it were live now, otherwise they would have to trawl through metadata they stored to see if that yielded anything. They wouldn't be able to recover content but they would establish usage. She was putting the word 'toast' into their Star system. Charles looked up again. They'd probably get as many hits in the next hour as he could see stars in the heavens. He briefly considered waking Jeremy and getting him to check his laptop but didn't want to alert him. After all, he could be part of it. Unlikely, but anything was possible.

Before six, it was possible to move on the M25 and he made good time. But when he turned into the Office underground car park, shared with an insurance company, a firm of solicitors, a department store and a company that made porn films, the barrier stayed down. He waited, knowing he was on camera. No-one came. He didn't want to leave the car blocking the ramp so he reversed and parked on double yellow lines over the road.

The guard in the entrance hall was an overweight middle-aged man. He did not put aside his newspaper.

'Have to use your swipe card,' he said.

'I don't yet have one. Could you open it for me?'

'Need it in writing from your line manager to park without a swipe card.'

'I don't have a line manager. I'm the boss.'

'Still need written permission.'

'From whom?'

The door behind the desk opened and another over-weight man appeared, looking as if he had swallowed something unpleasant. 'Got to have written permission,' he said.

Charles was patient. It would be undignified for the Chief to get into a row with the guards. 'Can we do it retro-spectively? I'll get someone to write it for me when the staff arrive and send it down.'

'Long as your car stays outside.'

He had another idea. 'Let me just check to see if I've got something.' He sat in the waiting area and took some Foreign Office headed notepaper from his briefcase. He wrote to the effect that the bearer had permission to park pending issue of his swipe card, signed in his own name and dated it the week before. The second man had dis-appeared when he handed it to the guard. 'I found I had got this.'

The guard put his finger on Charles's signature. 'Who is this?'

'The line manager. The top one.'

The guard handed it back. 'You can lift the barrier your-self. It's broken.'

The cleaners were still there, chatting in the open-plan area outside his office. It had been suggested that he would set a good egalitarian example by making his office part of the open plan. He had tried to think of plausible reasons for not but now, energised by what was happening and what he was about to do, he decided he would simply say no. He would say he didn't want it, with no further explanation. Attlee was like that, he remembered reading. When a sacked minister asked why he had been dismissed, Attlee had reputedly replied, 'Because you're not up to the job,' and carried on writing. Charles had a weakness for grand historical comparisons.

He had brought his mobile in with him because that was the number Cheltenham would use but still he hesitated to ring Sarah. He would give her another half-hour. There was power today so he made a coffee and turned on his computer, only to realise he could not get into the system. So far Elaine had logged him on before he arrived. He didn't know his user name or password, though he had an uneasy feeling he had been told them, and couldn't access even his diary. He sipped the coffee, staring at the screen-saver and recalling Sarah's recent scolding about his futile resistance to the computer age. He was in fact less resistant than he allowed himself to appear but took a private pleas-ure in being the object of protest and concern. Now, cradling his coffee in both hands, he reflected that if his theory was right it was no bad thing to be out of the system. He would be the only person whose thoughts and actions were unreadable.

At half past six he got out his address book. There were no numbers stored in his phone, something he could now present as a security decision. He rang George Greene first, hoping he held to the working habits of his youth. In Vienna he always did two hours' work before the rest of the embassy was awake, which meant he could have long lunches and give the impression of being effortlessly on top of things.

It was no different now; George was at home in Pimlico, working on his red box. 'Even earlier these days,' he said. 'Competition from the Prime Minister. He rises at five, into his box by 5.30. Not one of your vices, I seem to remember. Must be world war three to have got you out of your cot at this hour.'

Charles explained. When he finished there was a pause.

'Did I meet Peter Tew?' asked George. 'Name's familiar.'

'Not through me. After your time. You probably read about him.'

'Got it in for you, by the sound of it. Two down and one to go, if your theory's correct.' He chuckled. 'Vintage Agatha Christie.'

'You're the third person who's said that.'

'Won't be the last, especially if he tops you.'

'But will the warrant be okay? Will you authorise it?'

'Suppose so, though it may not be for me. Sounds more like one for Five and the Home Secretary.'

'That'll take for ever, especially if it has to go up to the Prime Minister.'

'All right, I'll do it and square him when I see him this morning. You just make sure someone sets it in motion. Get Angela on to it. You'd better tell her what's going on anyway, otherwise she'll throw all her toys out of the pram when she finds out.'

Charles wasn't convinced that George appreciated the full import of his theory. 'You do see that if I'm right about all this it could be the answer to our cyber attacks as well—'

'Interesting if true. Keep your head down.' George Greene never found it difficult to end conversations.

Charles caught Angela as she was about to leave for work. She cut him off soon after he started. 'Charles, can't this wait until I get into the office? Also, should you be talking about it over the phone?'

'No and yes, Angela. I can't get in to explain and we've got to set things in motion quickly.'

She heard him out and sighed. 'Oh God, this is all we need. Sorry – not your fault, I know. We'd better have a

COFE later. I hope to God Tim Corke is in London. Will you be able to get to it? I take that back – you will, you'll have to, just have to. I'll get my office to set it up.'

'Make it this afternoon.'

'George Greene having a word with the PM is all very well but we've been here before on other matters. Neither of them will put anything in writing or even think to tell anyone unless they're asked. And then they'll give wildly different accounts. It's no way to run a country.'

'We're not running anything, we're being run. Up to now we've been reacting, that's the point. This is our chance to get ahead of the game, provided we act fast.'

He next rang Sarah. There was no answer from home or her mobile. He tried her direct line at work, finally her secretary. She was baffled. 'Can't find her anywhere, I've tried everywhere, she was to chair an early meeting that was supposed to start ten minutes ago and I've had to put every-one off, including two people over specially from New York about the London Bridge project. It's a nightmare, I can't think where she is, I'm sure she'd have rung in, she's so – you know – thoughtful and organised. The log at reception says she had two visitors yesterday evening when she was working late. She saw one of them but the other left with-out leaving a name and didn't come back. Then she left. Did she not come home, then?'

Her office night guard was at home asleep and couldn't be disturbed. The CCTV system was controlled by security who were difficult about access. Charles told her to keep trying and to keep in touch. He meanwhile would go home to check. His unspoken thought, which he sensed the secretary shared, was that Sarah might have fallen ill, or even died. Things happened, including unlikely things. He had an image, more vivid than he wanted, of her sprawling on the bathroom floor. His other unspoken thought concerned the mystery caller. So far the outbreak of war had been theoretical, his own theory, not proven. But if this was what he feared, it was war.

Elaine arrived just as he was packing up. She had a black eye. He hurried out, giving her instructions as he went and saying he was off to an urgent Cabinet Office meeting. She tried to pass messages lurking in his emails and wanted to know when he'd be back. He was abrupt, telling her he couldn't say and that she was to sort out what she could. By the time he got downstairs he felt guilty and rang her from reception.

'Sorry I was short with you. It's just that something urgent has come up and there's not time to explain. I'll call in later. Meanwhile, get me on the mobile if you need me.'

'Of course, yes, I'm so sorry, I—'

'Don't be. All my fault.'

'There's a message for you from Sussex Police, a DI Whitely wants you to ring her.'

'Good, thanks. Bye.'

'And your car keys are on your desk. At least, I assume they're yours. I'll bring them down.'

She was still flustered and concerned when she arrived. He put down his briefcase. 'Elaine, this just proves I wouldn't get anywhere without you, not even out of the building.'

'Michelle Blakeney – director HR – has been back to me already about the OFRA meeting – Open Plan For All. I said you'd had to postpone again this morning. She sounded quite cross, actually – well, it is the third time – and wants to know when there's going to be a decision.'

'Tell her it's just been made: no more open plan.'

'She'll be awfully cross.' Elaine couldn't hide her smile.

'I know. And meanwhile you and I will just have to cope with our mutual distress at this announcement. Tell her I'll discuss with her later.' He picked up his briefcase.

'I hope everything's all right?'

'Thanks, so do I. I'll explain as soon as I can. If by any chance Sarah should ring, let me know straight away. Keep in touch. And Elaine – the eye. You'll have to say something about it.'

'I box.'

'Of course.'

'I won.'

Charles nodded. 'Good. We'll go into this later.'

It would have been quicker into Westminster by train but he reckoned he might need the car. When eventually he turned off the Embankment he idled into Cowley Street, postponing in the last minute what he had raced for in the last hour.

Her car wasn't in sight and the door was locked. He closed it quietly and walked from room to room, as he had in Viktor's house. There had been no more unpacking, the bathroom was as he had last seen it, her clothes were hanging as he remembered, the dishwasher was still only half full from when they had last eaten.

There was a message on the phone from 2.14 that morning. For a few seconds there was silence, then her voice, speaking slowly and sounding flat. 'Charles, it's me. I'm all right. I'm with Peter Tew. He wants to meet you, to exchange me for you. I'm on my mobile but there's no point ringing it. We will call you again on yours.' There was a pause, murmuring in the background, then, rapidly, 'If you try to involve the police or anyone else, he says he will kill me.' Then a click and silence.

He listened again, saved it and stood staring at the receiver. He was calm. Not the calmness of detachment, still less of indifference, but of calculation; so long as he could see a way to act, he would focus on action. Everything else would come later.

His mobile rang. DI Whitely sounded excited. 'Prisoner friends of your friend,' she said. 'Three names stand out. One's still inside, another was released early eighteen months ago because of health problems and may be dead but the third is on our doorstep, just up the road from here. Michael John Swavesy, aged forty-seven, fourteen years for armed robbery, supply of firearms, possession of a firearm, receiving stolen goods, got off a murder charge on what sounds like a perverse jury verdict. Said to have been a professional hitman. Good behaviour, trained as a clock and watch repairer, released after eight years three years ago, so out well before your friend. No indication whether they kept in touch. Sounds promising. Took a swing past his shop this morning, doesn't look as if he does much business. Want us to have a look at him?'

'Thanks, Louise, that's very helpful.' Charles thought. 'We don't want to alert him. We want to watch him. I don't suppose you've got the resources to—'

'Not without my super's say-so and even then only for a short time for something specific. I dare say the Met—'

'Let me get back to you. Meanwhile, find out everything you can about him – cars, phones, family, contacts, habits, everything. Take your watch in.'

'So long as you get me a new one if I don't get it back.'

'Two for a conviction.'

'Deal. Oh, and your friend – he's got cancer. Terminal, they say.'

'Does he know it?'

'Think so, yes.'

Hence Peter's urgency, why he was doing it now, why he had absconded. 'Anything else?'

'That's enough to be going on with, isn't it? I mean—'

'More than enough, it's very helpful. I was just – where was it, his last prison? Open prison.'

'Not far from here. Old army camp. Holiday camp now, they come and go as they please. Do courses to prepare for outside, bed their visitors if they can. Live pretty much as if they're out already except they don't have to pay the rent.'

'Did my friend have any visitors?'

'Dunno, not sure it says. Let's have a look.' There was a pause. 'No, doesn't seem to – yes, hang on. A Mrs Chester.'

'Katya Chester?'

'Mrs K. Chester, that's all it says.'

'How often? More than once?'

'Doesn't say. Just says when permission was first granted.' She gave the date. 'May have been just that once.

You think he had something going with this married lady, then?'

'Something, yes, but not the usual thing. Not his style. Anything else? Did he do any courses?'

'Hang on, let's – sorry, gone past it. Here we are – trades, vocational, education. No, nothing listed, unless – no, he didn't do any courses but he took one. I mean, he taught one. Computing skills. Taught it to other prisoners. So they could get up to date on fraud for when they come out, stuff like that.'

'They had computers in prison?'

'Unless they did it with matchsticks.'

Afterwards Charles started to dial Michael Dunton's number but changed his mind and rang Graham Wood of the Civil Contingencies Unit. He was less likely to ask questions. 'When did the CNI attacks begin?'

Graham drew his breath. 'Well, that's the thing. We can't say for sure. They might have been into our systems some time before we knew about it. First indication we had on the GSI network was in May. I can look up the actual date if you like.'

Charles didn't need that. The dates were close enough. Katya's permission to visit had been granted in April.

The COFE meeting was again in the COBR. Charles had got Angela to bring it forward to later in the morning.

Because of that there were only Angela, Tim Corke and Michael Dunton. It took ten minutes to bring them up to date.

As soon as he finished Michael Dunton said, 'We must tell the police. I don't know whether the Met still have their specialist kidnap squad but they've got the expertise anyway and the sooner they get on to this the better Sarah's chances.'

Charles reverted to his usual tactic, nodding agreement. 'Of course. The only reason I haven't got on to them already is that I wanted everyone to know where we are and whether Tim's people have had any luck with what I asked for during the night. Because that might help steer the police investigation.'

'Some, but not necessarily anything that's going to be any help with Sarah,' said Tim, speaking faster than usual. 'At least, not yet. We got into Jeremy Wheeler's laptop straight away, thanks to the details you gave and to the fact that he leaves it on. He wasn't using it for any nefarious purpose but simply to play chess. Seems to be a protracted game but we don't know who with, except that he calls himself Toast, as you said. We won't know where Toast is until he goes live again and comes back with his next move. If he stays live for long enough we'll get a fix but it can take time, especially if he's on the move. What we have established, however, is that Wheeler's and Toast's chess games coincide with our cyber poacher's access to the MI6 system and from there to the others. They – whoever they are – are piggy-backing on Wheeler and Toast to get into our systems.'

'That ought to be impossible,' said Michael. 'The laptops issued to Wheeler and other ISC members have no access to the sealed systems within the agencies. There are no links. The information we supply electronically to the ISC doesn't come from within our own systems. There are simply no bridges back to us. You know that, Tim, your people set it up.'

Tim shook his head. 'That doesn't mean that someone couldn't contrive it, given the expertise. If your Jeremy Wheeler—'

'I don't think Jeremy could do that,' said Charles. 'But his laptop is the one he was issued with in the old SIA and maybe it could, without his knowing. If he uses it to communicate with people within the Office – as I suspect he does because he's always trying to find out about things – then he might be opening a pathway that a sophisticated cyber thief could exploit.'

Angela held up her hands. 'And so who is this Toast character who can wreak such cyber havoc simply through moving his knight to pawn four or whatever? He must be a computer prodigy beyond—'

'Toast is Peter Tew,' said Charles. He explained. They looked doubtful.

'That's your main reason, the anagram?' asked Angela. 'That and coincidences of timing? What makes you think Tew is capable of—'

'Peter was a cyber evangelist from the days when MI6 first started using computers seriously and in his last gaol he taught some sort of computer course. Maybe he also updated himself. But you're right, Angela, he wouldn't be able to penetrate and threaten our critical national infrastructure unaided.' He nodded, reinforcing his reasonableness. 'But if he affords access to those who can and if he has sufficient ill-will – as his kidnap of Sarah surely demonstrates – he could make his cyber connection available to the Russians or Chinese, or both. He lets whoever it is use his chess games with Jeremy as their bridge and I guess they've captured Jeremy's computer, or are on their way to doing so.'

'We must get it off Wheeler straight away,' said Michael. 'Close it down.'

'Why don't we use it first, play it back at them? Misinformation. Get their submarines off the scent of *Beowulf,* for example. Make them think she's back. Also it would help us locate Peter Tew which would lead us to Sarah—'

Angela shook her head. 'Too many hidden ifs, Charles.

Of course we've got to get Sarah safely back, that has to be our number one priority but it's for the police—'

'Definitely,' said Michael. 'The police. It's got to be the police.'

'– and for our part we can't for the sake of some hypothetical advantage allow these power cuts and cyber failures to continue an hour longer than necessary. The government would fall if it got out that we'd let them run on for nefarious purposes of our own. If we can stop them we must. We stop them dead.' She slapped her palm on the desk.

Tim caught Charles's eye. 'Why do you think Tew wants to speak to you?'

'He wants to exchange me for Sarah. Sarah's the bait.'

'What does he want you for?'

'To kill him,' said Michael. 'As he killed Configure and Frank Heathfield. He wants revenge on those who put him away. That's why Charles must be under police protection from now on. Another reason to involve the police immediately.'

Tim was still looking at Charles. 'But if you're assuming he found out where Configure and Frank lived by accessing the MI6 database via Jeremy Wheeler, why couldn't he do the same with you? He could just turn up on your doorstep and shoot you instead of going to all the trouble of kidnapping Sarah.'

'He wouldn't have found me on it. Fortunately, I've been very remiss, haven't yet told them where we now live.' It was not going as he wanted. His aim was again to leave the meeting with his freedom of action intact while preserving his access to intelligence community resources. 'Best thing would be to wait till he rings again on Sarah's phone so that you can monitor live and get a location fix. At the same time we should get Jeremy to resume his chess game so that you can get a fix on Tew's computer. It and Tew might not always be in the same place.'

Michael and Angela were shaking their heads before he'd finished. 'Absolutely not, no playing those games without police say-so,' said Michael.

Tim said nothing, which Charles felt – hoped – was an indication of complicity. They were right about the police but he didn't want them yet. 'I'll tell the police when I leave here.'

'Why not before?' said Angela. 'You don't want to get home and find Peter Tew on your doorstep. And every minute counts for Sarah.'

The last was true; it was why he wanted to act now and not wait. But he needed Tim's help.

'They'll want to come to my home, to help secure it. I may as well meet them there.' As he stood to go he said to Tim, 'I discovered last night I must have mislaid your mobile number.'

257

Tim gave it to him and Charles hurried out.

He walked back to Cowley Street. His mobile was cluttered with messages from Elaine, which a quick trawl showed to be about briefings, missed meetings and diary queries. He ignored them all but felt guilty about the trouble she was going to. If he rang now he'd have to explain, and there was no time for that. Once inside the door he rang Tim Corke, reckoning he would have had time to get back to his London office.

'Thought I'd hear from you,' said Tim. 'You're about to hear from the police. Michael and Angela got on to them after you'd gone, not trusting you to do it. Which you haven't, I imagine?'

'I shall but I haven't quite worked out how to put it so that they don't rush into action too quickly. I was wondering if you could—'

'I think I know what you want, Charles. But are you sure this is what's best for Sarah? It's pretty high-risk and if it doesn't work God knows what he might do to her.'

'If it doesn't work he's still got me. He'll let her go in exchange, I'm sure of that. I know him. It's me he wants.'

'Yes, but—'

'How long d'you need to set it up?'

'Well, it's all there already. They'll pick up your call and

Wheeler's laptop but for live monitoring it would be help-ful to have estimated times. My worry is that—'

'I know, I know. Look, I'll ring the police now. I'll also ring George Greene so that we're covered, at least to a degree. Give me,' – he paused – 'give me a two-hour win-dow starting one hour from now. And then can someone ring me with the results? You've got my numbers.'

'That's leaving it a bit long, isn't it? Who knows what sort of state she might be in.'

'He won't do anything until he's spoken to me. She's a bargaining chip, that's all. Her value is as a hook for me and he won't want to harm her while she can still be that. He might kill her if she ceases to be of value which is why I have to make sure he thinks it's going to work. If he gets the faintest whiff of police involvement she loses her value and probably her life.'

'But what happens to you when he's got you?'

'I happen to him. That's what happens.'

He rang DI Steggles. If he had paused he would have begun to imagine what Sarah might be going through. Imagination, like thought for Hamlet, could be the enemy of action. Also, it was essential to delay the police.

'I was about to ring you,' said DI Steggles. 'What's all this about? Bit of a garbled story here about your wife—'

Charles explained, trying to get them to focus on the

scene of the crime and on finding Sarah's car. DI Steggles was pleased by the prospect of action. 'Where are you now, sir? We'd better get round to your home straight away. It and you will need guarding—'

'Surely the main thing is to get any street camera footage from around her office to show what happened and maybe follow the car through London. I'll be dashing about today. I've got to head south now, I should be safe enough there. Let's keep in touch and meet later.' He rang off, hoping they would interpret 'south' as Croydon. Then he threw some old clothes into a holdall and unlocked his gun cabinet which was temporarily in the utility room. He took out his guns, mostly sporting guns inherited from his father, wrapped them in blankets and locked them in the boot of the Bristol. Then he drove round to the Westminster underground car park to ring DI Whitely in Hastings. He didn't trust the police not to come screeching round to his house; once under protection he'd have no freedom to act.

'Your man, your local friend you were telling me about. Any chance of trying for surveillance again, including phone tap?'

'Not without someone putting up a case to the super. Unless the Met have one already and they ask us. What's the urgency, anyway? Have you found out something?'

He gave her the edited version he had given Steggles. 'Do

what you can to keep an eye on him. I don't know whether he's involved but he could be and if he is we need to be on him. If I hear anything I'll let you know, so keep your phone on. I may be in your area anyway, in which case we should meet.'

'Great. But your wife, where do you think—'

'I'll let you know.'

Next he rang Jeremy Wheeler, hoping he would be in Sussex during the parliamentary recess. He got Wendy, who sounded hollow.

'Yes, he is here, yes.'

'Are you all right?'

'I'm all right, thank you. We are just having a disagreement, that's all. A marital tiff. I'm sure you'll soon know what I mean.' She laughed unconvincingly. 'I'll just get him for you.'

There was an indistinct exchange in the background, during which he heard his name repeated. Eventually Jeremy came to the phone. 'Charles, how very nice to hear from you.' His oleaginous tone was as unconvincing as Wendy's laughter. 'What can I do for you?'

'Two things. I'm coming down later and would love you to show me how you play chess on your computer. Unless you're in the middle of a game now? I don't want to interrupt.'

'Well, it's a – we're a bit tied up at the moment – perhaps—'

'Don't worry, I'll ring before I get there.' It was exhilarating to feel free of the usual obligations of social intercourse. 'And the other thing is your secretary and researcher, Katya Chester. Is she at work today and if so could you give me her number? There's something I want her advice on.'

He could sense Jeremy's baffled tension. It was doubtless not a good time to mention Katya, but he didn't care. 'And if you could ring her to warn her I'll be badgering her that would be very helpful.'

'Well, yes, of course, but what is it—'

'It's advice on Russian protocol, what's polite and what isn't. Won't take long. But I'm in a bit of a hurry, sitting here with pen poised.'

He rang Katya a minute or two later. She had not been forewarned.

But that was no problem. Her voice swooped in surprise and delight at hearing from Sarah's famous husband. Wonderful Sarah, she was such a wonderful person, it was wonderful to do a favour to anyone connected with Sarah. She would do it immediately, whatever it was.

'I want to meet your friend, Mr Mayakovsky,' said Charles. As with Jeremy, the silence that followed was eloquent. 'In one hour in your office.' He spoke quietly and precisely. 'I shall explain why when we meet. If he is otherwise engaged, tell him from me that it is in his interest to break off his engagement immediately. Not only in his personal interest but in the interest of his friends in Moscow. Do you understand that, Katya?'

His words and tone were calculated to set the terms of the relationship he was about to have with Mr Mayakovsky. Given the political culture they had grown up in, Katya and her sugar-daddy were bound to overestimate the power of his position. They would never really believe that the Chief of MI6 had no executive powers outside his own organisation, nor that the implied menace of his remarks was incapable of fulfilment.

'I can ring him now, yes,' replied Katya, no longer gushing but picking her way carefully. 'But perhaps it would be better to meet him at his house, more private—'

'Your office in one hour,' said Charles.

The atrium in Portcullis House, the newer parliamentary offices linked by tunnel to the Victorian chambers, was a palace of light and talk. With the recess about to end, MPs, officials and visitors thronged the benches and coffee tables, people hurried through, greeting or avoiding with a wave of the hand. The controversially expensive trees forming the centrepiece were now taken for granted. Charles, once through the glass security tubes, recognised two ministers emerging from the escalator to the tunnel before he had hung his visitor's pass around his neck. Katya, who met him, was breathlessly explaining that Mr Mayakovsky was here already, sitting at one of the tables, and that they would collect him and go up to her office.

'This will do, we can talk here.'

Mr Mayakovsky was at one of the round tables near the trees, reasonably distant from the others. A good choice, thought Charles, though the hubbub of conversation would make overhearing difficult anyway. Mr Mayakovsky looked self-possessed. He rose without a smile and his handshake was limp, as Sarah had said.

'My office is on the next floor,' said Katya. 'It's very private, we can easily—'

'This is fine.' Charles sat.

Mr Mayakovsky did the same after a glance at Katya, who was hovering. Not entirely self-possessed after all, thought Charles.

'Shall I get some coffees?' asked Katya.

'Not for me.' Charles leaned forward, elbows on the table. Katya hovered another second or so, then sat. Almost everyone who passed glanced at her. He stared unblinkingly at Mr Mayakovsky's thin lips, knowing it would appear he was looking him in the eye. 'I have a message for your people in Moscow.'

Mr Mayakovsky raised his hands, looking from Charles to Katya. 'I am sorry, I am not understanding—'

'You understand English perfectly well, Mr Mayakovsky. I am sure you will also understand the implications of what I am about to say. I know exactly what you do here, I know all about your business and your relations with important people in Moscow who sometimes ask you to do things, such as talk to my wife. I know all about that. I have an important message I want you to pass to Moscow as soon as you leave this building. Whether you do it directly or via your contacts in the Russian Embassy is up to you. But it must be done quickly and accurately. If it is not, or if you prefer not to do it at all, I advise you to pack your bags and book your flight tonight, before my colleagues in the organs of state security take a serious interest in you and your business.' He turned to Katya. 'That applies to you, too.'

It was nonsense, of course; he could do nothing about either of them and MI5 would not recommend deportation to the Home Secretary without a serious case. He also knew nothing of what they were doing, beyond surmise. But they both stared solemnly back at him, Katya in surprise and shock, a rabbit in the headlights, Mr Mayakovsky like a dog that would like to bite but daren't.

'The message is simple. A department in Moscow has intermittent access to a computer here which in turn has access to sensitive government systems. Your specialist people outside Moscow have used their access to the first computer to get into these British government systems.' He held up one hand as if to forestall questions. 'Don't worry, we have known about it all along – and you can tell them, by the way, they are wasting time with their submarines – *Beowulf* is safe and on her way home. But mainly you must tell them we are closing this operation down because the Chinese also gained access and are proving very disruptive. You must also tell your Federal Guard Service – FSO, I think you call it, your computer security people – that we have reason to believe that the Chinese are, by some clever reverse engineering, attempting to access your own systems. The origin of these attempts is People's Liberation Army unit 61398, based in a twelve-storey building in Shanghai. Moscow will know about that unit but you may wish to note it.'

Mr Mayakovsky's expression did not change but he took out a notebook. Charles repeated the details. 'I will try to pass message but of course I know nothing of these matters.'

'Of course you will pass it and of course you know nothing. I think we understand each other. Your people will also wish to know why we are doing them this favour, this enormous favour.' He paused until Mr Mayakovsky looked up again. 'They know that their former agent, my old friend

Peter Tew, is out of prison. I suspect they also know it is through his and Jeremy Wheeler's computers that they get access to our systems. They wish to find Peter Tew, as you know. So do we. It would help us if they could tell us the coordinates of the computer he was using when they last accessed it. He is engaged in other criminal activities and we are bound to catch him but we will do so sooner if they help us. If they do help, they can have him when we find him. We know how much it is a question of honour for them to recover any spies who are caught. Especially as he has been useful to them again recently. That is my message. Do you understand?'

Mr Mayakovsky asked only to confirm the spelling of Tew. 'I need to know today,' said Charles. 'Otherwise I cannot guarantee that they can have him.' He could not guarantee it at all; it was so far beyond his authority as to be incredible to anyone who did not come from a system where people holding positions such as his could indeed make such promises. But problems arising from that could be dealt with later. 'I will give you and Katya my mobile number. One of you can ring me. Have you any questions?'

Mr Mayakovsky looked as if he were full of questions, but none he felt he could ask. Charles left without waiting to be escorted out.

17

He was back. She could hear him coming down the brick steps and could sense, beneath the rim of her hood, a slight lightening of the dark. He was moving about in the next room, probably with a candle again. She was hungry and thirsty, having had no water since breakfast, and still cold, though not as cold as during the night. She shifted on the bed, carefully lifting the chain so that it did not clank against the metal frame. One end of it was padlocked to the pair of metal handcuffs on her wrists, the other to the frame. The handcuffs weren't too tight but they still chafed. Her back was stiff and it hurt to change position. Thank goodness she had worn jeans to the office yesterday evening, nothing that mattered. Although her captivity had been only a night and part of a day – one day, surely, though it was impossible to know how much of it in the dark – she felt demoralisingly dirty, her head itched and she feared she was starting to smell. She would ask if she could wash. Perhaps he would let her brush her hair – there was a brush in her bag, assuming he still had her bag. It would be heaven to brush her hair. The thought of it made her feel she was going to weep again.

She heard the lock turn and sensed a further lightening from beneath her hood, much more than when he had come before. 'Food and drink, Sarah,' he said. 'And some exercise afterwards. I hope you haven't perished with cold? I've got another blanket for you.'

He put something down and moved closer. She bent her head submissively as she felt his hands around the back of her neck, undoing the hood. He was physically gentle with her – had been throughout, once he'd got her into the car – and spoke in the tones and terms of normal social inter- course. That was at once reassuring and difficult. If she responded in kind she felt she was colluding, whereas if she didn't she felt – however absurdly – ill-mannered and ungrateful. Also, not responding might prompt him to become nastier. She said as little as possible, confining her- self to matters of fact.

When he eased the hood off she winced at the brightness of the hissing gas light on the floor. She could see much more of the room now. It was all rough, discoloured, damp

concrete – walls, floor and ceiling – and there was no furniture apart from the iron bed to which she was chained.
There was an iron door in each side wall, at the far end. He
had come through the one on the right where, she remembered, there was another room. They had come down steps
into it. The other door led to a room like her own, unfurnished save for an uncomfortable bucket contraption
which, he said, was a chemical loo. She had used it twice
while he stood holding the candle in the doorway, looking
away from her but able to glance back if he wanted.

He had a plastic tray with a plastic mug of water, an
apple and a Yorkie bar of chocolate. He pointed at the
chocolate and smiled. 'They used to have "Not for Girls"
written on them but I thought that wouldn't worry you.'

She got into a sitting position on the edge of the bed and
held out her chained hands to receive the water. It was
almost like taking communion.

'Don't worry, you don't have to talk to me. But you do
have to listen.' He took the cup as from a patient and
unwrapped the chocolate. 'Eat this first. It'll give you
energy. Then the apple to clean your teeth.'

She didn't realise how hungry she was until she bit into
the chocolate. He squatted on the floor before her, watching. 'When you've finished we're going for a walk in the
woods. Not far, just far enough to get a signal on your

phone so that you can ring your husband again to arrange a hand-over meeting.'

'Hand over what?'

'You. You for him.'

'Why?'

'I want to talk to him.'

'What about?'

'Friendship and betrayal. The ethics of using people. Responsibility and justice. Big things.'

The chocolate seemed to have given her energy already. She felt more confident. 'Why? Do you blame him for what happened to you?'

'Not wholly, and not only him. There were others too.'

'So you blame others for what you did?'

She was more used to the glare of the gas lamp now and could see that he hadn't shaved. The light put his eyes in shadow but showed up his teeth and the lower half of his face. 'I don't so much blame them as want them to face up to their share of the responsibility. As I have mine for the past many years.'

'And what are you going to do to Charles if he agrees to meet you?'

'I told you, talk to him.'

She bit on the two last squares of chocolate. 'Not kill him?'

He smiled. 'It would give me no pleasure to kill Charles Thoroughgood, Sarah. We were friends.'

'And what if he won't meet you?'

He took the chocolate wrapper from her and passed the apple. 'I think he will.'

She raised her eyebrows as she bit into the apple. The longer they talked the better, she thought. It established a relationship, perhaps making it harder for him to do anything unpleasant. Perhaps. But given what he'd done already, nothing could be guaranteed. It also gave Charles and the police more time to find her.

He folded the chocolate wrapper into a precise square. 'He wouldn't want to risk receiving one of your ears in an envelope, still less a second ear.'

Later, he stood in the door while she squatted on the repulsive chemical loo. He had taken the handcuff off one of her wrists to enable her to wipe herself and he watched, with clinical dispassion. Perhaps he wasn't thinking of her at all, she thought, as she stood and fastened her jeans. Perhaps he was thinking about what he would say to Charles, or do to him. She tucked in her blouse, reflecting that there was one thing to be said for this regime: the longer it went on, the better for her figure. After rubbing her hands in the bucket of water he had thoughtfully placed near the loo, she held them out for him to refasten the handcuff.

Then, without a word, he took hold of the chain linking the cuffs and led her out.

They went through her chamber to the one containing his camp-bed, some clothes and other bits and pieces she couldn't identify before he extinguished the gas lamp at the foot of the brick steps. Still without speaking, he led her up. It was completely dark and she had to feel with her feet from one step to the next until he told her to stop. He let go of her handcuffs and she could hear him unbolting something above, then suddenly there was light. He carefully lowered a pair of metal trap-doors and waited, listening. Immediately above them was a roof of brambles with patches of blue and white sky showing through. She could hear birdsong and the sound of an aeroplane. The light was wonderful, too much for her eyes at first, and the cool air on her face soothing and enlivening.

He stood looking down at her with his backside pressed against the dirty rough wall. 'Follow me and keep quiet. Don't try to run because you won't get out.'

They crawled on their hands and knees through a winding tunnel in the brambles. She'd done it the night before, blindly, and again it was difficult with handcuffs because she could move each hand only a few inches at a time. Brambles in the ground hurt her while those above caught her hair. She lowered her head and followed the soles of his trainers. Everything smelt damp but fresh, beautifully fresh, after the bunker. They reached a curtain of ferns where he paused to listen before continuing through a narrower tunnel of green. When they reached the end he took hold of her handcuffs again and stood, pulling her up beside him.

They were in a small clearing among broad-leafed trees, the ground covered by ferns, young birch and brambles, some of the latter above head height. Lying immediately before them was the elephant-grey trunk of a beech tree that had come down. Sarah's jeans were wet on the knees and her hands hurt. He led her around the fallen tree and uphill to the edge of the wood. He walked at a pace, causing her to stumble several times.

'Can you slow down? It's difficult, I can't—'

He held up his free hand. 'Quiet.' He waited for her panting to subside. 'We'll go more slowly but no noise.'

He led her to the crest of the ridge just inside the wood, where he turned and looked back. She could see through the trees that the ground below the wood fell away into fields and hedges before rising to another wooded ridge. She couldn't see the track they'd taken last night after he'd dragged her out of the car. It had been level walking until the brambles.

He made her sit on a damp darkened stump. Her watch

said ten past three. He took her mobile phone from the pocket of his jeans and fitted the SIM card, which was in his shirt pocket.

'I want you to ring your husband. Tell him you're all right, that I want to speak to him and that he's to listen to what I say. Then you give the phone to me. Don't say or do anything else. D'you understand?'

She nodded.

He stared at her. 'Sarah, I hope you also understand that I mean you no ill-will. Under other circumstances we might have enjoyed a pleasant social relationship, perhaps even a friendship as you're the wife of my old friend. Instead, it's my duty to ensure that the principles of justice, violated many years ago by an issue that does not concern you, are reasserted. Just do what I say, help bring Charles and me together, and you will come to no harm, I promise.' His grey eyes were almost tender.

'And what about Charles? Will he be all right, too?' In the clear air her voice sounded sharp.

'That's up to him.'

'Why? What do you want from him?'

He handed her the phone. 'Ring now. Remember what I said.'

She dialled in full in order to give herself time to think but when Charles answered immediately she couldn't at

276

first bring herself to speak. He said 'Hello' twice before she said, 'It's me.'

'Where are you?'

Peter was standing next to her, one hand gripping her wrist and the other poised to grab the phone.

'I'm – I'm all right.'

'But where? Where are you?'

'Just wanted you to know that I'm all right.'

He said something else but she didn't catch it because Peter took the phone from her. It was uncomfortable, sitting with both hands held up, but when she made to stand he pushed her back down.

'Charles, this is Peter Tew. You've just heard from Sarah that she's okay. It's my intention that she should remain so until you and I meet, when she will be freed.' He paused, listening. 'I'll tell you where and when in a moment. Have you got pen and paper?' He paused again. 'We can discuss all that when we meet . . . it must be obvious to you, if you think about it . . . let's just say there are unresolved issues . . . no, just you . . . because you're the only one left and it's the only way I could find you in a hurry. I don't have much time. Me personally, that is. I'm dying. Cancer. Are you ready now?' He let go of Sarah's wrist and took a piece of paper from his pocket. 'I'll give you the grid reference.' He read it twice. 'There's only one way of approach, along the lane. Leave your car where the tarmac ends and the unmade bit begins, where it turns down to the right. Park near the gate but don't block it. Then walk up the track and across the fields to the barn. Alone. You'll be watched all the way. If there's anyone with you you'll never see Sarah alive. Do you understand me, Charles? ... Eight. On the dot.' He ended the call and let go of her while he removed the SIM card. 'Sorry, Sarah, but I had to say that, to make sure there's no funny business. You'll be all right, I'm sure. He won't want anything to happen to you.'

He took another phone from his pocket. 'Eight o'clock,' he said into it, and put it back. He took hold of her wrist again and pulled her to her feet. 'We're going home now, back to the bunker. A little primitive, these wartime bunkers, but well hidden. It won't be for long. You'll be out in time to meet him.'

Charles put down his phone. He was at the desk in the study at Jeremy Wheeler's house in Battle. There was only one chair and Jeremy leant ostentatiously against the windowsill, arms folded, his gaze fixed on a hunting print. Charles looked again at Jeremy's laptop.

Sarah's call had cut Jeremy off in mid-sentence. 'As I was saying, I don't accept it's my fault,' he resumed. 'Firstly, I had no way of knowing that Toast was Tew. Secondly, I had no way of knowing that he could use my computer as a Trojan horse. Thirdly, it's not my fault if government systems are so poorly designed that once someone gets on the inside track they can get everywhere. It's clearly something the ISC—'

'You should have returned the computer when you resigned.' Charles spoke while staring at the screen, which was showing the daily briefing for the ISC.

'No-one asked me.'

'And you should never have used it for non-official business.'

'That was never made clear, I—'

He paused as Wendy passed the open door, her heels clicking on the parquet floor and her gaze resolutely straight ahead. The front door opened and closed with a bang. 'She's like that all the time now.'

'That was Sarah on the phone.'

'Doesn't seem to feel any guilt at all about knocking off your friend Klein whenever my back was turned.'

'May I use your landline?'

'Of course, if you'd let me know who he really was I might have been able to look after him, help out a bit. Then she might not have—'

'What's Katya's mobile?'

'Katya? What do you want—'

'Just the number.'

Jeremy bristled with further questions but Charles's tone silenced him. He gave the number.

Katya sounded harassed. 'Jeremy, I am sorry, I cannot speak now, I am—'

'Katya, it's Charles Thoroughgood. Have you an answer for me?'

There was silence, then, falteringly, 'Oh, Mr Thoroughgood, Mr Mayakovsky—'

'Tell Mr Mayakovsky you have two hours from now. Otherwise you're out.' He cut her off and dialled again before Jeremy could resume. Tim Corke's secretary said Tim was in a meeting. Charles told her Sarah's mobile number had been used in the last ten minutes, probably in Sussex or Kent, and asked for location. His own mobile on the desk before him showed messages from Angela Wilson and Michael Dunton.

Jeremy moved away from the window. 'While you're faffing around here I suppose I'd better see what I can do about saving my marriage.'

Charles picked up his own phone. 'But she's just gone out.'

'I know that. I might go and get some flowers or something.'

'D'you want to save it? You've got Katya, haven't you?'

'Not if you have your way, by the sounds of it.'

'I can't kick her out. You know I can't. It's all bluff.'

'Anyway, it would look bad in the constituency. Also, after all this' – he waved his hand – 'and with her being Russian and whatever, I'd be off the ISC, wouldn't I? Wouldn't look good. An embarrassment to the government.'

'Sounds like the whole flower shop, then.'

Jeremy snorted. 'Don't see why. She's as much at fault as me. More than. Been going on a year or more, whereas Katya and I, we – you know – were still only talking about it, really.'

He was suddenly a schoolboy, fat, crestfallen and puzzled. Katya had clearly played him along, never quite giving him what he wanted. Perhaps nobody ever had apart from Wendy, at first. There wouldn't be any more of that now. Charles was surprised to feel a spasm of sympathy. The past was a bond; knowing each other over decades, even though they had never been close, created a hinterland of acceptance, if not always forgiveness. Self-important, unaware, unappealing, pompous and naïve though Jeremy was, he had no malice, was too sorry for himself to hate others, only ever wanted to be part of it all, whatever the 'it' was. As had Peter Tew. And Charles himself, perhaps. But Jeremy was not vengeful.

'What about some coffee?' said Charles. 'I've got a couple more calls to make. Then there's something you can do to help, if you want. Leave the flowers till you're talking to each other again.'

The messages from Angela and Michael were essentially the same, Angela's the more peremptory: where was he? The police were looking for him, protection was ready but they couldn't find him. His office didn't know where he was. Would he please get in touch. Charles put down his phone and picked up Jeremy's landline again, dialling DI Whitely.

'Any news?'

'Nothing much." She sounded flat. 'He was in his shop when I swung by this morning. Been trying to get a mobile team on to him but there's quite a bit going on today, big drugs push, and I daren't raise it again without the super wanting to know more. I've been sort of half-promised a team for a couple of hours later, depending how things go. Thought I might go up there myself, depending what you think, though it's not an easy area to hang around in. He had a call this afternoon.'

'Who from?'

'Hang on, made a note of it somewhere. Couldn't get him on live monitoring, as I think I said, but he's on instant call-check read-out. Here we are. Incoming call, three seconds. Not a very chatty lot, are they? From a mobile.'

He noted the number. 'Someone needs to be on him now. How soon can you get up there?'

'Ten minutes. But I can't stay for ever. I've got to pick up from the childminder's. Want me to check that number?'

'I'll get it done from here. Get up there as soon as you can and stay as long as you can. Let me know before you leave. I'll try to find someone to take over.'

He left the number with Tim Corke's secretary for urgent checking, then rang George Greene's office. George was in the House and couldn't be disturbed.

'Milk and sugar?' called Jeremy from the kitchen.

'Just milk, please.' He rang George's parliamentary secretary, who said he was in her office drinking whisky with his constituency chairman. George came to the phone laughing.

'Charles, what can I do for you? How's it going?' Charles told him what he proposed. 'Jesus Christ, going out on a limb a bit, aren't you? Why not wait for the police?'

'He'll be looking for tricks like that, he knows the terri-tory he's chosen and he knows the way we work. The slightest hint of company and he'll kill her, then me. I know Peter, he's dedicated to whatever he does. And we can't expect the police to mount a decent stakeout on unfamiliar ground with no notice. No-one could guarantee that. The only thing is for me to go unaccompanied, make sure she's released, then keep him talking.'

'Until he shoots you. Great idea.'

'Just wanted you to know, George, you don't have to approve. If it all goes wrong, say you ordered the opposite and I disobeyed. Also, could you get your secretary to tell Angela that I've got her message and will get back to her as soon as possible. She wants to imprison me in protection. Tell her what I've just told you if you like.'

'When's all this supposed to start?'

'Now. When I put the phone down. No good thinking about intervention.'

There was a pause. 'I can't stop you, then?'

'No. Have it in writing if you want.'

'You're off your head, old son. Good luck.'

Jeremy returned with two mugs. 'No milk. Well, no proper cow's milk, only that red-topped stuff she has with her gnat's pee tea. Seems to have gone on strike, domestically.'

'There's something you can help with.'

'Probably gallons of real milk in Klein's fridge. I bet she kept him well supplied.'

'Something that might redeem you in the eyes of the ISC after the scandal of your computer misuse. If it works.'

18

The cottage smelt damp. There was no time to light a fire. Charles spread his Ordnance Survey map on the table and followed Peter Tew's directions. It told him more than his phone could. The grid reference was a small building – Peter had mentioned a barn – in a field about three-quarters of a mile from where he had to leave his car. No doubt the site was selected so that Peter could watch him in and check that he was unaccompanied. The stated time – less than two hours away now – would leave no time to insert surveillance in advance. As for where Peter was holding her, the barn was surely too obvious; more likely it was simply for the hand-over. She would be held some-where nearby, within reach on foot. The barn and its fields were surrounded by hundreds of acres of woodland. He had no idea why Peter had chosen Sussex, unless it was because it was near his hitman, Michael Swavey. Knowing Peter, it would have been carefully worked out.

His phone vibrated on the table, the screen proclaiming 'Unknown number'. At first there was silence, then a foreign male voice said in careful, heavily accented English, 'Mr Thoroughgood, it is a pleasure to speak with you. We believe you are seeking the location of a special computer. I am happy to tell you that it was last turned on at 15.37 your time. I shall give the location on your English map.' He read out a grid reference. 'It was turned off at 15.41. We wish you luck and look forward to receiving our part of the agreement.'

Charles noted the grid reference. 'Thank you, I hope I shall be able to deliver but I cannot promise. That's not Mr Mayakovsky, is it?'

There was a pause and what might have been a chuckle. 'No, Mr Thoroughgood, it is not. Goodbye.'

The grid reference was the middle of a wood across the valley from the barn, about equidistant from where Charles was to park. There were no buildings or paths marked. For once he regretted the lack of a computer, though Google Earth would have told him less than the map. Perhaps Peter was based in the barn after all and simply went into the wood to use his computer, except that the footpath near the barn would make it an unsafe hide.

He rang Tim Corke again. This time the secretary put him through, saying, 'He was about to ring you anyway. He has news.'

'Charles, where are you?

'Sussex.'

'The phone that made the three-second call you enquired about made it from Sussex but we didn't have it on tap so couldn't say precisely where from or what was said. But there's since been another call and now we can. Got a pen and paper?' The grid reference was the one Charles had just received from the unknown Russian. 'Want to know what was said in the second call? I'm breaking all the rules, of course. Doesn't mean much here but it might to you. There were no names. Caller says, "Just to confirm, the barn at eight. But you need to be in position well before." Distant: "With my gear?" Caller: "With your gear. But use it only if we're interrupted while I'm talking to him." Distant: "Which one first?" Pause. Caller: "Him, then her." Distant: "What if they get you? How do I collect?" Caller: "Collect from the bunker. It's here now." Ends. Make sense?

'Sounds as if you need protection after all. I'm going to have to pass this on, you realise that? It's a police matter, I can't withhold information about serious crime.'

'Protection is trying to find me now.'

'You're not waiting? You're going ahead alone?'

'Not entirely.'

He next rang DI Whitely. 'Where are you?'

'Down the road from his place, in my own car. No movement.' She spoke softly.

'I think there soon will be. Heading out towards the country, Ashburnham area. Are you able to go with him? I'm sending someone to join you who'll take over when you have to get to the childminder's.'

'I'll see if they can have her for the evening. They've done it before in emergencies but I don't like to push it.' She paused. 'Hang on, there's movement. He's coming out. I'd better go.'

Charles next went to the cupboard under the stairs where he had hidden the guns he brought down from London. It was not secure – the police would seize them if they knew – but it would have to do. He didn't shoot regularly any more but always assumed he would in some imagined leisurely future.

He laid all five carefully on the dining-room floor. He still hadn't admitted to himself that he had decided to go armed – a serious and illegal escalation which at the very least would cost him his firearm certificate– but knew he would. Choice of weapon depended on which circumstances he thought he'd face. The two shotguns were ideal for close-quarters work, one to one, but too indiscriminate if he were trying to shoot Peter without hitting Sarah. The .22, with telescopic sights and silencer, would be fine for distance work but that was unlikely in a wood and anyway he'd need to be sure of hitting a vital organ to stop some-one. He hesitated over the Savage, a useful .22 and .410 rifle-shotgun combination, something of a favourite. But he chose the last, the Winchester 30-30, his father's quixotic purchase, justified by the alleged need to cull muntjac in the Chilterns but never, so far as Charles knew, used in anger.

Until now, perhaps. He worked the under-lever action familiar to viewers of a thousand ancient Westerns. It was a compact weapon and although over open sites he wouldn't trust himself at more than eighty to a hundred yards, it fired a heavy enough round to ensure that what it hit stayed hit. Bush guns, they were called in America, ideal for close country. He remembered an idle day on leave from the army, knocking the tops off old iron fence posts with it until his mother protested at the noise. Like much of the past, it seemed so innocent. Especially now, as he also remembered showing the gun to Peter during that weekend.

He loaded four rounds, pushing each into the magazine with the snub nose of the next. The mechanism reminded him of Dante's medieval popes in hell, crammed one on top of the other for – what was it – simony? Thinking of other things was a refuge, he knew. If he stopped to think about what he was doing – a semi-public official taking the law into his own hands, going to kill or be killed by an old friend, hazarding his wife's life without waiting for the help that was on its way – he would not act. But waiting meant leaving responsibility to someone else, another form of refuge. The only alternative would be to go naked into Peter Tew's trap, hands in the air, agreeing to anything, including his own immediate extinction, provided he saw her walk free.

So why didn't he? The question hovered unanswered as he wrapped the Winchester in a sleeping bag and laid it on the floor of the Bristol.

DI Whitely followed Michael Swavesy's white van into the industrial estate. There was enough traffic for her to keep two or three cars between him and her Corsa, also enough to keep him from pulling out of sight. But in the estate she had to let him go when he turned off towards the garages behind the tower blocks. It would be too obvious to follow, especially as there was no clear way out. She turned round farther down the road and parked outside a car parts business, facing the way they had come. Her phone rang while she was still debating whether she had enough things with her, ideally a bag she could bulk out, to pass as a woman from the tower blocks walking past the garages with her shopping.

It was Charles Thoroughgood. 'Where are you?'

She told him.

'Okay. I'm in my car, parked up, not far from where I think he's going. Have you got a map?'

'I've got a phone.'

'I don't know whether grid references are any help but I'll give it to you anyway.' He described what he thought she would see on her phone. 'It's a barn by itself in the corner of a small field, with the footpath branching off and running right past it. You have to go through some woods to get to it. I think he said it was thatched. I'm pretty sure that's where your quarry is headed but I'm not sure whether he'll hide himself in the barn or stake it out. He's almost certainly armed. Don't go near him, just do enough to confirm he's in the area.'

'Is the armed response unit on its way? Do they know about it?'

'They'll have been told and may be on their way but they'll almost certainly be too late. Any worries, pull back. It's not worth risking your life. As I said, I'm sending a former colleague to help you. He's local so he knows the area but it's a long time since he did anything like this and he was never much good at it anyway. But he's another pair of eyes and has his own vehicle which your quarry won't have seen. I've told him you're in charge so don't take any nonsense and if he's no use, send him home. He's waiting to hear from you.' He gave her Jeremy's name and mobile. 'As I said, Louise, don't take any chances. If in doubt, drop out.'

She appreciated his use of her first name and smiled despite herself. This was better than recording burglaries and break-ins that were never going to be cleared up. 'You'll square this with my super, will you?'

'The Foreign Secretary knows about it. The Home Secretary soon will.'

When Jeremy joined her, Michael Swavesy had still not reappeared. The year-old silver Range Rover, the most conspicuous vehicle in the estate, had to be his, she thought. He sounded like a Range Rover on the phone, grand and all-encompassing, assuring her as if she were a frightened little girl that he would be with her 'Asap – that is, as soon as possible'.

She wasn't reassured when he squeezed into the Corsa and she felt the springs go down. His palm was clammy. 'Good to be back on the street again,' he said. 'So where's our quarry?'

She told him.

'Well, I can walk in there, can't I?'

'Not without a garage to go to. It would look odd. One of us might be able to walk past the turning but we wouldn't necessarily be able to see which garage he's using or what he's doing.'

'I can if I'm the local MP out canvassing.'

'But you're not.'

'I am.' His smile was surprisingly gentle. 'Not quite my constituency but close enough to feign confusion. I've got some leaflets in the car. Always keep a few, just in case. I'll walk round.'

She watched his bulky figure approach the tower blocks, survey them proprietorially, then disappear in the garage turning. He reappeared after a couple of minutes, still unhurried.

'Did you see him?' he asked. 'The motorcyclist?'

'That was him?' A motorcyclist had emerged not long after Jeremy went in but she had been looking only for the white van.

He gave her the bike's number. 'His garage is number seventeen. His van's in it. He'd done the change-over with the door closed, which is suspicious. I was walking past when he opened it to push his bike out. Slapped a leaflet on him which he didn't want, of course, but he couldn't say no. Then I stood in the way asking about local issues. He was obviously in a hurry, didn't want to say anything. When I asked in a friendly way where he was off to he was stumped for a moment, then he said, 'Battle, I go for rides in the country outside Battle.' So I kept him a bit longer, talking about how lovely it is, then let him go. We've lost him now, of course, but we know where he's heading and might be able to pick him up out there.'

They took both cars. Jeremy knew the lane but not the barn. At his suggestion they left his Range Rover at the Swan, where he and Charles had dined, and headed down towards the wooded declivities of Ashburnham.

'First on the left,' he said, then began telling her about his career.

The lane was narrower even than the one they'd left. 'How far until it becomes unmetalled and there's the track to the barn?' she interrupted.

'About a mile.'

'But if that's where he's going we'd better not drive up there, had we? He'll see us. We should park somewhere here and walk across country.'

Jeremy looked as if the thought of walking was un-congenial. 'How would we know he's there when we get there? We can hardly call out for him.'

She had to brake hard as they rounded a bend into a pack of bloodhounds that surged like a good-natured sea around the car, their ears flapping and jaws slobbering. One stood on its hind legs at the passenger door, its paws on the roof.

'God!' said Jeremy, leaning heavily on her. 'I don't like dogs, I've got a thing about dogs.'

A man on a tall grey horse shouted and cracked his whip at the hound, which immediately rejoined the pack as he edged his horse past them. Bringing up the rear was a woman on a bay horse.

'Ask her if she's seen a man on a motorbike,' said Louise.

'Not with all these dogs, I'm not getting out.'

'How come you did all those things you say you did then?'

'Not many dogs on the diplomatic circuit.'

The woman was helpful. Yes, they had seen a man on a motorbike, he'd almost come off when he saw the hounds. Luckily he wasn't going very fast. They were crossing the lane in front of him then and he'd carried on up the track towards the farm. But he hadn't gone to the farm, she knew that.

'Where did he go?'

'To the barn along the footpath. He's parked round the back and gone inside. The doors are open. Can't think what he'd be doing in there, he was quite alone so he's obviously not doing what some people go there for.' She laughed. 'It's open to the public, you see, it's a very old barn, restored for local people to use, parties or picnics or bird-watching or whatever they want. Must get on, sorry.' She edged her horse past the car.

'How d'you know he's in there?' called Louise.

The woman pointed her riding crop at the hounds. 'They told us. They always know where people go. We came back down past the barn and they milled around, pointing. It couldn't have been anyone else because we'd have seen them come up. And his bike's round the back. I might be wrong of course but they were definitely telling us there's someone in there.' She wheeled away. 'Sorry. Bye.'

Louise got back in the car. 'They stink, those hounds.'

'I know.'

She rang Charles but there was no answer.

'Where is he?' asked Jeremy.

'Somewhere near here, he said.'

Jeremy shook his head. 'Communication was never Thoroughgood's strong point.'

A text came through from Charles, telling her to communicate by that means. She told him what she'd heard. He told them to stay in the area but to keep well back, not to approach the barn. 'We'd better find somewhere to park up,' she said.

'Anyone who sees us will think we're a courting couple.'

She said nothing to that but drove on until they came to a wide gateway into woodland, with heaps of logs piled just inside. She reversed into it and switched off.

'Unless I'm recognised, of course,' Jeremy said. 'That wouldn't be so good.'

'Not very likely here.'

'Don't suppose your husband would approve, either.'

'Haven't got a husband.'

She was aware of him glancing at her, so she took an interest in the nearest logs. She wouldn't have minded if he'd been more attractive and a bit less obvious about it. Could be fun to have an MP, a change from the unlamented father of Tilly.

He turned to her with a solemn expression which she imagined was meant to convey understanding and sympathy. 'Tell me about yourself, how you became a policewoman, life and everything.'

'I was thinking we might take a discreet walk around to get the feel of the area, off the road and not too near the barn, of course. Just enough to direct the armed response unit when they come.'

Jeremy grunted as he released his seat belt. 'Be more helpful if Thoroughgood could bring himself to tell the world where he is and what's going on.'

They cut up through the woods parallel with the lane. It was heavy going at first, a mixture of bracken and brambles, but easier as they got farther into the wood. When they were parallel with the point where the lane turned down to the right and became unmetalled, while the track to the farm went straight on, she said, 'The barn should be ahead and off to our left.'

Jeremy was breathing heavily. 'May as well take a look as we've come this far.'

'Not sure we should. Don't want to alert him. Or get ourselves shot. He's got form, this man.'

'Useful to be able to tell the armed response unit how close they can get in vehicles.'

He had his good points. 'As long as we're careful, then.'

Still under tree cover, they made their way down a hill, across a boggy valley and up through a neglected strip of alder and willow. 'That must be the field with the barn,' she whispered, pointing to the green through the trees. 'The footpath runs along the side of the wood in front of us. If we turn left we should come to the edge of the wood where we might be able to see it.'

They picked their way through a thicket of fallen trees and branches. She led while he grunted and wheezed behind her. Every so often she stopped to check her phone and let him catch up. Eventually, after crossing a deep ditch and scrambling with too much noise up the other side, they crouched a few yards from the edge of the wood, within sight of the barn.

It was small and thatched as Charles had said, with black weather-boarding and brick steps up to the wide doors, which were open. It was too dark inside to see anything. On the grass outside was a round plastic table with two white plastic chairs facing a small grass-grown pond. About thirty yards down the overgrown slope to the side of the barn were the remains of an old brick building, a few small apple trees and three beehives.

'What could he be doing in there?' whispered Jeremy loudly.

She held up her hand to quieten him. 'If it is him. He may not be alone. Maybe Tew and Mrs Thoroughgood are in there. It's probably the place where Charles has got to meet them.'

'But where is he? What the hell's he doing?'

'I'll text to tell him what we can see. Then we'd better pull back.'

'Better than that, stop what you're doing and stand up, hands above your heads.'

The voice was behind them, low but with no attempt at concealment. 'Now.' The word was emphasised.

A spasm seized Louise's shoulders at the first words and

at the word 'now' the skin on her neck tightened. She felt Jeremy flinch beside her. He turned his head.

'Do what I say and don't look round or I'll take your head off.' It was louder and rougher this time. Jeremy obeyed. They got up awkwardly, hands above their heads. She was holding her phone and could think only of Tilly; whatever happened she must get back to Tilly, Tilly mustn't be left motherless, she would agree to anything to make sure Tilly was all right. She could feel tears welling behind her eyes, almost as if it were Tilly being taken prisoner.

'Walk towards the barn,' the voice said. 'Keep your hands up.'

It was difficult to get through the undergrowth and in the field, with their hands raised high, they stumbled on tussocks. When they reached the pond it occurred to her that he might be bluffing, might not have a gun at all. But she daren't look round.

'Stop.'

They stopped, facing the brick steps.

'You – fatso – lie down where you are, face down.'

At least he hadn't meant her. Jeremy knelt. With his hands above his head he had to roll half onto his side to get onto his belly. She had a glimpse of his face, which showed no hint of a message or even of recognition; he seemed wholly concentrated on manoeuvring his body.

300

'Now you, go over to the table, turn and face me and empty your pockets. I want everything on the table.'

The man she saw was close enough to the photograph of Michael Swavesy: average height, forty-something, greying brown hair, jeans and trainers, a black biking jacket. He was not bluffing about the gun, a sawn-off shotgun pointing at her. Jeremy was on the ground between them. There wasn't much to empty from her pockets as her handbag was in the car, just handkerchief, keys, purse and warrant card from the pockets of her gilet. Too late, she thought she should have kept the warrant card back. He told her to lie down beside Jeremy, then walked over and examined what she'd left.

'Copper, eh?' he said, smiling. 'Let's have a look at your boyfriend. Come on, fatso.' Jeremy got awkwardly to his feet and went to the table. His sports jacket and cavalry twills seemed to have many pockets, with something in each.

When he had finished he stood facing their captor, his podgy hands hanging limp. 'You should know that I am a member of parliament. You'll see my Palace of Westminster pass here.'

'Are you now.' The voice was flat. 'Get back down with your girlfriend. Any funny business and they'll be calling a by-election.'

ALAN JUDD

Louise lay with her head facing away from Jeremy, the grass damp on her cheek. She could see Swavesy at the table again, facing them, the gun in his right hand and resting on his thigh while with his left he picked through their belongings. He took a mobile from his bike jacket, put it on the table and pressed once with his left forefinger. He picked it up and after a pause said quietly, 'You're breaking up. You must be down there, are you? Yeah, that's better. We got two visitors, lying down before me. Not very innocent visitors. One's a bitch copper, the other's a fat-slob member of parliament. They look like friends of your friend, the one you're meeting, both got notes of his name and number. What do you want me to do with them?'

Louise tried to think of any bargaining chips she could conceivably hold, threats she could credibly make. Perhaps she should break down and weep, throw herself on his mercy, tell him about Tilly. Perhaps Jeremy was planning something. She could hear his breathing beside her, like an unwanted intimacy. Perhaps she could persuade him to offer himself instead of her. But if Swavesy were to kill either he would need to kill both.

Michael Swavesy chuckled into the phone. 'Could – yeah – could do that. Wouldn't say no. Depends what your plans are now – does this alter anything?' There was another pause, and then, 'Sure. Will do. Give me twenty minutes.'

She could say she wanted to go to the loo and escape while doing it. But maybe he'd make her do it in front of him and Jeremy.

'Okay, ten,' Swavesy said into the phone.

19

'Stop. Stay where you are.'
    The voice was clear, somewhere behind and to his left. Charles lowered the Winchester into the ferns, straightened and put his hands on his head. He hadn't been told to do that but it might put Peter – assuming it was Peter – at his ease.

He could hear movement in the brambles behind, a large clump occupying much of the clearing. According to his map and his phone, this was as close as he could get to the site of Peter's last transmission. The clearing was almost on a ridge in the wood and when he entered it he could see across to where the barn must be, shielded by trees bordering its field. He had planned to surprise Peter in his lair.

He stood waiting but heard no more. Hands still on his head, he turned, very slowly.

'Don't move,' said the voice. There was no-one. But there was movement in the brambles downhill to his right. The voice said something he couldn't catch, then quietly but still clearly, 'You'll have to do them both, get rid of them . . . No, quicker, ten minutes, they must be on to us. Then pull out and go home.'

He recognised Peter's voice after all this time but Peter wasn't talking to him. He took a chance and lowered his arms. There was no response. He stooped to pick up the rifle but as he did so found himself staring into Peter's face at about waist height in the brambles. Charles froze, his knees still bent, the rifle not yet to hand. Peter was quicker. He pushed himself free of the brambles and straightened up, pistol in hand.

'Stay where you are,' he said loudly, half turning his head to speak behind him.

There was a log just by Charles. He lowered himself onto it, keeping his hands at shoulder height. He was closer to the rifle now, which Peter, downhill of him, could not have seen in the ferns at his feet. He crossed his legs and then slowly lowered his hands and hooked his arms around his knees as if for a chat by a camp-fire. 'Hello, Peter.'

'All right, come out now. Slowly,' said Peter.

The brambles rustled and shook. Sarah crawled out, awkwardly, head down because of the handcuffs. She did not see Charles until she straightened, still kneeling.

'Over there, where I can see you.' Peter pointed to a spot in the bracken between him and Charles.

Sarah bent again and crawled forward, using her fore-arms. She knelt upright and faced Charles. She looked pale and tired, a strand of hair had fallen in front of her face and she had to raise both hands to move it. She tried a smile. Charles tried one back. Neither spoke. She was all right, that was what mattered. So far.

'Turn and face me,' said Peter. She inched round on her knees. Peter looked back at Charles. 'What are you doing here?'

'Come to do a deal with you, I thought.'

'I told you to go to the barn. How did you find out about this place?'

'Your Russian friends told me. They'd worked it out.'

'Why should they tell you?'

'They want you back. We did a deal. They're offering you a home.'

'If I give myself up, you mean? Come quietly with you, back into the British justice system, so-called. Very likely. You'll have to do better than that, Charles.'

It was, and was not, the Peter he knew. He was gaunt,

unshaven, older, with a pallor, but it was his manner that had most changed. The younger Peter's charm and flexibility, his desire to please and accommodate, had been worn down by prison and age – also perhaps by illness – to a spare and hardened core, like the remnants of a broken jetty.

'Why are you doing this, Peter?'

'You know why. You don't need to ask.'

'First Viktor, then Frank, now me. That's it, I assume? Or is there anyone else?' It would take a fraction of a second for Peter to pull that trigger; he had to engage him, keep him talking.

'I can't wipe out the whole Service, or a whole governmental culture. You'll have to do.'

'Don't be ridiculous,' said Sarah, her voice sharp in the stillness. 'You don't have to do anything of the sort. There's no point. Better do nothing at all.'

Charles kept his eyes on the squat black pistol. The barrel's small mouth was unwavering.

'Why now, Peter?' he asked gently. 'Is it only because you're ill?'

'Always did your homework, didn't you? Knew that already? Thoroughly good Thoroughgood.' He nodded. 'I haven't got long so it's now or never.'

'But what's the point? You can't undo the past.'

'I can tie a knot in it, staunch it, that's the point. It's all

I've thought about for years now. Every day. You have no idea what that's like.'

'Because you think we let you down?'

'Because you betrayed me. You, Matthew, Frank, Viktor, the Service, the government, the Americans, everyone. I cooperated because I believed I was saving Igor. But once you'd got what you wanted you told the Americans and they told the world and the Russians did what they did to him.'

'Which was?'

'I don't know.'

'I do.' It was a lie. He spoke without knowing what to follow it with but it achieved its end. Peter was engaged, his attention now on what was being said. 'But that wasn't really the point, was it, Peter? It wasn't our betrayal, as you call it, that got to you.'

A pheasant called and faintly, distantly came the throbbing of a helicopter. 'You don't know what you're talking about,' said Peter.

'I'm talking about Igor. It was Igor who betrayed you. That's what you can't accept, that's why you're so bitter with us.'

'Bollocks.'

'Think about it, Peter.' Charles continued to speak gently. 'What you couldn't bear was the idea that Igor targeted and recruited you, that it was all a ploy, that he was an SVR officer all along and that they sent him after you, trading on his homosexuality which would otherwise have got him sacked. And did when the case collapsed. You fell for him, as they hoped you would. But you couldn't bear the thought that he never really loved you, that he was using you, doing what we were all trained to do.'

Peter shook his head. 'I told you, you don't know what you're talking about. There's no point trying to make out it wasn't your fault. I trusted you and you let me down. That's what happened.'

'We weren't to know the Americans would leak it.'

'But you told them.'

'They'd have worked it out anyway. And we owed them.'

'What's happened to Igor, then?'

'He was allowed to leave the SVR and was given a job with a bank, a Russian bank.'

In Charles's perception the movement of Peter's arm and the sound of the shot were simultaneous, as were Sarah's gasp and the convulsion in his breast as the sound passed through him. But nothing else did, the bullet thudding into the earth by Sarah's knee. Peter was grinning, his gun still pointed almost at her but his eyes on Charles. 'You're lying. Igor's dead. They kicked him out and abandoned him and he took to drink. That's why death is the only answer now.

For all of us. Death the great equaliser. You don't seem to get it, Charles. This is not a negotiation. There's no solution to be had, only an end.' He looked at Sarah. 'But not for you, if you do what you're told and don't make a fuss. Stand up.' She got awkwardly to her feet, facing him. 'Turn to your right and start walking. Keep going and you'll come to the lane eventually. There are some cottages down there. You'll find someone to help you.' She didn't move. After a few seconds he added, in a kindlier tone, 'Don't be silly, Sarah. Off you go.'

Still she didn't move. 'You don't need to do this, Peter. There's no point. Walk away. Go and live in Russia. Do something for Igor's family.'

Charles couldn't see her face but her voice was controlled. Peter shook his head. 'After having two people murdered and then kidnapping you? They're never going to let me go to Russia, Sarah, but thanks for the thought. Now, you can walk away or stay here and watch. It's up to you.'

Charles edged his feet forward until he was nudging the Winchester. He knew where it was without having to look down. He had cocked it after leaving the car a mile or so away and making his way across country, keeping to hedgerows and woods. There was a round in the breech, the hammer was back, he had only to pick it up and point it, pushing the safety catch with his thumb and squeezing

311

the under-lever, the secondary safety catch, as he fired. Between two and three seconds, he reckoned. But that was long enough for Peter to get the same number of aimed shots off. They had to keep talking.

'It's better you go, Sarah,' he said.

She turned her head. 'I'm not going, I'm not going any-where. I think this is completely ridiculous and unnecessary.' She looked back at Peter. 'You'll have to shoot me too, I'm afraid.'

Charles was exasperated, fearful and grateful. Anything to keep the conversation going. 'Sarah, please go. The only reason I'm here is so that you can go.'

'I know and I'm not going.'

She looked from one to the other. Perhaps she realised it too – anything, including a marital tiff, to keep Peter from his purpose.

It didn't work. Peter Tew pointed the gun at Charles, straightened his arm and fired.

'All right, stand up. Hands on your heads.'

Michael Swavesy's voice was flat, as if weary of repetition. He was still at the table, shotgun on his lap, mobile at his elbow, cigarette in his left hand. He watched them get up, raise their hands, hesitate as to which way to face, then turn towards him. 'Cigarette?' he asked.

Jeremy shook his head but Louise nodded. It was a sinister offer – the last smoke before execution, perhaps – but it was engagement of a sort and it might delay things. Swavesy pocketed his mobile, threw away his half-smoked cigarette, shook another from the packet, put it in his lips and lit it. His right hand still rested on his gun. Then he put away the packet and walked over to her. At arm's length, holding the gun at waist height and pointing at her belly, he took the cigarette from his own lips and put it between hers, grinning. His brown eyes were friendly, almost caressing. 'You can use one hand to smoke it. Keep the other on your head. Turn round, both of you. We're going round the back of the barn.'

'Where are you taking us? What are you doing?' Jeremy's voice was hoarse.

'I'm going to tie you up, leave you where you can be found. Nothing to worry about.'

Being told there was nothing to worry about made it worse, Louise thought. That was just what you would say. They followed the track around the barn. There was his motorbike, a patch of rough grass, a wooden shed and beyond it a fence and stile. Beyond that was a clump of bushes, then the field above. There was no sign of rope to tie them with.

'Okay, that's far enough.'

313

'May I finish my fag first?' she asked.

'Course you can. All the time in the world.'

That convinced her. She listened for the click of the safety catch. It might be off anyway. She took a pull on her cigarette and looked at Jeremy. He was staring down the field towards the beehives and the old brick privy. He seemed self-absorbed, or perhaps catatonic with fear, certainly not heeding her. 'When I chuck my fag away, run for it,' she murmured. He gave no sign of having heard.

She was going to do it, but stopped. She couldn't bring herself. The small of her back felt horribly vulnerable, the muscles quivering. 'One other thing—' she called. Then she did it, tossing the cigarette straight up and breaking to her right.

There was a loud bang and a shout but it wasn't her. She was on the stile and then off it, out of control, tripping on brambles and falling in the bushes. There was another bang. She got up and ran stumbling to her right, the bushes tearing at her feet and arms. Then she was in the field out of sight of the barn, running uphill by the hedge as fast as she could.

It was Michael Swavesy's uncharacteristic hesitation that saved them. He was creeping closer, so as to get a more concentrated blast in the back of each head, when she said something and tossed the cigarette in the air. His eyes followed that, only momentarily but enough for her to have started her break to his right. His gun was still at his waist and if he had swivelled after her immediately he'd have cut her in half. But the man started running too, straight ahead and downhill. He was heading for the beehives, might very soon be behind the privy and then out of stopping range, whereas the girl was closer and had nowhere to go, just the fence and the stile. He could take her second. He stopped his swing towards her, pulled back round to his front and let the man have it. The man went down with a cry, knocking one of the hives over.

When he turned back to the girl he couldn't see her. Then he saw the bushes move and fired into them. They quivered and were still. It looked as if he'd got her. As he broke open the gun to reload and follow up on her the man got up and started running again, but limping and slow. Michael Swavesy left the girl for the second time and ran after him, holding the gun in his left hand and fumbling in his pocket for cartridges. He had one cartridge in and was reaching for the other when he realised the man had stopped running and was waving his arms around. He closed on him, slowing to a walk, thinking it might be delayed death spasms. He slotted the second cartridge in, checked it, snapped the gun shut and looked up to see the man's blotched and bloated face looming towards him. He had no time even to bring the gun up before the man fell on him, gasping and shouting incoherently. Swavesy went over backwards, with the great sprawling weight on top of him and a bit of masonry digging painfully into his kidneys. The gun was knocked out of his hands, falling between his legs. There was sudden stinging on his face and neck and the backs of his hands. For a moment he couldn't struggle free and then the man was off him and running away again.

Swavesy got to his feet amidst a swarm of bees. There were dozens of them, inside his shirt collar, in his hair, up his sleeves, in his ears, stinging, stinging, stinging. He heard himself shouting, ran a few yards towards the barn, then back to pick up his gun, then down into the field away from the barn, trying to leap the broken stone wall but tripping on a strand of barbed wire and falling, winding himself, then up, gasping and flailing, still holding his gun, running haphazardly down the field.

He could not have failed to hear the helicopter but he failed to heed it. Louise, from the top of the field, panting and exhausted within the safety of the wood, heard it only seconds before it arrived. It came in very low and fast, a violent, overwhelming intrusion, buffeting the tree-tops and blasting warm air on her upturned face. Seconds later it landed in the field below the barn and three or four helmeted armed figures leapt out as the wheels touched.

Swavesy, she could see, was running haphazardly across the field as if dodging invisible obstacles. The figures from the helicopter ran after him, then stopped, kneeling, as the rotors wound down. There was shouting followed by a clattering of sharp cracks. They didn't sound much – less than Swavesy's shotgun or the other shots she had heard from across the valley as she fled – but they were sufficient. He crumpled like a puppet whose strings were cut and lay still, a small dark lump in the middle of the field. On the far side of the barn another figure stopped its slow stumbling run and turned to watch. When the shooting was over it began to limp back towards the helicopter.

Seeing the spurt of flame from the small black hole and hearing the shot told Charles that he must be all right, that Peter had missed. Pretty inexcusable from ten yards, he thought afterwards, though with a pistol anything was possible. But the noise and shock of being shot at at close range paralysed him for a second. That was the time for Peter to get another shot off, the one that shouldn't have missed. Instead, he was distracted by two shots from the direction of the barn, as if in answer to his own. He looked round.

It was enough. Charles had the Winchester cocked and in his shoulder in one movement. He had forgotten how loud that .30 round was, how solid the kick. You knew you'd fired a grown-up gun. It took Peter in the middle of his chest, flinging him onto his back in the ferns. His pistol flew sideways and fell across Sarah's foot.

Charles was on his feet without thinking, the gun re-cocked and pointed at Peter. Sarah had not moved. She stared at the body. 'Are you all right?' he asked.

She turned towards him almost reluctantly. 'Yes. Are you?' Her voice sounded remote.

He stepped through the ferns towards her. He knew he should be overwhelmed with relief but couldn't yet feel it. He wanted to say so much more than ask if she was all right but the words wouldn't come, for either of them.

She turned back towards the body. 'Hadn't we better see if we can do anything? He might be still alive.'

'He's dead.' Something about the newly dead told you they were dead, an absence, something not there, even while the body was warm. He had witnessed it first with his father in the hospital. It had been impossible to mourn just then because it was no longer his father, just a body. Whatever had been, wasn't.

'You can't be sure. He might be alive.'

'He is dead.' He eased the hammer forward, laid the gun in the ferns and knelt at Peter's side. There was a small hole in the chest, slightly to the left, where the heart would be, and virtually no trace of blood. There would be a bigger and messier hole in the back. Peter's eyes and mouth were open to the sky, as if in surprise. He might just have had time to see, as he turned back from the distraction, that Charles had a gun; it would have been the last thing he saw. Charles started going through his pockets.

'What are you doing?'

'Looking for the keys for your handcuffs.'

She made a sound that was half laugh, half gasp. 'How can you be so – so practical? No, that's not what I mean, that's not the word.'

It was, and it was because there was nothing else to be. Consciously irrevocable actions were rare and the full sense of what he had done he would feel only later. Something of himself had died with Peter, albeit something that had died in Peter long before. But to act was necessarily to disregard.

The clattering roar of the helicopter made them look up. They saw it land, a handful of figures disembark and run down across the field and out of sight, shielded by trees. Then they heard the shooting.

'That'll be his number two, his wing man,' said Charles. 'The one who was probably supposed to shoot me. And maybe you if necessary.' He found the keys and went over to her.

She held out her hands. 'Would he have shot me, d'you think – Peter?'

'I doubt he intended to unless' – the handcuffs fell to the ground and she stood rubbing her wrists while he put his hands on her shoulders – 'it seemed practical.'

20

George Greene's parliamentary office was one of the larger panelled ones at the back of the Commons chamber, behind the Speaker's chair. It was near, not too near, the Prime Minister's office. There was room for his desk, a small round conference table and another desk in the corner for his parliamentary secretary. George, Angela and Charles sat at the conference table with coffee cups, scraps of paper, glasses and two-thirds of a bottle of Laphroaig.

The debate on what had become known as the Barngate affair had just ended. To viewers it had been acrimonious and noisy, with George and the shadow foreign secretary at each other like a pair of Jack Russells. The Prime Minister had been solid, if not overly demonstrative, in his support of George; the leader of the opposition almost incoherent with righteous indignation. It had ended, as everyone expected, with a comfortable majority for the government and, away from public gaze, equable private exchanges between opponents.

George Greene was pleased. 'Stupid of the opposition to take the shameful-treatment-of-gays angle. We're fireproof on that – all in the past, changing social attitudes, couldn't happen now and whatever. Whereas we are actually vulnerable on the competence angle – porous computer systems, lack of controls, inexcusable post-Snowden – even though none of us was in charge when it all started. Lucky they swallowed the idea of Charles as computer-savvy new broom, incredible as that may seem.'

Angela's smile was wintry. 'Your media reputation as action man hero and husband of beautiful, brilliant and brave lawyer has made you invulnerable to criticism. For the time being.'

Charles shook his head at George's proffered whisky but George poured anyway. The weeks since the shooting had been a whirlwind: the police investigation, the referral to the Crown Prosecution Service, public speculation about his future, media stories about an action-filled past that was unrecognisable to him, press harassment of Sarah for an interview, the suggestion – hastily withdrawn – that he might have murdered his predecessor, accounts of his and

Sarah's Oxford love affair with ancient photographs of them at a ball, his appearance before the ISC, Jeremy Wheeler's elevation to national hero for having tackled the professional hitman, saved Louise's life and endured hundreds of bee-stings and a leg wound, the request – easily refused – that he cooperate with a film based on Peter Tew's life, the safe return of *Beowulf* with the news that she had suffered a communications failure but could receive signals all along, and eventually confirmation from the CPS that he was not to be prosecuted for killing Peter. The police hadn't returned his guns, though, and there was a struggle to get the Home Secretary to prevent Louise's superintendent censuring her for departing from normal police procedures.

'That and the fact that the lights are back on,' said Charles. 'Not that that was really my doing.'

Angela nodded. 'We know that, of course, but the focus on you helpfully distracts people from asking how we could have been so vulnerable in the first place. For once it's useful to have a high-profile C.'

'So long as you don't blather all over Facebook about it and keep your tweets under control. Assuming you'd know a tweet if it sat up and bit you.' George topped up his own whisky again after Angela put her hand over hers. 'Useful, too, that that prat Jeremy Wheeler is hogging so much of the limelight. We're going to have to do something for him, I'm afraid. Something harmless, anything to keep him out of the Cabinet. I'll leave Angela to fill you in. Main thing is this competence issue. They're bound to return to it once the personality hysteria subsides and it's vital we maintain public confidence in our ability to protect ourselves from cyber attack. At the moment, people – our enemies and the public – thinking we can is in fact our best protection. But it's not enough.' He looked at them both. 'Now, this request from BBC *Panorama* for MI6 cooperation with a programme on the subject – quite right you turned it down flat, both of you – but it could actually be very useful if it helps us perpetuate the myth of invincibility a little longer while we do all this clever stuff to make sure we are indeed less vincible. If you could bear to do it, Charles. You'll hate it, of course.'

Charles had been waiting for it. When accepting the job he had neither expected nor wanted to become a public figure. Still less had Sarah when agreeing to marry him. 'When you appointed me you said I and the Service were to keep mum, shtoom, say nothing in public.'

'But that was then. This is now. Things are different, with all that's happened. When the facts change I change my mind and all that. You know what Keynes said, I'm sure.'

Charles knew it was a losing battle, which is why he made only a token effort. There might even be some benefit if it took attention away from Sarah, who hated publicity more than he did. 'Yes I will hate it and yes I will do it.'

'Thank you. In public life you should never become a slave to consistency. You always end up on the rocks. This will be appreciated, I promise you.'

'One condition.' They looked at him. 'We leave Croydon and return to Westminster.'

'Not possible,' said Angela, 'there's neither the budget nor the—'

'Agreed,' said George.

Angela bristled. It was as if they were all young and back in Vienna, decades before. 'George, you simply can't say that. You can't possibly promise it, it's not in your gift, it's—'

He topped up her glass before she could get her hand over it. 'I'll get the Prime Minister to order it.'

Back in Cowley Street Charles edged past the packing cases in the hall to find Sarah in the kitchen opening a bottle of champagne.

'Home early? Only a ten-hour day?'

She nodded and smiled. 'The only good thing to come of all this publicity. They felt shamed into promoting me and giving me a pay rise.' She popped the cork.

'That's wonderful.' He kissed her, thinking the last thing he wanted was champagne on top of whisky.

'But I'm not the only one with good news.' She watched him. 'I'm afraid we've had another invitation. From Sir Jeremy and Lady Wheeler. Still together after all these years. Wonderful what a title can do. And he's to be the next chairman of that committee you complain about, the ISC.'

Charles leant against the door jamb. Anything was possible in this world, anything at all. 'Just hand me the bottle.'